I0600131

Blood Veil

Red Masquerade Duology

Book Two

Shaye Madison

SHAYE MADISON

Copyright © 2025 by Shaye Madison

ISBN: 979-8-9930054-0-9

All rights reserved.

No part of this book may be reproduced in any form or by any electronic or mechanical means, including information storage and retrieval systems, without the prior written permission from the author, except as permitted by U.S. copyright law.

No generative AI training use. No AI was used in any part of the creation of this book.

Cover Art & Design by Dayna Watson

Proofreading by Emily in the Archives

For those who watched Nosferatu (2024) and thought, "why he kinda...?"

Author's Note

Blood Veil is a darker novel than Red Masquerade.

Content warnings include: blood and gore, loss of pregnancy (not the main character), characters bitten against their will by vampires, threat of assault, cannibalism?, physical and emotional abuse by a family member, and explicit sexual content.

For a complete list, my website has all updated content warnings here: https://shayemadisonbooks.com/pages/rm-2.

PROLOGUE

The Devil stood before me.

How terrible his grin, twisting his face into a grotesque mask of joy, when what simmered underneath, I knew, was a cool rage. A demented sort of glee lived there, festering, a bit of hellish pleasure seeping from dark pools of rage.

I knew this devil: he was determined to crush the heart beating in my chest, turn it to stone and crumble it within his fist.

"Is he dead?"

The air vanished, my heart ceasing to beat at his words. *Is he dead?* His gaze darted between me and my captor.

And next to him, waiting, the haughty man to whom he'd sold my hand.

My lungs struggled to work around the noxious truth poisoning the underground tomb, the air a thick sludge, an echo repeating in my mind: *he's a vampire, he's a vampire, he's going to kill me at last, he's a vampire.*

"No." Marcel's lip curled. "This was entirely too simple. We must go."

"And why isn't Thornton dead?" The Devil, my brother, slid his black stare to the vampire standing at my back. Oh, how our mother would weep at the malevolence in his eyes.

Marcel's fingers tightened on the soft flesh of my arm—a warning. I was a rabbit moments away from the snap of a wolf's slobbering maw, teeth digging in with the urge to tear through sinew and bone, held back only by the promise of my submission.

Dead. They wanted him *dead*.

The backs of my eyes burned, the instinct of prey begging me to go limp.

At the defiant silence, Lucas smoothed back a stray hair that wasn't there. His evening suit, a striped dark gray, the tie at his throat perfectly hugging his neck, was unrumpled, ironed, each pinstripe straight as a ruler. No shining marks at his neck, no obvious difference to his eyes; they were as stony as always.

"Lloyd Dixon is taking care of it."

A hum of displeasure. "Later, then."

Wright Highsmith, baron-heir, lounged in a wooden chair across from my brother. Silent thus far, hands clasped in his lap, eyes wandering: from my thighs, my neck, eyes shining low in the dim light. Rancid possession wavered there, irises dilating as they skimmed along my exposed skin beneath the short dress I'd worn. Our stares met, mine frightened, frozen in shock, his carnal, and I knew that not two, but three wolves circled me now.

He'd wanted me weeks ago; with my refusal he only coveted more.

Lucas sighed, waved a hand toward the crumbling hall whence Marcel and I appeared. "I assume we cannot go above ground?"

A shout sounded out in the distance, dust raining, disturbed, from the earth above us.

"What is this?" I heard myself say, my voice thin and pitched, crackling like through a radio. "What is happening?"

"Let's go, then," my brother said, as though I hadn't spoken at all.

"You're lucky I was able to make Dixon *agreeable* at all, what with the state Thornton is in." Marcel's growl dripped with disdain.

He began to pull me toward another dark doorway cut into the wall of stone across the room as the other two men followed closely behind. I couldn't feel my fingers, couldn't command my limbs to resist, observing the scene play out before me, and I was no longer part of it, a specter floating, only watching through this body's eyes, hearing through this body's ears. Until Marcel's grip became bruising, bolts of pain rocketing down through my palms.

I clawed at his fingers, hissing through my teeth. "Wherever you are taking me, I can walk on my own."

The darkness swallowed us whole, each step carrying me further and further from the party above. My friends—missing, unconscious, brawling—would Dixon really kill Vince? Surely not, it was unthinkable—

My heart rended in two, each half fluttering a rabid pulse in my ears.

At my first stumble, Marcel pulled me along, his grip so

strong my knees did not have the chance to hit the uneven ground. "Careful," he taunted, hot breath caressing my ear.

The men moved with haste, no sconces to light our way, no cracks for moonlight to claw its way through. We were surrounded on all sides by stone, damp clay, the must of decay and dust worsening as we encased ourselves in that spiraling darkness.

The phantom pain of his fingers in my hair, wrenching my head back, neck exposed, a blanket fear urging me on, because now he could sense the blood in the artery with precision, could rip apart my flesh with his teeth.

Vince's blue-black veins, hands like claws, a demon within him, clawing its way out.

No, he *was* the demon. That monster had always peered out at me, gazing with curiosity and hunger and lust for my blood, but tonight it had cleaved itself free from Vince's mortal guise.

There had been so much blood—*too much blood.*

Marcel's grip was unrelenting, fingers prying into muscle.

A cruel sort of torment, to force me to walk towards my demise. I'd rather he threw me over his shoulder once more, took away my ability to run, to dig my heels into the soft silty ground.

But what good would it do to refuse?

Lucas always got what he wanted.

It was a lesson I'd failed six years ago, and failed again tonight.

"How many of *them* are there?" Wright asked. So close, he could wrap an arm around my waist and wrench me away, take me for himself, gloat about how he'd fooled me with his facade that first night we met, force me to look in his eyes as his fingers wrapped around my throat. "I'd prefer not to run into Thornton and his ilk if we can help it."

"Then move."

The foolish, hopelessly girlish part of me still thought it possible that Vince would appear; this could not be over yet, it could *not*. He would bare those teeth and rip out their throats, and in their gore we'd be painted with freedom, finally, *freedom*.

"Please," I whispered, knowing Marcel could hear. "I—"

"Hush." Talons digging into my skin, a vise-grip pulling me along.

Roots grabbed at me, scratching my ankles, the dirt under my feet wavering with stones, my shoes slipping and tripping through the debris. That we were under the tomb, traveling in a tunnel under the graveyard, I could not forget, and I ignored my wild imagination that insisted I was kicking bones with each step. Corpses reaching out for me, wanting to pull me under the cool soft earth until my own flesh mottled and dissolved.

The sound of dirt cascading from the ceiling above us made the men pause in their steps. Marcel's fingers twitched on my arm. The dust rained down, landing on my bare shoulders, in my hair. A thousand tiny spiders, my nightmares screamed—or worse, wriggling maggots from bodies suspended above—

"*Go!*" A growl erupted from Marcel, before he was pulling me further, over the finger-like roots, the fabric of my dress snagging on the walls.

Shouts echoed in the distance, voices echoing down the

stone hallway, still so far away yet—but they were coming, and the threat of the chase spurred my captors on.

Wright cursed, the sound of a rock skittering across the tunnel.

Like he tripped.

Still *human*, I realized; blinded in the pitch-dark, guided by my brother's hand.

My brother wasn't struggling in the dark.

My brother wasn't struggling in the dark.

I couldn't catch my breath, couldn't calm my racing heart, with that sickly sweet smell invading my senses.

We were flying down the hall. Marcel's steps were confident, seemingly dodging every root on the ground, every stone.

And then—

Up ahead, a glow surfaced from the earth.

"Finally," Wright said on an exhale.

The shouts behind us continued, drawing nearer.

So close—

If I could stall for time, fall to the ground and slow them down—

The glow grew brighter, until I could see a single lit torch, waiting for us far ahead. The air became salty, the humidity cloying, the clay turning to mud beneath our feet.

The stench of rot intensified.

And then we were at the end of the tunnel. The dirt path led to a little stream, where a small wooden boat rocked against the current, tied to a wooden post. The torch glowed along the wall, lighting the small space.

Except as we neared, the image of the wall wavered, and—

An emaciated corpse slumped against the damp stone. Jaw hanging, eyes empty and staring straight at us, the torchlight flickering in the still-wet eyes. A guest from above, dragged to the depths of the tomb and *ripped apart*.

His neck was destroyed—his throat and his chest, bloodied and raw and torn open in jagged slashes.

A scream ripped from my throat before I could stop it. Marcel grabbed me, covering my mouth and carrying me the rest of the way to the little boat.

Mortals are dying left and right, Dixon had said, only days ago in the city. Saying, without words, that Marcel was responsible. But—

His ribs were cracked, the center of his chest missing. Like some beast had torn him apart and *taken his heart*.

The organ was missing, his intestines and other gore spilling out onto his lap.

I was going to be sick.

The voices down the hall were drawing ever closer, words becoming recognizable, bouncing off the walls, echoing, louder and louder, frantic shouts, the shuffling of feet turning to rapid footsteps.

Marcel caged me tightly against his chest. Wright and Lucas clambered on after us, the edge of the boat rocking dangerously close to the water, before my brother used a booted foot to push off from the makeshift dock.

His heart is missing.

I slammed my eyes shut.

This was a nightmare. It *had* to be.

"Let's hope the current takes us out to the Sound before they round that corner," Marcel grumbled.

The boat swayed. My stomach churned along with it, my

tongue going dry, dizziness sending every sensation into a tailspin.

No, no, no no no—

And when I opened my eyes again, Lucas was looking at me, grinning. A sharp fang—stained red—glinting in the low light.

PART ONE

DOWRY

ONE

ONE WEEK LATER

Like a headstone emerged Whitrow Estate from the hills of central England, a shock of white against the dull emerald hues of the plains. The seat of the Whitrow barony, its shape loomed as we drove ever closer, a long stone drive lined with budding trees ushering us onto the property.

"Finally."

Wright Highsmith lounged on the seat next to me, a spark coming to life in his eyes at the sight of his home.

For seven days, stuck together on an ocean liner, he'd watched me with what I could only assume was dissatisfaction, or maybe even resentment, and I had the constant feeling some sort of admonishment was on the tip of his tongue. But he kept quiet, if stern, in laying out his expectations for my future—*our* future.

We were to marry in another week's time.

I had seven more days to settle into my new life before I was stuck here forever, till death do us part.

He said nothing else as the car continued along the drive. My brother and Marcel were following behind us, and another driver took up the back with all of our luggage. The closer we approached the house, the more I hoped I could blink and be transported back to the Sound. That it wasn't Whitrow, but Vince's mansion that loomed ahead.

Perhaps in another life, I would have marveled at the rolling hues of mossy green, the winding paths between fields, the occasional farm, each catch of my breath in my throat an offering to the fae that lived amongst the hills, according to every fairytale from my girlhood. In another life, I'd have savored the crisp air, the lilting accents. I would have wondered at the novelty of it. I would have wanted it for myself, until the feeling faded, until I coveted the next shiny, new thing. A new house, dresses from a French designer—whatever Wright would give me.

But after being forced onto an ocean liner across thousands of miles of water, in this foreign land I loathed every inch of grass, every chirping bird, every rock, every reminder that *this was not my home.*

The driver stopped the car at the foot of the entry way, a dozen or so steps leading up to a porch where the front doors sat ajar. A handful of servants awaited our arrival, but —the Highsmith family was nowhere to be seen.

I'd had a long time to think the past week at sea: about everything Marcel had said, about the scheme to find me and bring me to England, about the barony Wright was set to inherit, about his parents, the current Baron and Baroness, and what *they* expected from me. Wright had made it clear in the garden of my family's house in New York that I was to bear his children, his heir—that was my purpose. No doubt a sentiment shared with his family. And though I loathed the thought, if I was not in the Baron and Baroness' favor, my life at Whitrow would fall to an even deeper circle of hell.

But Baron Whitrow and his wife were missing.

Wright exited the car, not waiting for the driver to open his door.

"Welcome home." The man who I presumed was the butler stood at the end of the line of servants, inclining his head in deference as Wright approached.

"My father?"

"In his quarters." The butler's face remained pensive until Wright disappeared inside the house.

Each and every one of the servants stared at me, expectant. Waiting to see the girl their baron-heir would soon wed. I'd had seven days to prepare for this, seven long days—in which I'd been locked away, alone, in a small cabin room— to steel myself against the scrutiny I knew was to come.

As Wright disappeared inside, the driver opened my door, offering me a hand. I swallowed around the lump of apprehension stuck in my throat, easing myself onto my feet.

The other cars pulled to a stop, wheels crunching on the gravel before they parked. Lucas and Marcel stepped out a moment later, my brother looking the slightest bit dazzled at the house before us, no matter how he schooled his features and tried to hide it.

Or maybe it was jealousy. Wright came from old money. *Powerful* money. Even if he was just the next in line for a barony, there was pedigree in his bloodline missing in the lines of new-money families like ours.

I watched my brother warily, half-expecting him to lunge

at one of the servants. An easy meal, and what could they do? Wright had welcomed the vampires into his home. How easily Lucas and Marcel could take the house over and Make everyone within. All these humans, easily overpowered, and none of them knew it.

It had taken me days on the boat to come to terms with this new reality: that my brother was a vampire; that he was somehow in league with Marcel—had maybe even been *Made* by Marcel, they would not tell me. And if I were honest, denial still pounded its fist against my heart, bruising my ribs from the inside out.

And Wright, still austerely human, this entire time had cared nothing for the blood-thirst of the two, as though this quality was no worse than a gentleman's penchant for liquor.

The footmen sprung into action, unloading the trunks and hauling them into the house. A young maid broke from the line to greet me. She was only a little older than myself, I guessed, with light hair under a cap and the accent of the region. A slight, nervous incline to her head, as though unsure if she should show deference to me as well. "I will show you to your room, miss."

"Thank you." Because I didn't know what else to say.

I was corralled inside, Lucas and Marcel ahead of us, walking into the massive house like they knew its layout well. Before I even met Wright, my brother had visited the house, setting up the deal that would sign me over to him. And I had been blissfully unaware in the city, drinking away the nights until the sun rose, dancing with Flora and any man who offered.

Until that party when Vince found me in a crowd of hundreds.

"What is your name?" I asked.

"Anna."

"It's nice to meet you, Anna."

She bit her lip.

"How long have you been a lady's maid?"

"A few years, miss, but I was just hired on here at Whitrow a bit before your arrival. During Mr. Quintrell's last visit." She looked blankly ahead as we walked, but a muscle feathered in her throat. "Miss."

I looked around at the high ceilings, the grand stairs, the paintings lining the halls. "And where did you work before?"

"At Berrymore." The name meant nothing to me. She paused, eyes narrowing. "I assure you, I've been well-trained and should you need anything—"

"I didn't mean to question your abilities," I said, turning to her, wondering just what I'd said to sour her opinion of me already. "I believe we can get along just fine."

Again, she didn't reply, pressing her lips together and walking on.

We rounded a corner, the sound of our footsteps dampened by a long runner. Mahogany doors appeared every few feet on both sides of the hall. My room was at the end of one long wing of the house, the floors made of the same polished stone, the walls papered, old landscapes hanging in between each door. The sound of our steps was muffled by plush rugs. The vampires' voices had faded away into an echo.

Did the inhabitants of Whitrow know what sort of creature they'd welcomed inside?

"This is Mr. Highsmith's wing of the house. Your room

is here." She reached for a door handle, which opened up without a sound. She led me inside, going to the window and drawing the curtain open a foot or so, just enough to illuminate the room with the waning sunlight.

"If this is his wing, where is his room?" I asked. The walls were paneled, the lights all gilded, the bed a four-poster with a canopy.

"Right next to yours, miss."

And then I noticed the door to my left, a few feet away from the stately wardrobe, right along the wall to the next room.

He could come in whenever he wanted, then.

There was a chill about the room, a foreboding, like ghosts were watching me enter, a specter sitting in the corner, invisible and vexed at my intrusion.

"Come, Miss Helena." Anna gave me a short smile that didn't reach her eyes, standing by the vanity and wardrobe. "I am to ready you for dinner."

Dinner. I was torn between making a good impression, if just to make my time here more bearable, and becoming even more of a thorn in Lucas' side.

I wasn't sure how I'd get out of this. I didn't know how to get home.

"So early?" It was half past four in the afternoon.

"The family has taken to retiring early as of late. The Baron is not in good health—"

"He's not?"

She blinked. "No, miss. Baron Whitrow has been ailing for quite some time." She hesitated, her voice softening. "It won't be long now, we suspect."

"How terrible." Though as I said it, the words came

wholly unconvincing. Perhaps if Wright had spent the last week attempting to make a friend of me, then I'd be swayed to sympathy.

If I hadn't been taken from my life in New York, then maybe I'd be pleasant.

Perhaps that was the strategy: to be so unbearable that Wright wouldn't have me.

But, no, my brother—some number he'd done on me. Maybe he had whipped me into shape, after all, if I was considering stopping myself from drawing out his anger now.

Anna began brushing through my hair before finding some pins to hold it in place, putting it into an elegant, if nostalgic, style. The strands were growing long, longer than I'd kept it in a while.

I watched her reflection as she worked. "May I ask you something?"

"Yes." Her brows furrowed in concentration.

For the briefest second, I was reminded of Séra. "How many live here? The family, I mean."

"Three: the baron, his wife Lady Whitrow, and Mr. Highsmith."

She undid a pin, adjusting the lock of hair before securing it into place again.

"Some advice, Miss Helena."

I found myself tensing at her clipped tone.

"Mr. Highsmith prefers you call him 'lord' in private. He has not yet assumed his title, but he has directed the staff to call him such."

"Yes, I'd noticed," I said.

"But not around his mother. She would not react well."

"Noted."

"And—"

"You know quite a lot about *Lord Highsmith* for someone who was only just hired." My eyes narrowed on the girl.

"One would think you should know as well, seeing as you are about to marry him. I am only trying to help." She looked down at me through the mirror. "*Miss.*"

I bit my tongue. No good would come from having a spat with my maid. "Tell me more, then. What do you know of Wright?"

Her eyes widened for just a second at my using his first name, though she recovered quickly. She cleared her throat, continuing to mess with the pins in my hair, voice light. "He's been married before. Twice, miss, in fact."

The realization was like ice down my spine, not for jealousy, but—"Twice?"

I was not to be Wright Highsmith's first wife. I'd suspected he was a few years my senior, given the crow's feet at his eyes and his worldly arrogance, but I'd chalked it up to his being a rich Englishman, an aristocrat. The exact type of man this world was built for.

Anna raised a brow. "The last one was a bit ago, though. A few years. He was not considering remarrying until Mr. Quintrell began visiting—at least, not that I *know* of."

"What happened to her?" I regretted the words as soon as they were out.

Anna met my eye in the mirror. "She's dead. Both of them are."

After being dressed in a sapphire number with short lace sleeves, and thoroughly groomed and rouged so that any evidence of traveling the past week had been wiped away, I was led down the stairs to a grand dining room. Anna was quick to disappear, either unnerved by our conversation or an enemy of mine, already. Before I could take a breath, the doors were pushed open, I was ushered through, and my name was announced to the family within.

Five sets of eyes turned to me, stopping mid-conversation.

Clumsily, I inclined my head to the family, unsure what I was to do. No one had told me how to act, if I was to curtsy —did you curtsy for a Baron? I swallowed the lump in my throat, staring at the floor. "Baron Whitrow, Lady Whitrow."

I felt so completely like I was messing this up already.

The man had graying hair, slicked back, and looked the mirror image of Wright, only a few decades older. His rheumy eyes were kinder than I expected—a soft expression, maybe even the beginnings of a polite smile. His skin was a blueish gray, spots along his temples, and his hands trembled, though he couldn't have been more than sixty years of age. He sagged in his seat, fatigued. "Ah, there she is."

His wife, to his side, dissected me immediately, her gaze a scalpel on my skin. Her lips were pinched, her brown hair in a wavy bob, and at my entrance, she scowled.

Two enemies I'd made thus far, then.

Wright sat on the baron's other side; next to him, Lucas. Marcel at the end of the group. All of them, staring right through me.

"How good of you to join us." My brother broke the

silence. I suddenly felt as though I were being tested, and I didn't know the correct answers.

I held my head high and sat in the chair pulled out for me by one of the footmen tending to the table. "Apologies for my delay."

"Mother, Father, this is Helena Quintrell," Wright said, irritation already wrinkling the space between his brows. "I'm sure she just needed some extra time to prepare after our long journey."

His wives were dead.

"Of course." The Baron gestured to the butler, who was already stooping to set a plate before me. "A pleasure to meet you, dear. It goes without saying that should you need anything, let one of the servants know."

"Thank you."

I wasn't sure how I'd stomach the salad that had been set on my placemat, much less the courses that were to come soon after.

"We've heard much about you," Lady Whitrow said, looking down her nose. "Mr. Quintrell spoke of you during his previous visits. We hope that your marriage with Wright is... prosperous."

I willed my heart to calm. Straightened in my seat. Tried a polite smile. "Thank you, my lady, and Baron Whitrow, for —for welcoming me into your home."

How had Wright's wives died?

"We are just looking forward to all the future has to hold." The Baron smiled weakly, kindly. "My wife has been hard at work planning the celebrations."

"Yes." Her eyes flicked over to me. "We have much to discuss tomorrow."

"I look forward to it." I lied through my teeth. "My lady."

"And while you ladies are busy, I am taking Quintrell and Brancato into town in the morning," Wright said, looking at me over the rim of his glass. Eyes lingering on my lips, my neck.

I pretended not to see.

Abruptly, the dining room doors opened once more. "Mrs. Quintrell," the butler announced.

And a very round Lucy walked into the room.

I nearly dropped my fork.

She moved slowly, a maid offering her support under her arm.

Glittering blue eyes, a face like a rose, and golden hair curling around her ears, her hands rested on her belly as she entered, already smiling. But when our eyes met, she lit up, and a delighted gasp slipped from her lips. "Helena!"

I stood, immediately, not caring about the old rules of propriety, and rushed to hug my sister. "*Lucy.*"

Her hands were delicate, gentle, wrapping around me, and I was taken back to New York, to safety, to comfort and happiness and nostalgic summers in the city where we giggled over our hands at teas with Mother, conspiratorial glances during dinners with Lucas.

Lucas hadn't spoken hardly a word of her on our journey. But there she was, miraculously, thousands of miles away from home, and positively glowing.

She laughed, inspecting me up and down. "You've made it."

"I can't believe you are here." I gaped.

Maybe I was not so alone as I thought.

She quickly glanced at the family, flushing, and greeted them. They had visibly softened, even Lady Whitrow plastering on a smile for Lucy. She had an ethereal quality to her, a brightness that infected the entire room, and maybe her current state amplified that brightness, like a kernel of sunshine radiated from within her chest. A servant helped her into the seat next to me.

Lucas remained sitting, propping his jaw on his fingers, watching.

"I'm glad you are feeling well enough to join us," Lady Whitrow said.

"I am very well this evening, my lady." Lucy smiled, though her shyness began to rear its head when she remembered she had the attention of the whole room.

"Any updates from the doctor?" Wright asked. He sipped from his glass.

Lucy averted her eyes. "No, sir. It is a waiting game at this point."

Wright's eyes narrowed. Was that envy?

You only need to have one, he'd said. *Then you can take whatever man you'd like. So long as you're discreet.*

"You must be thrilled, Mr. Quintrell." The baron gave another weak smile.

"Elated, my lord." My brother donned his facade. His sharp teeth stayed hidden. "It feels like we've been waiting forever."

Lucy's blush deepened.

And Marcel said nothing, fingers swirling around the lip of his glass, observing.

All the comfort I felt at seeing her washed away, realizing

she was soon to become a mother amongst this family. And that Lucas had brought her here—

He was a monster, now. Those teeth were deadly. And a child was on the way.

Did Lucy know?

I struggled to swallow the one bite of food I'd eaten.

Marcel caught my eyes, his brow arching almost imperceptibly, the corner of his lips twitching.

He was *enjoying* this.

"Well, your family is welcome to stay with us as long as needed," the baron said. "We will keep the doctors on call, and I do insist that you remain until everyone is well. You are about to become our family, after all."

Lucas grinned. "Thank you, my lord."

The next course came and went, and if Lucy noticed her husband's near-full plate, she did not comment on it. Nausea roiled in my stomach at the thought that deep red liquid in his glass, in Marcel's glass, was not wine. And if they were drinking blood, from whom had it been harvested?

Surely they wouldn't—not in front of so many.

Lucas, prompted by the baron, detailed his projections for the company. Wright added his piece, how advantageous to both families this deal was. They went on, until Lady Whitrow insisted that speaking of business was not for the dinner table, instead once again asking Wright about his visit to New York.

"I cannot say I'd like to visit again," he said, eyes flicking over to me.

I pretended to be engrossed in my food, pushing the roasted vegetables about my plate.

"Maybe after you and Helena get settled, perhaps after an heir or two, then you can come visit Lucy and I in the summer. New York is the best in the warm months." Lucas spoke to Wright, though his stare lingered on me.

"Maybe." Wright didn't sound convinced.

"But how was the city?" Lady Whitrow asked. "All the papers say it is *chaos* over there."

"In truth, I don't care for the city," Wright almost sneered. "I was a bit preoccupied. There was not much time for leisure, Mother."

I realized she must not have known that I ran, because she didn't look at me with suspicion at all. They'd not told the Baron and his wife how *difficult* I'd been.

But maybe it was the way Marcel was watching me, never saying a word, but waiting, as though he knew I'd crack at any moment. Dark eyes observant, looking too closely, and I thought for just a moment that maybe he had the power to read my mind, how intently he looked at me.

I was an outsider here, and my maid, the family, *everyone* seemed intent on reminding me.

"Excuse me." I pushed away from the table, shocking everyone into silence. I dipped my head again. "I'm afraid the day is catching up to me. Goodnight."

Before I could be stopped, I slipped from the room. My lungs begged for air. I couldn't be moved to care if it was improper, if I needed to be given leave before making my escape.

The stone lodged in my throat ached as I tried to remember the way back to my bedroom. And the entire way back, my slippers padding across the marble floors, afraid I'd slip, I feared a certain heir would follow and give me a shaking. Or my brother, to set me straight.

I rang the bell inside the bedroom door once I was alone. I was at the vanity, pulling pins furiously from my hair when Anna arrived. Neither of us spoke a word, even though I was burning to ask more about his previous wives and what trouble I'd found myself in.

Lucas must have known.

He hadn't cared to warn me.

And now I was mere days away from resigning myself to my unknown fate.

Pulled from the nothingness of sleep, I awoke with a gasp. Knowing, down to my bones, that something was wrong. My every hair stood on end, echoes of a warning ringing in my ears.

Swearing that when I opened my eyes, I heard the soft *snick* of a door falling into the latch.

The moon cast midnight blue beams of light across the room through the curtains, the dark forms of the furniture still indistinguishable in the inky black. The hearth had long since died. A cool breeze unsettled the air, even with the windows sealed tightly shut. The clock on the wall read barely past three in the morning, each *tick tick tick* fainter than my heartbeats.

Sitting up, the covers falling to my lap, I saw—nothing.

No one was in my room.

Yet when I moved, my fingers brushed against something silky soft on my pillow.

Just like—

I lifted the rose to the light. Deep red petals, black in the darkness, in full bloom.

The flower tumbled from my fingers, dread chasing away all traces of sleep from my mind.

I wanted to believe there was an explanation for this gift. Wanted to believe that it was some sign Vince was here, with me. That he'd found a way. A signal that only I would know —that he'd been watching over me this entire time.

That he was going to save me.

Didn't you know he's been threatening your family all along?

And that's when I heard it: the low moan, coming from the other side of the wall.

From Wright's room?

Was he....

I held my breath, the silence ringing louder.

Another moan echoed through the hall. A low, agonizing sound that had come from somewhere distant in the house, wracking through me like a specter's terror.

I slipped from bed, feeling every bit like I was the only soul awake. It was unwise to rise during the witching hour, to investigate strange sounds, to look deep into the shadows, and yet, my pulse quickened as I approached my bedroom door.

The sound came again; it was a woman's voice, this time so soft, but surely just down the hall.

Pressing my ear to the wood, I heard the low rumble of it. Like an animal in pain, caught in a trap they knew they'd never escape.

I turned the handle—but it stuck.
I was locked in.

Two

"I was hoping we could start anew."

Wright sat across from me, not in the stately dining room from the evening before, but in one of his private rooms, with only a footman standing to the side, waiting for his command. After an evening tossing and turning, Anna had arrived early with an order to ready me for breakfast with my soon-to-be husband.

I didn't know what to say to him, whether to curse at him or hold my tongue.

Someone had locked my door. Someone had come into my bedroom while I slept and then *locked the door*.

"I'd like to come to an agreement. Our previous discussions have not been entirely... productive." He eyed me, unreadable.

We hadn't *talked* much at all on the boat, but when I had been let out of my room, I'd been subjected to his lecturing, my brother's goading. Reminders to *behave*.

"I'd like to make a few things clear."

We sat at a dark mahogany table, a spread of eggs, sausages, toasts, jams and jellies, and freshly cut fruit laid out before us. A steaming breakfast tea filled the room with its warm aroma.

Exhaustion weakened my limbs. My eyes burned from my lack of sleep.

Disdain for me lived in him, I knew it was there, just like I knew it simmered under Lucas' skin, too. Wright hadn't cracked—yet—but I knew that within him was that capacity for violence, just like my brother, just like Marcel, just like all the men who believed they could impose their will upon me. The men I'd met at midnight parties, wanting a taste; quiet fury at being told *no*—they were all the same.

He cleared his throat at my silence. "Very well. I want you to understand the magnitude of the favor I am doing for you."

"A favor?" I bit out. "Or just part of the deal you struck with my brother?"

He brought a cigarette from its case to his mouth, using a lighter to spark the flame. Taking his time, pulling a few puffs before he answered me. "I am in need of a wife, and you, a guardian."

A guardian, but I was not a child any longer.

I couldn't hide my scowl as I finally faced him. "I was managing just fine."

The pleasant facade he'd shown me that first night we met had been washed away, and a cold, dutiful man stood in its place. "Not according to Quintrell. I'm told you are a wild one."

I did not like the way he called me *wild*.

He glanced at the footman, who then ducked his head and quickly made his leave.

"Your brother told me you were a whore. Only after," he waved a hand in the air, "all of this." Fingers coming up to the cigarette, he pulled it away from his lips to tap it on an ashtray and raised a brow. "Should I believe him?"

As though he hadn't *kidnapped* me and forced me on a boat across the ocean to marry him.

But was it even a crime, if he and Lucas had signed the contract weeks ago?

"I don't think anything I say would sway you."

He exhaled a disappointed laugh. Crossed his legs and leaned back. "So you admit it?"

"Does it matter?"

Wright flashed a brief grin. "I suppose it does to certain men. It does to your brother." The cigarette's smoke swirled in a tipsy dance before rising to the ornate ceiling. "I only want an heir."

"You want *me* to give you an heir."

"All great men want their bloodline to continue."

I barely stopped myself from scoffing. "But why do you want me? Why go through all this trouble—"

"It's a matter of principle, Helena." He gave me a look like he almost *pitied* me, the poor, naive girl who didn't understand how his world worked. "You were to be my wife. That doesn't change because you ran away. Your brother and I have an agreement."

"And does he have the right to just *sell* me to you?" I asked, my tone rising.

I didn't care if any of the other servants heard in the hall, didn't care if I drew attention. I had no allies in this house, that much was clear.

The question sat in the air, unanswered. He only dragged on his smoke once more.

"Why *me*?" I repeated.

A muscle ticked in his jaw. A warning. "I told you. We came to an agreement."

"But—"

"*Enough.*"

It lingered heavily in the air, echoing off the walls.

Wright's brow twitched, and he didn't move for a moment, rigidity to the muscles of his neck, his shoulders.

Frustrated tears had begun to line my lashes, but I blinked them away because I would *not* cry in front of him. Forced myself to choose from the dishes, to make myself a plate and eat. I did myself no favors by giving in to my lack of an appetite; I needed my wits about me if I was to figure out how to get out of this mess.

"I will not have you performing your melodrama in front of my family," he continued after a deep breath, a drag on the cigarette. "In fact, I'd like to make sure you are over this irrationality, as it were. There will be no running away. No throwing these tantrums. It's unbecoming of a future baron's wife."

"Is it?" I was biting my lip so hard, a rage trembling through me.

He glared. "So I hope we can come to some agreement. Put this senselessness to rest."

A deal with a devil.

I swallowed down all the things I wanted to say, because I saw that wretched disdain beginning to surface in his eyes.

"You are unafraid of them," I said. "Lucas. Marcel."

Wright looked at me, silent for a second: perhaps debating if our battle of wills should continue, until he could get me to submit, or if it was better to let the matter go.

"I must admit I was surprised when your brother revealed himself to be something more than human. Fascinating, isn't it? To acquire a hunger so disgusting?"

I exhaled, slight relief at his attention turning away from my reluctance.

"No, I am not afraid of them. They've shown their cards without even realizing it: to be motivated by such a base urge, is to be easily misled. Easily *controlled*." He adjusted the way he sat in his seat, reclining, stretching his ankle onto his knee. "Did mankind not put lions on display? Can we not cage falcons?"

I frowned. "Yet *we* are vampires' prey."

He shrugged, bringing the cigarette to his lips. "Don't show them your back, then."

And what of Lucy, who roamed the house unaware? What of the Baron, who was already on his deathbed, weak and vulnerable? They walked amongst monsters, and did not even know it.

Was it a blessing, then, that I *did* know?

There was no convincing my soon-to-be husband against his new partners; whatever deal he made with Lucas, whatever bargain he'd struck with Marcel, had him right within their grasp.

Or—were they in his?

Breathing deep, trying to settle the shaking of my hands,

I crossed my arms. "You want to come to an understanding with me. Tell me what I must know."

Knowing, I decided, was better.

He blinked. Tapped a finger on the table. Exhaled a plume of smoke. "What you *must* know?"

My face heated. "At the very least tell me what I should know about your family. About... I don't know, what I should expect. Lucas has told me nothing."

"Perhaps because you ran away before we could."

"You cannot expect me to go into this *happy* if I don't know what I'm walking into," I argued, ignoring his jab.

"Happy?" He scoffed. "Who said anything about happiness?"

His finger continued to tap as he studied me, eyes lingering on mine.

"And I can't say I understand it," he continued. "Your refusal to marry. Your refusal of my hand, my name."

I glanced toward the window, to the rolling clouds with patches of blue sky peeking through. I bit my lip; I'd angered him enough.

"What have you been up to these past weeks anyway?" He looked at me through hooded eyes, reminiscent of the leering gaze in the tomb, his lecherous stare as Marcel dragged me into the dark. "How do you know him?"

Him.

Vince.

Adam.

"I—" My throat constricted, grabbing the cutlery before me, busying myself. "We met at a party."

It was true enough.

"A party." He gave me an incredulous look. "And—you

saw something in him all of a sudden that made you want to run away from me? Or was it something else? Perhaps he *wooed* you with his money? If that's all it took, I could've listed all my investments when we met. I could've promised to show you my family's heirloom jewels. I could've told you all that I am set to inherit. But, no. That's not it."

He leaned forward.

"Perhaps his charm? Does he have a way with words?"

My tongue ran dry.

I decided not only did I hate this man, but I *loathed* him.

"I just find it peculiar," he continued. "The evening I arrive, you succumb to your *hysterics*, and in the morning you're missing, right out of your bed. Window unlatched, like someone stole you away."

I said nothing.

Maybe if Vince hadn't made his way into my life again, maybe if he was still dead to me like I'd believed him to be for six years, then I would have accepted the marriage contract with Wright. Maybe I would have been a softer woman, and one who could bear the expectations of being a wife and mother.

Someone like Lucy.

I wish you were like Lucille.

I surely would have avoided my brother's anger in this battle of wills.

Because really, would I not be cared for? Would I not still have the newest fashions, warm meals, and this extravagant house? Were I to accept this, accept Wright and the Highsmith name, I would be comfortable. I would still have more than most.

Lucas would never have married me off to a beggar in destitution, no matter how much he *wanted* to. It would not reflect well on the Quintrell name.

But I was cursed to know my alternatives: that Vince was still out there—*that Adam never really died*—and I could have *love*, too.

"It's almost as though it were planned," Wright said.

I shook my head. "It wasn't planned."

"No?"

"No. It just—happened."

I wasn't sure why I felt the need to explain myself, but I also wasn't sure how much Wright already knew. He was trying to parse *something* with all of these questions.

"So you jumped down from your bedroom one story high and, what, hailed a cab? To take you to the house of the richest man on Long Island and you assumed he would give you refuge?"

I squeezed the handle of the knife in my fingers. Shocked myself with the intruding thought to *use it*.

I looked at him then. "What do you want?"

The corner of his mouth lifted, just slightly, in amusement. "Trying to make sense of my future wife, is all."

It was a lie, I knew.

How naive, how *pitiful* I had been, thinking I had a choice.

I straightened my spine. "So you still want to marry me, even if I am a whore?"

"You won't be the first whore I've laid with."

That creeping sliminess seeped over my flesh, the same warning from the evening we first met. An uncanny feeling that something wasn't right.

But of course, *nothing* was right.

"Won't that tarnish your reputation, to marry one?"

He shrugged. "Who else will know? You don't have a reputation that precedes you. Not as Lucas fears, anyway. It will be no problem, long as you do as we advise you."

The pointed warning in his stare, the same look Lucas often gave me.

"In any case, you will be expecting soon after the wedding."

"Soon?" My stomach dropped. We were to marry in a week.

"Yes." He tapped the cigarette against the ashtray. "There is no need to waste time. Mother is eager to have a young one in the house, and the sooner, the better, really, once I inherit the title."

"But—"

"Oh, you must understand that this is imperative. Better to get it out of the way, yes?"

My body moved on its own. I stood, hands shaking, feeling every bit of disgust I'd felt that night weeks ago, when he'd brought this up, as though it were a natural fact of life.

"I—" The words caught in my throat.

His face twinged red. "Sit down. It's decided, and you cannot run from it this time," he said, voice low.

I cannot run from it this time.

His wives were dead.

"I'm sorry," I said, though it wasn't true. "You've misunderstood the type of woman I am."

"*Sit.* I will not ask again."

There was a flurry, a tempest, brewing within my chest, and it needed release. A fury, that felt only half mine, that heated my blood, whispered dangerous things in my ears. That gripped my heart, and tried to persuade me to do something I'd regret.

After a breath, I sat, if only to lessen his anger.

"I have not misunderstood," he continued. "I know what you are: this new century has women believing in some sort of liberation that defies the natural order of society. You've been led astray, and your brother has more important matters to deal with."

"And you think a marriage will change this?" I scowled.

The smile he gave me was sardonic, and I knew without a doubt we were enemies then. "No. But you are not the first woman I've had to tame."

THREE

The breakfast ended when Wright decided he'd had enough of me, checking his timepiece and announcing it was near time he, Lucas, and Marcel left for the day. And though the men were gone, the house still sat heavy, something oppressive and seething and dark seeping in the air as I was led back to my room.

I would suffocate here, I realized, if I had to endure the rest of my life with Wright.

Passing each window, I gazed at the outdoors as if there lingered my answer, my freedom.

Whitrow would be a veritable prison, if I let it.

Lady Whitrow appeared not longer after with Anna, some other maids, and a dressmaker in tow.

"Your role here is quite simple," the lady said as she sat upon the settee. "You keep the house in order, and in doing so, you keep the family in order. The Baron cannot see to his duties if the house needs attending to."

She supervised as the seamstress took my measurements.

The dress was already made, having been picked out and ordered a few weeks ago, within days of Wright leaving for America. Its silky form hung over a mannequin, modest in its length yet modern in its figure. I held my arms up for the seamstress to measure my waist and hips, the length from my shoulders to my knees.

"This is as easy as it will get—for now, you need not do anything but observe and learn. But when you and Wright settle into your own house, it will be up to you to keep things straight. Keep him happy, and I assure you, *you* will be happy."

I bristled at her words.

"Our own house, my lady?" I prompted, still getting used to addressing her correctly. I knew I did not have many chances to slip up.

Was that why the other women died, because they could not live up to the family's expectations?

I hadn't asked about the sounds from the hallway at night, admittedly too afraid for the answer.

I just needed to try my best, and one day, I'd be able to walk away from this place.

"Yes," she said, intently watching the seamstress work. "We own a few properties. There is a townhouse in London, if you'd prefer. It may come in handy if he is ever stuck working for long periods, and you'd rather not part. Otherwise, there's the house in Somerset. It's a quaint little thing. I never much liked it, but you may find a home there. Of course, it is up to Wright where—and when—he wants to settle. You will be here with us until then."

No one had told me any of this. I'd been under the

impression we would stay at Whitrow. Why wouldn't we, if the Baron was supposedly so close to passing?

But if we chose a different house, he'd likely leave me for the city often. I'd have numerous chances to slip away and be gone before anyone realized. A townhome in London—I could easily slip into a crowd and disappear for good, find some way back home.

Lady Whitrow went over the schedule for the wedding day. An early start for me, a breakfast alone while they readied me. The ceremony would be after noon, the reception and party in the evening and late into the night. She told me who was attending, a long list of names and their titles, but I retained none of it; I gathered she relayed all the information to remind herself, more than to inform me. And as she listed off the names, I felt myself shrink, the dread taking over.

The seamstress set about wrapping up, gathering her things, stating she'd return tomorrow.

Lady Whitrow decided she'd show me around the house, since I hadn't had the opportunity to tour the whole thing the day before. "The Baron and I reside in the opposite wing," she said. "There is no reason for you to find yourself on that side of the house. However, this entire wing, and the bottom floors, are open to you."

She went on, detailing renovations that the wings had undergone less than a decade ago to take the house into the new century.

And while she spoke, it was as though the ghosts of Wright's previous brides followed us through the halls.

Anna had refused to speak more on it this morning, and I didn't know who else to ask.

"Has he bed you yet?"

The air in my throat stalled, pulling me from my thoughts and stunning me into silence. I stopped in the center of the corridor, staring as the lady continued on, her footsteps soft against the rugs.

"No, my lady," I managed, resuming after her.

"Good."

She stared straight ahead, not meeting my eyes.

"And I trust that you've abstained prior to your engagement?"

"I—" Anger heated my blood.

She stopped abruptly, warning in her eyes. "I should not have to explain why I ask, because if you are with child, then we would have to remedy the situation."

I opened my mouth to speak, but nothing came out.

"Well?"

"No, my lady." I bit out, unable to hide how her words had insulted me. "I am not with child."

I saw it then, in her eyes, that she decided I was something to be wrangled into submission. Though I gave her the answer she wanted, her lip twitched with displeasure—maybe irritation that I'd not answered so readily, or maybe distaste that she knew I'd not kept my legs closed. I was to be the black sheep daughter-in-law, doomed to earn her disfavor.

She wanted a young girl who would gladly keep her head down and do as she was told. A girl who had no worldly knowledge until married.

She wanted Lucy.

"Well, it won't be long, now," she said, continuing down the hall.

I felt like I failed already, the finality of it sinking into me. The bride-ghosts grinned in anticipation.

"My lady."

She didn't look at me as I once more caught up to her long strides.

"Perhaps you can offer me some guidance," I said, softening my voice as much as I could. Let her think me meek and silly. I became the girl my mother always wanted me to be. "I find I am overwhelmed with *everything*—"

"Naturally."

"And I would be mistaken if I did not... heed your advice, my lady."

She stopped. Her eyes turned assessing, looking me up and down.

Let her believe me. Let her see a young, naive girl.

"This is all so strange to me." I stared at her through wide eyes. "But I'd like to do this well."

Lady Whitrow was not much older than my mother, but she held herself with a cool grace, an assuredness I'd noticed at dinner the night before. She knew who she was, and she wanted more than anything for her son to succeed.

In this, she was just like my mother.

I couldn't be Lucy, but I could make myself seem pliable.

She hummed. "I was wondering when you would admit it. Come."

FOUR
SIX YEARS AGO

The dull *thunk* of a stone at my window. Once, and moments later, again a second time, rousing me from sleep. It was late in the evening—the sun did not set til late in the summer, and it had long since passed over the horizon by the time I fell asleep. On the third stone, my eyes flew open.

I threw off the thin blanket, rushing to the window sill. Fingers fumbling with the latch, a grin already pulling at my lips, as I saw the man a story below, waiting. He glowed in the midnight hour, the only light coming from the moon high above.

The sight of him warmed me, sent my heart into a frenzy.

This was the third time this week. Madness, utter madness. But I couldn't fight my smile, the giddiness, all the same.

I held a finger to my lips, to which he nodded, before retreating back into my room and shutting the window softly. A dressing gown sat ready at my vanity. Slipping it on, I loosely tied the sash before sneaking from my room.

The house was quiet. Lucas had gone to bed hours ago, as had the live-in servants. The only sounds came from the occasional carriage outside, the creak of the house settling as the air cooled.

I had become good at this, walking on my toes to dampen the sound. I knew what steps to avoid, which floorboards creaked, as though I could float, silent as a mouse. It was an effort not to run, to keep my steps light while traversing the house, floating down the long hall that led to the garden outside.

The hall was pitch-dark, no candles burning, but I felt the latch of the lock, the large doors moving quietly against my weight.

Adam was on me in an instant, an arm around my waist before the heavy doors could close behind me. His lips found me, kisses against my cheek, my temples. Strong hands gripping my hips, pulling me further outside.

I sighed, suppressing a laugh.

In his arms, I felt completely whole, like Lucas and Mother and Father never existed. Like I was a sylph and there was nothing holding me to earth. The soil was damp beneath my bare feet, the stones of the path smooth and worn.

He still smelled like ink, like grease and solvents and all those chemicals that soaked into his skin, his clothes. His cap was missing, his auburn hair shining in the moonlight as he consumed me, my fingers tangling in the strands and gripping him to me.

He walked us backwards, knowing the route innately, his feet carrying us to the safety of the sycamore tree.

He laid me down, under the curtain of vines, the low-hanging branches shrouding us from the city. It was still warm, a certain mugginess to the air that pebbled my skin. Adam loomed over me, his features dark in these shadows. I reached for him, my hands finding his cheeks, thumbs racing along his lips.

"I love you," he breathed.

A laugh escaped me this time. "I love you," I exhaled, before he fell upon me, his lips finding my neck.

His teeth nipped at my skin and a gasp flew from me.

"We have to be quiet," I reminded him, though I knew it was *me* who needed reminding.

His breath was hot against my throat, stubble scratching at the sensitive flesh as his jaw moved. "I want to hear you," he murmured, low and gravelly.

This man did strange things to me, turning my heart into a bird fluttering, every bit of my flesh awake, something deep within me wanting him closer. Three times this week he had lured me down under the tree, whispering words, tracing my skin with his lips until the early hours.

He pulled away, just enough that I could see the devilish smile at his lips. The dark, masculine hunger as he gazed down at me. My fist clutched at his shirt.

I realized the dressing gown had fallen open, exposing the thin slip I had worn to bed. The peaks of my breasts pressed against his chest, every breath shifting the fabric against the sensitive buds.

"Do your parents not notice you're gone?" I whispered.

He shook his head.

"You must be tired in the morning, spending the midnight here with me." Reaching up, I tucked a lock of his hair behind his ear, only for it to fall again.

He shook his head again with conviction. "You invigorate me."

My face heated, cheeks flushing, even if he couldn't see it in the dark.

Months of this, of sneaking around, of meeting each other on the other side of the city just to steal kisses in alleys, never able to go any further. My desire for him had only grown, day by day, since we met. It was driving me mad, my want. Every time we met, I wanted to bring him closer, as close as we could be. I wanted his mouth on me, everywhere. I yearned for him, in a way I'd never yearned for anyone before.

"I want you." The words came from me before I could stop them.

Something flickered in his eyes.

He knew what I meant. And I knew the desire burned in him too, had felt his arousal against me so many times, but was never able to touch him.

The hunger written on his face flared. "Are you sure?"

It would be fitting, to give him this, under the tree. The only place in the whole world that Adam and I were alone, well and truly alone. I nodded, anticipation already twisting my stomach, sending shivers through my legs and belly.

When he came to me, and we spent the hours baring our souls under this tree, speaking of inconsequential things, of his family, of his time at work the day before, the teas I attended during the same time, and how we both wished for more, longed for more, I knew I wanted no one else.

When I was with him, nothing else mattered.

"It feels like I've been waiting eons for you," he said, mouth finding mine once more.

I melted under him, tasting the sweetness of his lips, the feel of his strong frame under my hands, a slickness growing between my thighs. My desire building, untamed.

His fingers raced along my hips, my navel, pulling at my slip, the silky fabric gliding along my skin, over my hip, my flesh exposed to the cooling air. I gasped at the feel of his fingers wandering, having touched me everywhere else but— *here*.

A cry slipped from my lips as he found the sensitive spot right between my thighs, sending bolts of pleasure through me.

He smiled against my lips, supporting himself on one elbow while his fingers found my pleasure, drawing it forth, his touch light like a feather. My back arched involuntarily, the new sensations sending my heart into a whirlwind. I clutched at him, my mouth falling open.

No one ever had—

Something built up within me, his thumb brushing against that sensitive spot, circling, circling, pressing harder, until I bit down on my lip to suppress my cries. My hips moved on their own, chasing the electricity of his touch. Higher, harder, until I was shattering and withering and imploding all at once. A whimper stalled in my throat, my head falling back against the soft earth.

"Adam," I whispered, chest heaving, his hand slowing.

"Yes, darling?" His fingers moved lower, massaging, finding the wetness between my thighs. He inhaled deeply as his fingers found how ready I was for him.

"I want more."

In a moment, he reached for his trousers and was free. I stared at the hard length of him, the way his hand gripped himself and guided it toward my entrance. The soft, blunt head nudged against my sex, an entirely new sensation, and a drop of fear infiltrated my mind—what was I doing? How would that fit?—before he was pushing, pressing himself into me, stretching my flesh in a way I didn't know was possible.

I shut my eyes against the feeling, my fingers tightening against him.

There was no going back after this. If anyone knew—

I was ruined.

Good girls didn't do this, didn't let a man they weren't married to do this.

But I burned for him, a fire lit in my chest that wouldn't go out without him.

"Open your eyes, my love," he whispered. He held himself above me, hands on either side of my head, as he pushed further inside.

I gazed up at him. His eyes darkened in lust after that first inch, the band of muscles resisting the intrusion. Tight, so tight.

My thighs burned, forced open by his hips.

It was too much—I couldn't—

"That I am the first to do this—" he groaned, sinking deeper. "I was made for you, Helena."

I sighed my agreement, eyes fluttered closed again. Every inch, every ridge burned, heat tightening my thighs, clenching and unclenching against my will. A pain so exquisite. My back arched again off the ground, pressing closer to him. I muffled the cries that wanted to escape, panting, squirming, trying to find relief at the immense pressure of his body within mine. Wrapping my arms around him, I buried my face in his neck, tasting the salt of his sweat and biting lightly, muffling the sounds that wanted to escape against his skin.

"*Fuck*, Helena," he exhaled, falling upon me again. And then he was fully seated, my thighs wide open, ankles falling around his hips.

I burned. The intrusion was too much, intense and agonizing and sweet all at once. I shifted beneath him, moving my hip, and suddenly he was nudging a spot within me that sent electric sparks through my nerves. A cry slipped from my lips, reverberating against his throat.

He withdrew, slowly, just a bit, the dragging making my toes curl, before he thrust once, as far as he could go.

"It feels like you were made for me," Adam said against my neck. One of his hands found my breast, squeezing, rolling my nipple between his fingers. I arched against him, the only invitation he needed to continue, to begin moving.

I was a succubus overtaken. Every thought had left me, save that I was meant for this, for him.

How could something so pleasurable be so wrong? My thighs shook with the ecstasy of his movements, slow and soft, until my pain ebbed away, and my head fell back against the soil beneath the tree. His thrusts plunged deep, hard, quicker when he realized my core no longer resisted him.

Never before had I felt anything like this—

An electricity shot up my spine.

Yes, yes, yes.

I realized I was chanting the words, his name falling from my lips.

"Anyone could walk out of the house and find us," Adam said through gritted teeth, but when I looked at him, a darkness smoldered in his eyes. Like he dared anyone to try and stop him taking me like this. "Anyone could walk by and see what I'm doing to you."

I nodded absently, mouth falling open. My hands clutched at his hips, pulling him closer, deeper. Lucas didn't matter at this moment, my mother, my father—no one but Adam, plunging into me over and over again, saying without words how much we were meant for each other.

"I told you I would ruin you."

All along, I knew he would.

All along I knew this was what we raced towards. I knew our joining was inevitable; I knew that I wouldn't ever look at any man the same, because none of them were *him*.

Adam slowed his movements, his face falling closer to mine, searching for protest, for any sign of pain. Then he grinned. "I'm inclined to do this all night."

My hands rested on his chest, right over his heart. The organ beat strong, rapid, pumping blood against his skin. His heart, which beat for me.

Just as mine beat for him.

"We could," I said, breathless. "But then I really would be ruined."

He leaned down and kissed me again, this time gentler, sweeter, as sweet as the ache between my legs. His mouth trailed along my jaw, placing soft kisses against my cheeks, my brow, the tip of my nose. "My only regret is that I am too hasty. A girl like you should do this in a proper bed, at the very least."

"I don't care."

"You make me wild, Helena." Adam searched my eyes. "You make me want to damn the rest of the world just so we can be together."

I leaned up and nipped his jaw. "So why don't you?"

His throat bobbed, his eyelids lowering. "Brave words from a girl who's sullying herself with a working boy." He thrust harshly once, twice, covering my mouth with his hand as I gasped, muffling the sound. "You have everything to lose."

I wound my hands in his hair, tugging at the strands. The sharp intake of his breath as I pulled, biting back. I met his fierce eyes. "So do you."

What could only be a growl loosed from his lips, and he flipped us over, and sullied me over, and over, and over again under the tree, until his body was fused with mine and I couldn't tell where he ended and I began.

FIVE

I awoke with a startle, gasping for breath. The ornate plaster ceiling above me was dimly lit by the moon streaming through the crack in the curtains, and all was silent, save for—

"You're awake."

Lucas.

He eyed me from the vanity against the far wall as I scrambled back to the headboard, the sheets tangling around my legs.

My mouth ran dry. An ache had grown between my thighs at the dream, my body reacting to the memory, a cruel type of torture. A moment from the past when I was so, so naive, ignorant of what was to come.

Lucas had thrown his jacket somewhere, his tie missing, the open collar of his shirt revealing the column of his throat, a honey-blond curl falling across his face. In his hand was the rose. Deep eyes peered right through me. "Who gave this to you?"

"I—What?" Sleep still addled my mind.

He twisted the flower, the dark red petals spinning in a pretty pirouette, the stem seeming too delicate, too breakable in his fingers, even as he ran his fingertips along the thorns. "Sitting here on the vanity. A gift for you, I presume?"

My heart was pounding in my throat. "I don't know."

He hummed, gaze lingering on the petals, the stem twirling slowly in his grasp. "Sleeping well? Pulled you from a dream, did I?"

My face felt hot. "What are you doing in my room?"

Tilting his head, he discarded the flower on the vanity once more. "Making sure you're getting your rest, *sister*." His eyes flashed in the shadowed room, zeroing in on me, seeing *through* me.

The men had been gone all day, and I'd retired early after a dinner with Lucy and Lady Whitrow, during which I'd been on my best behavior to convince the baroness I belonged as perfectly as the ideal wife she'd imagined.

"I'm fine." The hair stood on the back of my neck. Though Lucas didn't move, the feeling of being cornered had alarm bells going off in my mind.

He cocked his head. Listening, I realized. "Are you afraid?"

"You just startled me, is all."

I knew Lucas, knew his M.O. If he saw me rattled, scared, he'd revel in it, push me further, see how far he could go. But if I spat back, I'd only fan the flames of his anger. It was best not to react—

Do not react.

Not even when he stepped closer, staring right at me,

hearing every single *thump* of my heart, the traitorous rhythm betraying the fear racing through my veins.

I couldn't hide my terror from him any longer. He'd always know better, his senses sharpened and *deadly*.

When had my brother lost his humanity?

"I'm fine," I repeated, hardening my voice. *Do not react.* "You can go now."

My hands were twisted in the sheet. My limbs itched to *move*, and I was eyeing the door between Wright's room and mine. I was not my betrothed's favorite, but surely he'd take offense to his wife being attacked.

"*Are* you fine? We haven't had a chance to speak in private, since...." Something darkened, the shadows falling over my brother's eyes. "Since you were taken."

As though I hadn't made the decision to leave it all behind, no, I *must* have been *taken* by Vince.

"I can only assume that some wool was pulled over your eyes," he continued, meandering around the room. "You were deceived, it seems. *I* was deceived."

Biting my tongue, I willed my body to relax, to focus.

If I screamed, I would alert every soul in the house.

But there was a small part of me that didn't want to bring attention to myself, didn't want to be *wrong*.

Lucas liked to intimidate me; this could've just been his usual slinging of threats, and if I made a scene for no reason—

"Vince Thornton. That's who you prefer?" Turning to me once more, Lucas was unreadable.

Did he know the truth, now? That Vince and the young man he'd forced overseas were one and the same?

He studied me for a moment, eyes flicking to my throat for the briefest second.

Revulsion rushed through me.

He was dangerous before as a mortal. Now—

"Were you dreaming about him?"

My instinct was to lie. "No."

"That sound you made only a few moments ago would suggest otherwise."

Flames heated my skin, but I wanted nothing more than to shout at him to leave. I bit my lip so hard I began to taste copper.

Do not react.

Lucas shook his head, running a finger along the wardrobe door, as though inspecting for dust. "You disappoint me, Helena. Running from your duties to dally with a man who can't give you anything, not really. His name means nothing, his wealth will run dry, and soon he'll be a laughing stock." He turned to me.

No, Lucas decidedly did *not* know.

"I can't pretend to understand why one would consort with the likes of him."

"Have you even met him?"

Malice. That was what gleamed in his eyes. "I have no need—not when he's made sure to twist his way into my life —*our* lives—for the better part of a year. Did you know that, sister? That your dear Thornton has been conniving all along?"

My teeth ached.

Didn't you know Vince is the one that told Lucas to marry you off?

He grinned then, sensing my unease. "Yes, it's true. Vince Thornton has been a thorn in my side for many months now. He thought he could manipulate me in such a way he'd take over our holdings—take *everything* from us, sister, do you understand? He'd see to putting us on the street."

"How?" I could hardly exhale the word, my lungs tight in my chest.

"The vagrant trades in information." Lucas' lip curled. "Things you wouldn't understand. Deals made by Father long ago—no matter. I thought my hands were tied, but things seem to be falling into place for the better, as it is. He wanted you married, though he never disclosed why. And knowing now how he's had his fingers all over you, it makes even less sense. Should he not want you for himself? Though, I am nothing if not amenable."

He smiled in a move that bared his teeth in the low light.

"Highsmith had been reluctant to shake on our deal until I threw you in. How convenient."

He leaned forward suddenly, palms flat against the bedspread. Only feet away now. "How does that make you feel, sister? That the man whose bed you climbed into cares nothing for you?"

Do not react.

The words sent waves of hurt crashing through my heart, doubts scratching at the walls of my mind. The wounds of a young girl accustomed to the harsh words of her sibling, weathering the onslaught of suspicion and barbs until she began to believe them.

Six years ago, I believed it was my fault. I believed that if I weren't so foolish, I wouldn't have condemned Adam to death. Questioned everything, questioned him, *myself,* wondering if I could really love him if I had been so careless?

It was my fault Adam and I were caught.

It was my fault Adam was sent to die.

"This is twice now, yes?" Lucas continued, fingers like claws on the bedspread. "Two failed lovers, and no doubt countless others to whom you've given yourself. All for what?"

"Why does it matter to you?" I bared my teeth right back. I had no misgivings that my brother cared for my heart.

"Because *you are a Quintrell*."

Was that incredulity in his eyes? The breath in the few feet of space between us stalled, stagnant and churning in the silence.

Something primal within me was acutely aware of the danger before me. Hackles raising at the minuscule twitch of his brow, I was a mangled hare in a trap, bones crushed and writhing and waiting for my death blow.

"How many times must I spell out my expectations?"

"Fine," I said, ignoring how dizzy I felt, how my palms dampened with sweat. "You do not have to worry for me anymore."

"Of course I must. We are blood. Though things have *changed*, we are still very much family, you and I. Your well-being is of the utmost importance, my dearest sister. And I cannot protect you if you refuse to play by the rules."

Nausea rolled in my throat.

Get out, get out, get out.

My eyes flickered to the door once more, the bitter taste of fear saturating my tongue. The little girl within me was cracking, panicking at being cornered, knowing what this monster of a man was capable of—wary of what he was capable of *now* as this creature. Only a few feet separated me from the door, from the freedom of the hallway. The door handle glinted, taunting me.

He could grab me in a second.

His lips pressed into a firm line as he pressed his weight further onto his hands.

He'd given me that look before.

"I am your guardian until I hand you off to your future husband. Have I not been kind to you? I've found you the most eligible man—who has said nothing of your tendency to open your legs. Perhaps he's eager, knowing what he does about your past."

"Is this your plan, then?" I said. "Marry me off so I never step foot back in New York? So you never have to see me again?"

He clicked his tongue. "Don't sound so upset. I will not be abandoning you immediately upon your marriage. What kind of a brother would I be? Mother would not approve."

"Mother's approval means little."

She would always hold her tongue, no matter what he did. She was old-fashioned and my brother was head of the family. What he decreed was law. I wasn't sure he *could* disappoint our mother if he tried, her darling boy.

"Perhaps," he said.

He hitched his knee on the bed.

"Do you intend to Make Wright, too?" I swallowed the lump in my throat. Anything to keep him talking.

Do you intend to Make me?

Lucas' blond hair was dull in the dim light, though

messy like he ran his hands through it a thousand times, the pomade long gone. Maybe a trick of the darkness, but I swore I saw a scratch at his jaw.

"I've offered." He said nothing else.

"And?"

Even though Wright had told me how he felt about Lucas' vampirism, I wondered if he had said something to the contrary to my brother.

A minuscule shrug. "He's uninterested," he said, with a hint of irritation. "He only wants money—our deal. His title. And *you*." Another grin. "Serve him well, and you'll be rewarded, dear sister."

I shut my eyes, perhaps the most foolish thing to do in the face of a monster. He always reveled in my discomfort, my pain, my anguish. He had seemed completely human only weeks ago, when he brought Wright to our family's home: no monstrousness in his eyes that hadn't been there before, no sharp teeth.

Had I been too new to this world of blood-thirsting creatures that I hadn't noticed? I'd only just reunited with Vince, had only just been introduced to the dark world which mingled with ours. Had my naivete masked the signs of Lucas' change?

"Do you fear me?"

"What?"

He shrugged a shoulder. "You're like a frightened little rabbit. Shaking in place and eyes darting around everywhere. And I haven't the foggiest why."

"You don't—"

"Get over it, Helena." His eyes burned, suddenly sharp

and deep and black. "If I wanted you dead, you'd be dead by now."

I blinked.

"Surely I am no threat to you when you've been consorting with vampires all along."

"Who is your Maker?"

But it was the wrong thing to question. Though before he'd been still at the foot of the bed, he turned rigid, and the pressure in the room dropped.

I knew this game. Knew what came next.

My eyes widened. I put out my hands as if to stall him. "I'm sorry, I didn't—"

He was above me in a second.

A scream stalled in my throat. Grabbing my shoulders, pinning me to the spot, he was inches away, fingers roughly digging into my skin.

"Do *you* want to be Made, sister?"

A faint red streaked from his lips to his jaw. Dried, smeared blood that had been wiped away in haste.

"I—"

"*Tell me.*"

I flinched. "*No.*"

"Do you honestly think I'd believe that? That you've been around Vince Thornton all this time and never begged him to Make you?" Lucas' eyes burned, something fierce flickering behind them. His voice fell an octave, like this conversation was a secret, even though we were the only ones in the room. "Did Thornton give you a choice? Or was he going to decide for you?"

My head was shaking, back and forth, denying, and my

hands were fists against his chest, pushing with all my strength, but my brother was too strong.

"Tell me, did Vince Thornton ever drink from you?"

"I—I don't see how that's any of your business." My fingers twisted against his shirt, but he was an immovable wall, muscle and bone as unyielding as concrete.

"That's not a denial, Helena."

My anger burned, becoming tears at the backs of my eyes, threatening to fall.

I will not cry in front of him.

I wanted to shout the truth, that Vince was Adam, and that Lucas wasn't successful in keeping us apart. We were inevitable, no matter how much Lucas tried. No matter what he did. I'd found Vince again. *We'd found each other.* He'd sent him off to a fucking *war* and Vince had come back, stronger, more powerful, than Lucas could ever hope to be.

Blinking away the tears, I steeled myself, and I never wavered in looking right back at him.

Satisfaction, awareness of his evolutionary superiority reflected in his stare. Amusement, gazing at me, eyes landing on that spot on my neck that Vince always sucked on, kissed, claimed.

Like he wanted to claim it for his own.

"Do you think I will hurt you?"

I willed my voice not to shake, to no avail. "I think you want to."

"Do not be afraid, my dearest sister."

And when he grinned, his teeth were sharp like knives and glinting in the lamplight.

Razor-sharp, I knew. And inches from my flesh.

He gripped my jaw. Something wet smeared against my cheek—blood? Had he pricked himself on the thorns of the rose? Or was he smeared in the blood of whoever he had bitten? His hold on me unforgiving, he wrenched my jaw back, baring my throat to him.

I could not fight him. I may as well have been pushing against a boulder.

"Quintrell."

Lucas froze.

And foolishly, I couldn't have been gladder to hear that voice.

Marcel Brancato stood in the doorway, one shoulder leaning against the frame. Still wearing his evening clothes, his hair boyishly ruffled, arms crossed. He only glanced at me for the briefest moment.

"Your thirst has been sated, has it not?"

Lucas' lip curled, almost imperceptibly. "There is no such thing for our kind," he said, voice low, a warning.

But Marcel was unfazed. "Highsmith and I had wondered where you'd gone. While I cannot fault you for wanting a taste—" His dark eyes flickered to mine again, and in them, I saw it—perhaps some inadvertent admission of truth. "There is much to discuss yet between the three of us, and Highsmith grows impatient. One more smoke."

For moments, nobody moved.

But then Lucas pushed away from me, standing from the bed, leaving me in a heap upon the blankets: a mortified corpse, hands in rigid claws, my knees curled toward my chest, as my brother straightened his shirt, smoothed back his hair.

The blood on his cheek was unmistakable now.

"Of course," he said drily. "Cannot keep him waiting."

He didn't look back at me once, not as he stepped around Marcel and left the room, not as his footsteps faded down the hall.

Marcel lingered. I knew he saw the blood that wasn't mine smeared on my cheek, knew he heard the terror arcing through my veins.

I couldn't stop the single tear from leaking down my cheek.

"This is your fault," I whispered.

The only sound was his exhale, a sigh, before I heard the door shut with a small *click*.

Six

"You must tell me everything!"

Lucy's arm was in mine as we ambled through the extensive gardens of the estate. The morning sun was settling into noon and the weather was fair. I had asked her to meet me as soon as she was able for a walk along the grounds, hoping in privacy I could check on my sister, find out what she'd been told—or *not* told.

She wore a pretty sky blue dress that highlighted the near-white blonde in her hair and allowed her stomach room. Every time she flashed me a smile, I saw Flora for the briefest moment.

I held on to her tight.

"There is so much to tell," I hedged, guiding us along the cobble path. It was a true British garden, with so many flowers I couldn't even recognize, expertly manicured to appear as though we'd stepped into the scene of a fairytale.

I'd not seen any rose bushes, yet.

"How was your trip?"

"Dreadful." The admission felt like a weight was lifted from my shoulders.

She frowned, her delicate brow furrowing. "The ocean is not kind."

I paused. "No, it's not."

Lucy went on, ignoring my hesitation. "It was quite dreadful when I came, too, you know. I was sick to my stomach for days and couldn't much move from my bed. When I arrived at Whitrow, it took me some time to return to normal." She laughed to herself. "As normal as can be, I suppose."

The lightness to her steps, the flush to her cheeks, the brightness in her blue eyes.

She couldn't know about the manner of creatures who really walked the halls of this estate. She couldn't know about her *husband*.

At the beginning, when she and Lucas were newlyweds, she spoke little. She had only begun to open up to me in the last few years.

She had not told me in her letters that she would be going to Whitrow; then again, I hadn't written her, or received any of her letters, since running away to Vince.

"Were you not on bedrest at home?" I asked.

"Yes, but Lucas said this was important, and sent me over ahead of time. He needed to find you, and told me that when he did, we'd reunite here."

"You're so far along," I said. "You could have delivered without him."

She gave me a sheepish smile, her lips the same rosy pink as her cheeks. "It was possible. But I would have been alright:

they have doctors that check on me every day, and Lady Whitrow has been very *attentive*."

She lowered her voice, like she was telling me a secret. "It's any day now, truly. The doctors have said within the next few weeks, I can expect the baby to arrive."

Lucy'd told me in a letter—Evelyn for a girl, after her grandmother, and Thomas for a boy, after my father.

"Are you afraid?"

Our chaperone—in case of emergency, of course—lingered almost out of sight, but close enough that I worried she'd hear. An older woman, with graying hair, though I hadn't been told her name.

Lucy's eyes twinkled. "Afraid that I will not be good enough. But I am eager to have it done with." Her hand came to rest on her belly. "It is near impossible to stay on my feet."

"Let's sit, then." I pulled her over to a wrought iron bench amongst some leafy shrubbery.

Our hands remained interlaced.

"They didn't want to let me out," she said after some time.

"'They'?"

"The doctors," she corrected herself. "They want me to remain in bed. But I can't when you've just arrived."

It'd been my selfishness that had requested her company. I could've very well sat with her in her chamber, albeit with the threat of listening ears. "Don't tire yourself for me. We can go back."

She waved a dismissive hand.

We sat in a comfortable silence, wispy clouds over the plains gently rolling in, the midday sun bright, a warmth against my skin amidst the spring chill. The vague, sweet scent of grass from the fields carried on the breeze. I shut my eyes. Imagined each puff of wind was Vince, his breath trailing along my cheeks, his fingers tangled in the loose strands of my hair.

I thought I knew longing before, when Adam, to me, was dead. There's something finite in it, in the permanence of not-having. In knowing what I desired most was lost to me forever. The ache in me now was unbearable, as suffocating as smoke.

"Where were you?"

Lucy pulled me from my reverie, her fingers tightening on mine. I turned to her, and found her looking intently at me, a sort of scrutiny in her eyes.

"Lucas won't tell me," she added.

Glancing around the garden, the chaperone was still so far I was sure our conversation was at least obscured. I loosed a breath, watching as flowers swayed, the trees rustling with the new growth of early summer. Thought on what I was going to say, how much I was going to admit. Finally, "I met someone."

Lucy brightened. "You fell in love!"

I shut my eyes at the stinging of new tears. "This marriage—" And then I was choking on my words, my voice stolen, and nothing came out.

She squeezed my hand again. "It will be alright."

We breathed in and out with the wind which twirled its fingers in our hair.

"Was it the same man as before?"

My lip suddenly wobbled and I felt like I was eighteen again, my whole world coming apart at the seams, Adam walking out of my life forever, to a fate unknown. "Lucas thought I was better suited to a baron."

"Yes. Well." Lucy softly lay her head on my shoulder. "No one can be the judge of *our* own happiness."

I glanced around again, watching the chaperone, wondering if anyone else wandered the garden that we could not see through the greenery. With the breeze and the whispering of the leaves, our voices were soft enough I was confident they did not carry.

"Has anything odd happened?"

It was an effort to ignore the grief constricting my heart.

She gave me a funny smile. "Anything odd? Like what?"

I shrugged. A bee whizzed by, landing on the bush beside us. "I don't know, this house just gives me the creeps. Doesn't it frighten you? Even a little?" I watched for her reaction.

"Maybe," she said, brow creasing. "It's just strange to us, is all. Whitrow is old and drafty, and we're not used to the sounds it makes, or the people."

"Yes, I've heard sounds."

"Just the house settling." Her hand idly rubbed her stomach. "It was a week before I could sleep through the night here. Don't worry."

She smiled at me so pleasantly that I knew nothing troubled her, nothing like the sounds I heard at night, nothing like the fact that her husband was no longer human.

She knew nothing.

I wished, for a moment, to trade places.

"Ladies."

The peace of our morning was quickly sucked away as my brother and Marcel came around a hedge. The corners of

Lucas' mouth were quirked upward, something of a dangerous smile pulling at his lips. His eyes did not go to his wife, but instead, to me.

The breeze around us whirled, as though a tempest were brewing, despite the sunny sky.

"I hope you are not tiring my wife with your stories," Lucas said. I knew his concern was a facade.

But I could not accuse him of this, couldn't turn Lucy against him. I could not take her husband away from her, not now, even when I wanted nothing more than to shove her into the nearest car and drive us far, far away.

He only wanted to keep her in the dark. And she only wanted him.

"We were just catching up." Lucy gave the men one of her brilliant smiles, instantly placating. "Did your morning meetings go well?"

"Fine enough." His eyes slid to hers.

"Highsmith sends his regards," Marcel said flatly.

"Let us get you inside," Lucas continued, offering his hand to his wife. "I don't want you getting a chill."

She laughed. "It's nearly summer."

"Your health is of the utmost. I insist."

Lucy glanced at me.

"Go rest," I said, forcing my lips to smile. "We can have afternoon tea together."

She slipped her fingers through Lucas' waiting hand, not noticing the ease with which he helped her stand, as though he were moving a ribbon or some other weightless thing. He gave the other vampire, then me, one last look before Lucy promised to call for me in a few hours, and then they were gone. I noticed the chaperone no longer lingered, having disappeared herself, leaving only Marcel and I, alone. No witnesses.

I took a steadying breath.

"How are you?"

Glaring at Marcel, I stood to make my way inside. "You do not have to pretend to care for my wellbeing."

"And if I'm not pretending?"

A dry laugh slipped from me. "Right."

"Quintrell worries what it will do to her if she finds out."

I increased my pace, my hands in fists at my sides. "He worries for himself, not for her."

"You are having difficulty sleeping?" He strode beside me, hands in his pockets, unfazed by the speed of my steps. I wouldn't be able to lose him in this garden.

I glared at him. "Were you eavesdropping?"

"I can help you with that," he purred, "With exhausting yourself, that is."

And suddenly I remembered the firm touch of his hands, the unkind caress, gripping my body to his; his lips on my neck, scraping his teeth along my pulse, dragging me away from my home, his tongue taunting in more ways than one.

But then the memory of Vince doing the same thing replaced the vision. For a moment, I let myself linger there—the space in my imagination that was full of only him, his kisses, his body, the sweet nothings he'd whisper into my ear. The promises he made me. The dreams we shared when we were so young. The secrets I told him that no one else knew, because Vince *was* my heart, and I could not keep anything from him.

Only, that was a lie. Conspiring with Veronica had been my biggest mistake.

I should've stayed with Flora that night. Should've done what I was told and stayed in place where it was safe and I was out of Marcel's reach. He couldn't have stolen me away if I hadn't gone to the masquerade. He couldn't have threatened Dixon with Flora's life. We would've stayed cocooned in her room, chatting until the sun came up and we grew too tired. The next day, Marcel would have been long vanquished, and I would have been free to return to Vince. To my happiness.

Could Marcel hear how my heart was torn in two, beating along despite the agony ripping me apart?

"Leave me alone," I said, throwing as much venom into my voice, despite the way it wobbled.

"You're thinking about it, aren't you? About what I could offer you?"

His words brought forth a chill to my flesh, as though it were suddenly the temperature of winter. My nails bit into my palms, bright arcs of pain.

"You don't have to be so unhappy, my dear. Marriage is only a contract. Highsmith does not have to own you entirely."

I stopped, whirling to face the damned creature. "You're asking me to betray my husband?"

Marcel laughed in earnest this time, exposing his sharp teeth. There was no one else around to hide them from.

His dark hair ruffled in the wind. "Has he earned your loyalty already?"

"I'll tell him," I said, narrowing my eyes. "I'm sure he'll

be happy to continue on with whatever deal you've struck after learning you've propositioned his *wife*."

But—*You only need to have one. Then you can take whatever man you'd like. So long as you're discreet.*

Marcel took one step closer until we were nearly nose to nose.

Then, a pause, a breath lingering in the space between us.

"Tell him."

I dare you hung unsaid in the air.

I dare you.

I dare *you*.

"What happened to his wives?"

Marcel's eyes widened almost imperceptibly, the only indication I'd surprised him. "His wives?"

"He's been married before. Twice."

He was silent for a second, studying my face. Then, an admission: "You are not his first wife."

"What happened?" I asked again.

He exhaled through his nose. I knew he was debating what to reveal.

But should I not have known? Shouldn't I have known everything about my future husband?

"Bit of advice: don't turn your back to him."

A non-answer. And a chilling one, at that.

"Is he not human? Seems like I only need to keep my eyes on *you*." I turned, scoffing, continuing on the stone path. I didn't want him to know how much this troubled me. "I am not scared of him."

He followed me again. "I am serious, Helena. It would be unwise to lower your guard."

"And then what?" I argued, ignoring the chill down my spine. "He's been avoiding me, hasn't he? I think our interest is mutual."

Marcel's fingers wrapped around my arm, pulling, and I was suddenly off balance, my toes tripping over the uneven stones. "Wright Highsmith will eat you up if you let down your guard," Marcel nearly growled.

Stunned, I saw only grave sincerity in his face and it frightened me.

"Rich, coming from a vampire," I said.

His eyes searched mine, and for perhaps the first time, I was eye to eye with this vampire.

He had helped me.

For some reason, he had helped me last night.

Help, if it could be called that.

"A warning for you, then."

Marcel leaned, towered over me, invading every bit of my personal space. Improper—if a servant came, if they saw how close he stood, if they saw how his face was only inches from mine, his breath fanning my lips—

"Highsmith is crueler than I suspect you know."

"And you've told me I don't know Vince."

His lip curled. "You *don't*. Both men are the worst of our kind."

"I'm surrounded by cruel men," I threw back. "Why should I listen to you? Are you any better?"

A fang glinted in the low light, his lip curling. "No, I'm not. But I at least don't play with my prey."

SEVEN

Silk sheets a cool caress, our limbs tangled together, his lips came to my neck, his body cradling mine from behind. He was warm—he was *never* warm anymore—as his hand came to my hip, fingers pressed into the soft flesh there. I was roused awake, pulled from whatever nightmare, I couldn't remember, because he was mumbling into the pulse below my ear, fingers circling idly on my waist.

I arched into him, reaching up and tangling my fingers in his hair, holding him to me, sighing as he whispered against my neck. The familiar feel of him, the command he had over me, my body. Knowing it was him without opening my eyes.

"I've missed you," he exhaled, his tongue dancing on my skin.

"Missed me?"

But he didn't respond, instead moving his body against mine, fitting us together like two halves to one whole.

Maddening, how he could draw pleasure from me, setting every inch of my skin on fire.

"You've missed me, too." He was slow, his touch roaming across me, teeth nipping. My flesh was eager, each breath sharp, and he knew it, knew just how to play me like an instrument, how to tune me to his liking.

"Yes," I breathed. Already forgetting the strange thing he'd said.

And then he was rolling me onto my back, hovering over me with those icy eyes. Blood already stained his lips, my blood, and I wasn't sure when he'd taken it from me, but I didn't care, wanted to pull him to me, let him drink it all. He was heavy between my legs, hungry.

I wrapped my arms around his neck, near-blind with need, but he did not lean closer.

He gazed down at me, his broad shoulders blocking all moonlight from the curtains, his figure a deep shadow before me. But in my hands, his flesh felt as unmistakable as my own.

"Patience," he chided, and I saw the dim light glint on his teeth as he smiled. "You are a needy thing."

"Please." I fisted my hands in his hair, hoping to spur him into action, pulling at the strands. He hissed, and I was rewarded with a swipe of his fingers right where I needed him most.

"Say it again."

"*Please.*"

Then he was upon me, his lips inches from mine. I took him in eagerly, locking my ankles around him, reveling in his teasing, knowing how this game ended; he was prolonging our pleasure, pushing us both to the point of madness, so that the breaking was that much sweeter.

His lips brushed mine. "Patience," he said again. And I did not understand, because I was already beneath him, we were already careening toward that agonizing finale. "Only a little longer, my darling."

I kissed him, let him swallow my cries, tasted myself on his tongue. He took his time, savoring every second. With the curtain of midnight, we were entirely alone—no gods to shine light upon us, no wretched expectations to answer to. And as he moved, his teeth pricking my skin just so, electricity shuddering through my skin, I knew we were destined —or doomed—to dance together, like this, for eternity.

"Wait for me," he said.

"Yes." I sighed, tumbling toward ecstasy.

"*Promise me.*"

There was no Earl Grey waiting in a steaming teacup when I awoke as the sun rose. No pastries left out on the table, no fruit. It was barely dawn, the curtains drawn closed, and a deep silence stretched out across the house. I had been jolted awake, coming-to quickly with a heaving gasp, but I could not remember why. Only that there was supposed to be someone laying next to me, and they were not, the lingering touches of a ghost left behind.

My arm stretched across cold linen sheets, as though feeling for the warmth of *him*. I had kicked the blankets into a tangle around my legs in my sleep. Shivering, I stood and reached for the dressing gown strewn across the vanity chair.

The rose sat upon a mound of its own petals. Taunting me, mocking me.

My skin was too tight, my breaths coming in short pants. I couldn't get enough air into my lungs. My throat ached, my eyes felt swollen with tears.

And all I wanted to do was scream.

The door connecting Wright's suite to mine glared back at me from across the room. It was locked—I'd tried it before I went to sleep.

He could get into any room he wanted. I stared at the door. Waiting for the handle to turn.

He hardly looked at me at all since we'd arrived. It was torture, waiting for him to turn his attentions to me.

My throat itched with the urge to shriek, to stop shoving down my misery.

I threw open the heavy curtains, gasping for fresh air. The latch on the window was broken. I was trapped inside.

Do not cry.

I could make out the vague forms of the little houses of the village down the hill, gray smoke rising from the hearths, people starting their days of work, and distantly I thought I'd have turned out a lot better if my life was that simple.

I wanted to believe Lucy, that I was the beholder of my own happiness. I wanted to believe that I could make my escape, that I could bring her with me, and we would find our happinesses elsewhere. How simple a life we could have, if she and I could run away to some far corner of the earth, sisters once more, raising the child in her womb, so that it only knew softness. So that it could grow into a little girl with beautifully foolish dreams, none the wiser to the cruelty of the world.

But I knew my brother, knew the kind of men that he and Wright Highsmith were, and knew that they feasted on girls like us. We were an afterthought, an object for their appetites. Soft flesh to bite into, to bruise and mar.

In the growing light, my doom felt imminent.

It was only a matter of time before Lucas turned those teeth onto me, before Marcel decided he was done waiting for a taste.

And suddenly tears were falling. A visceral pain spider-webbed through me, starting at my breastbone and spreading to my fingertips.

Vince.

I should've listened to the Fates when they tore us apart. Now we were tangled up with vampires playing god, testing the boundaries of the threads that tied us together. Andreas, Marcel, Lucas.

I'd brought this heartache on myself.

But my heart sang for him. It bled for him now.

Promise me, he had said.

He'd made me swear to return. When I found him in the garden, when I finally gave myself to him again after six long years, I'd promised to come back to him. To let him back in.

But did I really even have a choice?

My knees met the plush rug, and I crumpled, gasping for breath. Sobs wracked through my bones, my tears blurring the image of my hand below me. Everything surfaced, every doubt I'd had these past weeks, every moment of pain, every tear, rushing past like a broken dam, until I was powerless against the onslaught.

I could not quiet myself, lungs heaving, my pathetic cries echoing in the room until I was sure someone would come knocking. Wright could no doubt hear me on the other side of that door.

But minutes passed, and no one came.

I pressed my cheek to the rug, my face wet, swollen. Shattering into pieces, my heart was cleaved into two, my limbs impossibly heavy. I wanted to melt. To shut my eyes and never open them back up to this horror I was living.

Happiness seemed forever out of reach—something I'd never find again.

Wait for me.

It felt so real. The warmth of his breath, the heady intoxication of his kisses. I cursed my psyche for conjuring up such a cruel dream.

I might never see him again if these three men had their way.

How easy it would be to give up. To let my brother sign me away to Wright. A life stuck within these halls. Marcel's offer—

No. I could not do this.

I'd die here. I would find my demise just as Wright's other wives. I would become a doll for him to show off, a shell of myself, only a cold husk while all the flesh and blood within me dried up.

It'd been nearly two weeks since I'd been taken. Two weeks of wondering where Vince was, if my friends were alive. Two weeks of waiting for these men to finally rip me apart—because it *would* happen. Lucas' slip in restraint made it blindingly clear.

But Marcel had stopped him. Had warned me about Wright. Insisted that Vince was not who he said he was.

It didn't make sense.

And I was tired of being subjected to the whims of these men. Of being left in the dark with no say.

The fury burned hot, roiling inside of me and wanting to claw its way out, a frustrated scream building up in my throat. This dangerous grief, this dismal rage, that was demanding to be let loose. It had always been there, lingering in the fibers of my being, even as a young girl. With each passing day, it grew inside of me, feeding off my misery, until it was a veritable parasite, making its home deep in my lungs, my bones. Soon it would take me over.

Soon, I could not be faulted for unleashing this fury.

And I was not sure that I wanted to push it down any longer.

Only when I could shakily fill my lungs, only when my weeping abated, did I right myself from the floor. I was a mess of tears, swollen eyes, shuddering breaths. My skin pebbled from the cold morning air. When I glanced at the clock on the wall, it was well past the time Anna usually came in—early enough the family was likely not yet awake, but late enough that the sun had crested the horizon.

I pushed to my feet, wobbling on unsteady knees.

The rose lost another petal as I plucked it from the vanity. The edges were drying, a soft rasp on my skin.

It'd come from someone in the house.

It was not Wright, that much I knew.

Leaving only one other possible culprit.

My fingers tightened over the bud, crushing the velvet petals in my fist, and I squeezed, and squeezed, the sharp points of the stem digging into the flesh of my palm, squeezing until my fist shook. Imagining that like a voodoo doll, he'd feel the pain of being crushed, too. I didn't notice the drop of blood until I dropped the rose once more, each petal raining down from my fingers in a cascade of deep burgundy. A line of red seeped from the center of my palm, dripping onto the scattered petals.

How easily I bled. They made me think that my blood was something precious, something to be coveted, when so easily could I slice open my skin and bring it forth.

When I rang the bell to call for Anna, it took some time for her to arrive. She rushed into the room, a muttered apology on her lips, as she set about drawing the curtains, pulling my dress from the wardrobe. She said nothing of the destroyed flower, or my reddened eyes, or the towel I clutched to staunch the blood, as she brushed through my dark hair and applied a soft rouge to my cheeks, probably hoping I'd not comment on her tardiness.

I avoided the gaze of the girl in the mirror—I didn't want to see the grief clouding her eyes, the pitiful state she was in.

As I left my room for the morning, Anna following closely behind, I hesitated at the sound of another door clicking shut, the soft sound echoing amongst the otherwise silent hall.

Wright paused, and so did I.

Our eyes met.

But then his gaze slipped past me, to Anna, who had just exited my room. She flushed under his stare, cheeks reddening, a sort of girlish blush, before she quickly turned away. Scurried off like a mouse under the eye of a hawk.

After a moment, my soon-to-be husband cleared his throat. "Heading to breakfast?" he asked me, and it was the most cordial thing he'd said to me since we'd met. He had shaved all but the thin mustache on his lip, his hair gelled back, dressed as though he planned to go out to the town today. He was the image of an aristocratic man who had nothing to worry over; no distress over his dying father, somewhere else in the house, no distress over the monsters that he'd invited in.

"I am."

I was tempted to ignore his proffered arm, but I accepted, sliding my hand along his forearm, keeping him close, and wanting to do nothing more than to dig my talons in. He seemed pleased, and our walk to the dining room was blessedly silent.

What he must have mistook as my acquiescence, my quiet obedience, was truly the moment I realized what I had to do: I came to the conclusion that if one of us would not escape this marriage alive, it would be him and not I that would meet his demise.

EIGHT

I snuck away after breakfast, when the rest of the inhabitants of Whitrow were occupied. The house seemed too large during the daylight hours. Empty halls and silent rooms, save for the servants ambling about, polishing silver, dusting every fixture. Outside, the sky was a deep gray, clouds having rolled in after sunrise. The only sounds accompanying me were those of my breaths, my footsteps along the rugs.

Wright must have had a study, a smoking room, *somewhere* I could find the contract between him and Lucas.

Just what had my brother traded me for? What was I worth?

One million dollars?

I only made it as far as the first door of Wright's wing, about to try the doorknob, when I felt eyes boring into my back.

"Lost, Helena?"

Marcel stood a few paces behind me, hands in his pockets. His dark hair was a bit untamed, as though he hadn't cared to do much else this morning other than run his fingers through it a few times. He looked at me with hooded eyes, glimmering with an inkling of smugness.

My heart skipped a beat at having been caught. "I was looking for the library."

He sauntered closer, his eyes never leaving mine. "Of course."

He could see right through me, I knew it.

"Will you show me where it is?"

"Trying to slip away with me alone?" He grinned, showing off his sharp teeth.

I rolled my eyes. "No, but I suspect you won't leave me alone now."

"Smart girl."

He led me away, slowing his pace so he could remain beside me. We passed no one as he brought me to a set of doors, painted a creamy white color, down an entirely different wing of the house. He pushed open the doors, holding them open for me to pass in front of him, and I could not ignore the fact that I was secluding myself with him in the quietest part of the house, this vampire who'd aided my brother and my betrothed in finding me.

"Now what's in this library that you are looking for?" He let the doors fall shut softly behind him.

"Nothing in particular."

I ran my fingers along the gilded spines on a shelf. General history books, a collection on ancient philosophers, some of the Romantic poets, all pristine and in their place. No layer of dust, even though I didn't think the books had been disturbed in years.

"I'd like to find something to read to pass the time."

There were shelves lining the walls, broken up by large windows overseeing the lawns on the far side. An unlit fireplace, a few dark emerald couches, unlit lamps stationed around the room. All seemingly for show, this collection of literature, and not for reading.

"Liar." Marcel had not stepped further into the room, watching me wander from shelf to shelf.

I read each spine, feeling foolish—there would be nothing in here to answer my questions. I was wasting time.

I faced him. "Who were you before the war?"

If I did not know my enemy, I could not move against him.

One of his brows arched, surprised, before he stepped closer, the shuffling of his feet sounding unbearably loud, and I wondered if he could hear my racing pulse. "Are you sure you want to know? Don't you want me to remain an enigma?"

"I asked, didn't I?" I didn't look away from his deep brown eyes, finding the flecks of amber within them.

He studied me for a moment. "You want something."

He only stopped once he was a few feet away, close enough to reach.

"I could have answered your questions there in the hall. What is it you *really* want?"

It was comical, looking up at him, and thinking about the man I'd met in a speakeasy not so long ago. He'd introduced himself almost as soon as Flora and I had walked through the door, insisting on buying me a drink, finding a table for us to talk. He'd known who I was, then—he'd known who I was to Vince.

He had been the one to find me first.

"Well if I am to keep you around," I paused, hoping he would hear the implication in my voice, "then I want to know more about you."

He could not hide the hunger in his eyes. He'd stopped my brother, he would not attack me now.

Right?

Or was it some sense of jealousy, some ownership he felt over me, that had him stopping Lucas from taking my blood?

I hummed, stepping around the corner of the shelf, eyes racing along the blur of letters, the different colored spines.

In a moment, he appeared at the end of the row, having moved across the room in a blink. Stood blocking my path.

"If you don't indulge my curiosity now, I will figure you out eventually," I said, forcing my voice not to waver. I gazed at him through my lashes. "You've gotten to know me, it's only fair."

His eyes gleamed from his spot at the end of the shelves, hands still in his pockets, but his jaw clenching as he mulled it over. "Fine. I was aged 26 years before my mortal life was taken from me. Second in line to inherit my family's estate before I was sent to die. Second-Made of Andreas, and now his heir, after we were abandoned by Thornton."

He stepped closer with every word.

"Does this sate your curiosity?"

"A bit."

He laughed low in his throat. "A bit? What, you want to know how many men I've killed? You want to know exactly how I died during the war? You want to know if there were any girls I fell in love with when I was still human?"

I flinched. I'd almost forgotten how cruel he could be.

His poor parents. And they didn't even know he was alive. Don't worry, Helena. I relieved them of their problem.

He stepped closer. "Or should I tell you about how I came from wealth? Though I was not a direct heir to my family's fortune—my brother was to inherit control of the fortune."

Lowering his voice to a murmur, so close—*too* close. "In another life, it could be *me* marrying you, not some English aristocrat."

I did not move as he stalked closer. "I would never marry you."

His eyes narrowed. "I quite think you find me just as interesting as I find you." His gaze flickered to my lips.

Everything within me recoiled, a heat blooming in my chest. "Perhaps in a morbid way," I glared. I was acutely aware that he blocked my way to the door. "You could kill me. It is a prey's interest in its predator. It's precautionary."

"Or something else."

He kept encroaching on my space, scrambling my focus until I was dizzy and discombobulated. I felt his finger and thumb at my chin, lifting my gaze back to his. "Tell me: do you wish for some power of your own?"

I shook my head, ignoring him. I needed to make him *talk*. "You have a lot of explaining to do."

"Do I, now?"

"You've brought me here. You've forced me into—*this*. You've made many claims. But you haven't explained any of them."

His eyes gleamed. "Such as?"

Anger coursed through me, my temperature rising. I

wanted to kick something, to throw one of these books at his head. "That Vince is behind all of this."

He smirked at the reminder of what he'd said before. His dark hair shined black in the sunlight filtering through the windows, almost a deep purple. "Ah, yes. That."

"If you're only going to waste my time, I'm leaving."

"What is there to explain? Vince Thornton is a grand schemer, a puppet master."

The urge to call him a liar burned in my throat. I bit my tongue. "You said Vince was paying my brother off, telling him to find me a husband." And Lucas had said as much.

Marcel nodded once, eyes skimming over me, inspecting me, *watching* me think about that night when he'd stolen me away from my one chance at happiness.

And he was telling me Vince was behind it all.

"Why would he do that?"

"Why do you think?"

I shook my head. "This doesn't make sense."

"You're a smart woman," he said, leaning forward, as though he was waiting for me to figure it out. "Think about it. It made you run to him, did it not?"

I hadn't stopped shaking my head. I forced my fingers straight from the fists they'd become, pressing them against my legs, my palms damp against the fabric of my skirt. "But how could he possibly know I would do that? How would Vince *know*?"

Marcel's eyes flicked to my chest for the briefest moment. To my heart. "Even I know what you would do."

He cocked his head to the side, dark locks falling boyishly over his face. "Would you not run to him now, if you could?"

"Of course I would."

But Vince wasn't here. In New York, the choice was simple, even if I had not realized it at the time: stay in my family's house and follow through with the engagement, or return to my love. I'd just been too afraid to run away. Vince showing up at my window was all I needed to realize that continuing on as I was meant heartache.

"That doesn't mean it was orchestrated."

Marcel waved a hand. "Believe what you'd like."

"How do you even know this?"

"Your brother made it clear to me how deep his hatred for Vince Thornton burned after he began draining Lucas' coffers dry. And I just so happened to know where Thornton lived. So, I offered my services."

The million-dollar reward had been a taunt, I knew that. Just like Lucas loved to taunt me, to torture me, to keep truths from me just to watch me squirm. But it hadn't been just for me—the message in the paper was for Vince too, that the game was up.

And Marcel had shown up just days later.

"You were the one to tell Lucas where I was. He knew all along."

Marcel lifted a shoulder. "You could say that."

"What do you even get out of this?" I demanded. "Why meddle?"

"Meddle?" He laughed again, but this time it fell flat. "I'm not *meddling*. I'm eliminating a problem."

The problem being—Vince? *Me?*

"Has it occurred to you *why* we're crossing the great pond?"

I swallowed the lump in my throat. "So Wright can marry me. So their deal does not fall through."

Marcel hummed. "Perhaps that's their goal, yes. But he could've forced your hand in marriage in New York."

My mouth went dry.

Whatever he was about to tell me, I did not want to know.

"Your soon-to-be husband will join us. He may be reluctant yet, but your brother will convince him soon. Think of it: the Whitrow Baron, a *vampire*. The Whitrow legacy—its power—immortal."

I was shaking my head, denying it all, my back running into the bookcase again, even as he drew closer. Trapping myself like the foolish girl I was. *I shouldn't have let him lead me in here.*

"I don't understand." Denying what Marcel was implying, denying the *truth*.

"My coven is small. An alliance between the Highsmith line and my coven—"

"Between the Highsmiths and Andreas?" The weight of it was immense, the possibility of so many vampires essentially allied against us—against Vince, against my friends back home.

Marcel's lip quirked, a manic gleam rising in his dark eyes.

Andreas wanted to establish a hierarchy. A crown. To rule over the undead amongst the living.

"A united front: your brother with his American connections, Highsmith with those in Parliament that may be willing, and myself. Imagine what we could do."

Our noses were nearly brushing now, his hands resting

against the shelf on either side of my head. I was trapped. I could not run, though everything within me told me to get as far away from him as I could.

But I could only stare at him, frozen.

"Your lover is a problem," he spat the word *lover*, "if I am to build Andreas' legacy."

"Just leave us alone, then." I pleaded, whispering, gripping the front of his shirt. "Bring me back home. We won't bother you."

"I cannot tell you what Vince's end goal is," he continued. "But I can tell you that there's a reason Andreas made him into what he is."

"And what is he?"

Marcel stared at me.

A monster.

I'd seen it well that night. Dark veins, black eyes. Some grotesque creature behind the mask, unveiling itself.

But when Marcel spoke again, he didn't voice what I was thinking, didn't mention the beast that we'd both seen at the masquerade. "Vince Thornton is not only playing as the Sire of a coven in America; he was once to be the head of another in France, as I'm sure he told you. He would be the head, now, if he hadn't left. But he did, and now he's gone and made his old coven *very angry*."

This had to be another lie.

But had Marcel lied to me at all?

He'll be glad to know you're doing so well.

"But—Andreas—he's the head of the coven."

Marcel shook his head. "No longer." A smile pulled at his lips again, something darkening in his eyes.

With the words, it was as though the air rushed out of the room.

"It's hard for a man to lead when he is not attached to his head. I do not think he even realized what happened to him before he fell into that great sleep."

He grinned now, sharp teeth shining, like he was brandishing a knife at me.

"Ah, because Vince *abandoned* us, left us all alone so he could run to *you*, the responsibility to lead fell to me. An honor I graciously accepted."

My blood ran cold.

Andreas was *dead*.

I stared at the vampire across from me with wide eyes, perhaps seeing the *true* predator that lingered below his charming exterior, the thirst that always simmered in the dangerous glint of his stare. He was just as dangerous as Lucas, whether he had attacked me or not. He'd been taunting me for my blood since the beginning.

To forget that I was unsafe around all three of these men was to guarantee my doom.

What had Marcel done?

And now he was scheming to take over a whole aristocratic human family line—aiming to convince and turn their heir into a vampire—would they turn *me*?

When Marcel had first come to Vince's to taunt us, he'd spoken as if Andreas was still alive, the threat of his wrath looming.

But how long had he really been dead?

"How can I trust anything you say?" It was all too much.

"Trust me, or don't." He shrugged. "But do remember that I am an honest man."

Honest. I wanted to laugh.

"Vince doesn't know," I said.

Marcel glanced around the room, indifferent. "If he did not know when I last spoke to him, then surely he does now."

"Then *he's* the one in charge."

A muscle twitched in his jaw. "No."

"If Andreas is dead, then Vince is the leader of your coven—"

"*No.*" The word echoed in the room, too loud for the small space. "He abandoned his duty."

"But—"

"I have the whole coven behind me, now. Twenty men. If he dares to show his face—" The shelf groaned behind my head, Marcel's fingers digging into the wood. "It will not end well for him. Or for you, I suspect."

I shoved against his chest, almost surprised when he fell back a few steps.

"He'll find me again," I said. "Or *I* will find him."

Whatever understanding we'd come to shattered between us.

"Perhaps I've been too *kind.*" He spat the word like it was a curse, anger burning in his eyes, but his voice dangerously low. "Your lover will not survive this. I will make sure of that, *personally.* And it is up to *you* whether you join him or not."

NINE

SIX YEARS AGO

The apartment was on the second floor of the four-story building on the East Side.

I'd gotten plenty of looks walking down the streets after hopping off the trolly. Wearing my plainest clothes, trying not to bring attention to myself. But this wasn't my neighborhood, and I must've looked like an outsider. I couldn't tell Mother where I was going, of course.

There was no doorman, just a hall that led to individual apartments and a slim staircase at the end to the next floor. The walls weren't painted, the plaster chipping along door frames and at the ceiling, where bare bulbs flickered dimly in the setting sunlight. No windows in the hall, either.

It was quiet, save for the sound of a baby crying behind one of the doors. The noise of the street was gone once the front door shut behind me.

I made my way to the staircase. Entirely out of my element, I felt like an intruder. Like someone would poke their heads out and tell me I didn't belong there. And perhaps it was true—I *didn't* belong here, and it was obvious.

Each door had a number nailed to it, with a name scrawled underneath on a piece of paper, some nearly illegible.

The stairs creaked beneath my feet. Butterflies danced in my stomach, the anticipation of seeing him, surprising him, yet the nervousness of being unwelcome. What if his family didn't like me? He'd hardly told me anything about them, just that his mother stayed home sewing and mending clothes, and his father worked in one of the factories. Would they even be home?

It was the first door to the left of the landing.

Vering was written in a feminine hand. Maybe his mother's.

The sound of my knocking made me cringe. Too loud, echoing down the hall, loud enough it seemed to alert the neighbors.

I didn't have long to worry about it, because the door opened just an inch.

And there he was.

A smudge of ink still dirtied his cheek, his hair wild. Only half his face appeared from the small opening, a chain across the door. Instantly, the smell of something savory wafted into the hall.

His eyes widened. "Helena?"

"May I come in?"

He stared at me for a moment, and it hit me, what this looked like. Me, a girl in a pressed skirt, a clean blouse, my hair braided into a crown on the back of my head. No dirt stuck under my nails, or staining the hem of my skirt. Knocking on the door of a working boy.

His family wasn't expecting me. *He* wasn't expecting me.

I shouldn't have done this. Absentmindedly, I took a step back as if to retreat.

Adam said nothing for a moment, his brow furrowed in shock.

"Who is it?" A woman's voice came from inside.

He unchained the door and tentatively opened it wider to reveal who could only be his mother. Hair a mousy, reddish-brown, graying, tied back but frizzy after the long day, her light eyes peered up at mine. She couldn't have been any taller than five feet.

"Who's this?" she asked again.

Adam's mouth opened, closed.

My face flushed. *This was a mistake.* "I'm sorry to intrude. I'll just get going—"

"No." The single word came out as a command, his voice firm and almost booming in the small hall. "Ma, this is... Helena."

"Oh." Her eyes widened, gleaming with life. She had a slight accent I couldn't quite place. "Would you like to come in for dinner?"

"Oh—"

"No. We were just going." Adam stepped out into the hall next to me.

"Going?" I asked.

"I forgot," he said to her. "I told her we'd go out."

A lie.

"Alright." She nodded, shuffling back into the apartment. From what I could see, it seemed small—the door opened into the kitchen, with a simple wooden table, where vegetables sat half-chopped and a pot boiled on a stove. "Bring her back sometime, your father would like to meet her." She gave her son a look, then shot me a close-lipped smile. There was kindness there, but a wariness too in the way she glanced me up and down. She turned to the pot on the stove and stirred. "Don't get into trouble," she threw over her shoulder.

I realized then, watching her hunch over the stove, I hadn't cooked a thing in my life.

"Of course," he said through his teeth, pulling the door shut behind him. He clutched his cap in one hand, running the fingers of the other through his hair. It shined red in the dying light.

"I'm sorry—"

"What are you doing here?"

My heart dropped. The accusation in his words struck me. He looked down at me, a wrinkle between his brows, mouth pressed into a firm line. He'd never looked at me like that before.

"I thought you were scared your brother'd find out?" he said, leading me down the hall, fingers encircling my arm.

"I am." It was a fear I never stopped thinking about. "I didn't—I'm sorry, I just wanted to see you. Your boss—"

He shook his head, a muscle ticking in his jaw.

I wrenched my arm away. "What's wrong with you?"

He blinked like I had struck him.

"I thought you'd be happy to see me. I thought—" Emotion welled up in my throat, a lump that made it hard to swallow. I was so suddenly and so wholly racked with rejection, it made my fingers tingle.

His hands hovered in the air, stalling between us, as though to reach for me. They turned to fists. "I am," he said, softer this time, his shoulders falling.

"Maybe I shouldn't have just shown up, maybe I should've told you, but—"

Suddenly his hands were on me again, gentle, pulling me closer. He smelled of ink and some chemical—he smelled like *him*. The way he always did when we met in the evenings. "I'm always happy to see you. I just—I wasn't expecting you, is all."

I shut my eyes, forcing the emotions away. Distinctly remembered him showing up unannounced on my street corner a few months ago, too eager to see me.

Adam sighed, his thumbs skimming across my cheeks. "There's not much to see, and my mother will only bore you with her chatter."

A not-so-small part of me crumpled in disappointment, a weight settling in my chest, that Adam didn't want to show me his life, his family, the place where he lived. Somewhere in that apartment was a bed, solely his, that probably smelled like him —were the sheets rumpled? Did he straighten the covers every morning? Did he shove his shoes half-under the bed frame, did his clothes hang in a wardrobe? We'd been seeing each other for months, and I hadn't yet even glimpsed his home. And the first time I meet his mother, I'm ushered away.

This was a mistake.

Adam saw it, a sort of displeasure darkening his features, but he linked his arm with mine and steered me back down the hall, guiding me down the slim staircase once more. The baby had stopped crying.

"Why don't we go for a walk?"

I said nothing, my thoughts spinning, tumbling in my head, wondering how I'd made such a mistake, how I hadn't realized that I was intruding, how I hadn't realized Adam wouldn't want me here.

"Hey."

His palm came to my cheek, gentle but rough all at once.

When I looked up at him through my lashes, he gave me a boyish half-smile, donning his cap and covering his dark messy waves.

"I'm glad to see you."

"Are you?" I asked, before I could stop the words.

"Of course."

"Are you, really? Because—"

"Stop," he breathed, shoulders falling, an exhaustion pulling them down. "Do you hear yourself?"

The front door at the end of the hall opened, and an old man stepped through. He paused when he saw us, and Adam cringed, like we'd been caught, before the man turned to a door and went inside, wordless.

Adam turned to me again, and suddenly we weren't just eighteen; a tiredness darkened his eyes, a grit shadowing the planes of his face. A small scar, almost too small to see, sat upraised next to his left eye—how had I not noticed it before? His shirt was worn, the leather of his belt cracked, and he still wore the same trousers from work with stains from the ink he wiped on his thighs.

"Do you think I wouldn't *want* to see you?"

There was concern there. An anger, almost, that I'd even assume as much.

"I just—" I started, then lost the words, sighing in frustration. "I'm sorry."

He shook his head. "Do not apologize for wanting to see me," he said. His eyes found mine, his fingers tightening on mine in a squeeze. "Do not apologize for wanting me. *I* will never apologize for wanting you."

According to men like Lucas, people like my family, like those in the society Flora and I dined with, I was off-limits to someone like Adam. Him touching me with those hands, stained with ink—I was sullied, that's exactly what it was. No one in our circles would ever want to marry me. Lucas' own reputation would be tarnished. Flora might be forbidden by her parents to see me. Mother would likely send me away to a distant relative in the north.

But the more we met, the further in love I fell with him, the less I cared.

I worried only what Lucas would do to Adam if he found out.

"I love you," I said, the words coming so easily, so simply.

Adam's eyes bounced between mine, searching, finding that I meant it, incredulously, even after all this time.

"I love you," I said again, "and I don't want anyone else."

The small smile he gave me, the easy lilt to his lips, made me want to throw my arms around him. "I only ever think about how I love you," he murmured, his hands falling to my hips.

I wanted him to pull me into an alley and ravish my neck with his kisses. I wanted him to hitch up my skirts and find how much I wanted him. I simply melted in his arms, under his soft, boyish gaze, the dimple in his cheek threatening to appear.

"You take up all my thoughts," he continued, leaning down, lips skating across my jaw. "I can't go a moment at work without thinking about you. About wondering where you are, who you're with. And thinking that if another man ever tried to win your hand, I'd kill him."

A laugh burst from me at the shock of his words. "How violent."

His fingers tightened. "I love you, violently. Completely. With my whole being, my whole heart." He grabbed my hands, flattening my fingers against his chest. "This, it beats for you. Only for you. So one day I can take you somewhere where no one else dictates what we do."

One day. Would it ever happen?

He had no money. I could devise a plan to cash some checks from Lucas' accounts, and get us as far as I could with it. Morocco, maybe. Some city along the Rhine. And we could change our names, and give ourselves some wonderful backstory, so no one could find us. He could be a world-renowned author, and I his muse, and we would be honey-mooning around Italy in inspiration for his next novel. And anytime someone asked about his work, we'd say he wrote under a pen-name, and they should guess which big name he was.

It all flashed before my eyes, images of us elsewhere, notions of a life that didn't exist.

When I blinked, it was all gone, and the ink was still smudging his cheek, and his arms were still around me.

"We should run away," I whispered.

He grinned. "Just say the word."

"I'm serious."

"I am, too." He kissed me, over and over, drawing giggles from my lips. "I'll go anywhere with you."

"But—" I exhaled a sigh as his lips found the sensitive spot under my ear.

"Let's plan it." Another kiss. "Let's make a plan, and in six months, we'll be out of here."

It was nice to dream, to imagine that wonderful life.

"What of your parents?"

"What of them?" He pulled away from me, a sort of frenzy in his eyes. "What of *your* family? Have they not held you back enough?" His desire was written all over his face, not just for me, but for the prospect of leaving, of changing this situation we found ourselves in. A sort of dark gleam in his cloud-gray irises.

I bit my lip.

Maybe in another world, another universe, we could marry. Lucas wouldn't care. And I'd be taken care of, even if Adam didn't come from money. No expectations, just bliss.

But in this world, it was impossible. It would be like asking to fly, willing my feet to hover off the ground and carry me into the air. It simply could not be done. Not in this world where my mother let my brother decide my future, and Adam could so easily be another man in our family's factories.

I placed my hands on his cheeks, the end-of-day stubble scratching my palms, and pulled him toward me, kissing him softly. His lips molded to mine, a familiar dance, his hands tightening on my waist.

"Just say the word," he murmured against my lips.

I didn't know how to tell him that I felt a ticking time-piece looming over me, counting down the days, the seconds —only, I was not sure how much longer we had left.

TEN

Preparations for the wedding were complete, and Lady Whitrow kept me busy fussing over the details, though I didn't have much to say about the bouquets and arrangements she had delivered, didn't care to argue about the dinner menu. She was more than happy to mold the wedding to her liking, as though it were her own and not her son's, though he hadn't cared to give any guidance, either. It was to be an extravagant affair, and the few guests had already begun arriving, settling into the spare rooms, keeping the servants busy from one end of the house to the other.

The dress was fitted, snug against my breasts and loose and flowing down my legs. Only once had I donned the veil, the headpiece, the satin slippers. Lady Whitrow insisted on making sure the whole ensemble was to her liking.

I couldn't bring myself to look at the gown in the mirror, at my figure dressed up like a bride—someone *else's* bride.

It was a betrayal to Vince.

It was a betrayal to the boy I fell in love with six years ago.

I was marrying another man, and I still had no idea how I'd get out of this. I knew what Wright expected of me on the wedding night, if he wanted an heir so soon. Bile rose in my throat at every reminder: that look Lady Whitrow would give me whenever my duties as the future Baroness were the topic of conversation, how eager she was to have "young ones" in the house.

And Wright avoided me most of the time, only speaking with me at meals; he was seemingly busy with his duties as the heir, taking on much of the responsibilities of the Baron, in anticipation of his father's passing.

I hadn't seen the current Baron at all since the night I arrived at Whitrow, and there were hushed murmurs between the servants, though he was never mentioned outright by Wright and the Lady, as though his ailing health would improve if no one acknowledged the tragedy that was soon to come.

There was something wrong—not the dying Baron, not that I'd been kidnapped, but an underlying affliction that permeated every room, thickened the air. An uneasiness that seeped through the stone walls, had the servants uneasy, glancing around with wide eyes. The guests that had arrived caught on to the energy, did their best to ignore it.

But I caught the way Lucas' eyes lingered on the new pool of mortals in the house. Flashes of hunger, unrestrained want.

Lucy was weakening and hadn't climbed out of bed for a few days. I sat with her, bringing her teacup to her lips, feeding her whatever she could bring herself to eat. She slept most of the daylight hours, while I paced her room, my heart fluttering in my chest like a rattled hummingbird.

Tomorrow, Wright and I were to wed.

I was hiding in Lucy's room, admittedly. No one would bother me as I cared for my sister. I couldn't stand the jeering of the guests, their curious eyes and invasive questions.

"Come here," Lucy said, voice barely more than a whisper. The only evidence of her exhaustion was the slight shadows under her eyes. She sighed often, complaining she could not get a full breath of air.

Both of us were suffocating in our own ways, it seemed.

I sat next to her, holding her hand tightly within my own.

She smiled a weak smile. "I can tell you are nervous."

"Of course I am," I said. "I'm about to sign my life away."

Even as I said it, my voice did not sound like my own. She did not know how I schemed, how I was mulling over my options, trying to quell the shouting rage within me, growing even louder, pressing against my ribs even harder, now that I was stuck in such a corner.

I'd only had a few days to come to terms with what I may have to do. A small part of me was still in denial, really, hoping that one day I'd wake up in New York and find this was all one bad dream. I couldn't plan it, couldn't think on it for long, or else I felt like I would lose my mind, descend into madness.

If I hadn't angered Marcel, I may have been able to

convince him to aid me in my escape, even by whatever means necessary.

"It does feel like that," she admitted, squeezing my fingers. "But I'm sure you will be alright. The Highsmiths will take good care of you."

"But are you happy, Lucy? I know what your marriage has been like—"

"I am happy enough," she said. She did not like to talk about my brother's darker moods. "I have everything I could ever want. Isn't that good enough?"

I didn't know how to answer.

"Besides, once this one is out," she patted her stomach, looking down at it with love in her eyes, "I'll be quite busy. I won't have time to worry about much else. Thomas. I just know it. It must be a boy."

All I could think is that *she did not know.*

Lucy did not know that her husband was a vampire. She did not know about Marcel's plan. She didn't know about Wright's dead wives. She did not know that I *refused* to be the next victim.

She was so lively and *human*, and she did not know she was surrounded by monsters—and that I'd become one of them, so entrapped in their web I was.

I sighed. "More tea?"

She shook her head. "No, I've had enough. I would like another scone, though."

I happily obliged, smothering it in apricot jam and clotted cream, and refilling my own teacup, just to give my hands something to do. I settled next to her again.

The door swung open.

"Ah, there you are." Lucas stepped inside, eyes narrowing on me. "Everyone's been looking for you."

"Me?" I asked, nearly dropping my teacup at his sudden intrusion.

"Yes. Lady Whitrow has been gushing about you to her family." He gave me a pointed look. "Don't be rude, you cannot avoid the guests forever."

I cringed, but held my tongue.

"And you," Lucas said, turning to his wife. "You should be resting."

Lucy had stopped nibbling at her scone, crumbs falling to the plate she held under it. "I've been in bed for days," she said, gently.

"And I'm sure my sister's chattering has tired you."

He took the plate from her, setting it on the side table, ignoring the crestfallen look on her face.

"Sleep. Someone should be up to bring you dinner later."

"But—"

The firm set to his features left no room for discussion.

She sighed, deflating against the pillows, but she did not protest. Our eyes met, her exasperation shining through, a sort of secret camaraderie between us. She could not argue that she was not tired, it was blindingly evident.

"Leave, Helena," my brother said. "Go entertain the guests. They're here for you, after all. *Lord* Highsmith requested your company."

I narrowed my eyes on him. "Did he?"

"What, you disdain the man before he is even your husband?" Lucas flashed his wife a smile. "I will be right back. Come speak with me in the hall, Helena."

Pressing my lips tightly together, I did not argue, not wanting to anger him in front of Lucy. I wasn't sure how *unpleasant* he was capable of behaving in front of her, but I did not want to worsen her condition, if I could help it.

He shut the door behind us. The hall was cast in shadows, as the mid-afternoon sun was on the opposite side of the house.

"Are you poisoning her against me?"

"I—*what?*"

Lucas stood between me and the door, as though to prevent me from reentering; his dark eyes held mine, all pleasantness wiped from his face. If I were none the wiser, I wouldn't be able to tell he'd been Made—his honey-colored hair gelled perfectly, that manicured scowl in its proper place, his clothing rivaling that of the Highsmiths', no doubt to show off to the wedding guests: he belonged here, he was one of them.

He let out a bitter laugh. "I know what you're doing. You're unhappy, so you must infect everyone else with your misery, so you're not so alone, huh?"

"I don't understand what you're talking about."

I was small in that hallway, a simple human girl, and I was so tired of being reminded of it.

He advanced on me, crowding me against the opposite wall until I could feel his breath on my face. "Just admit it."

"*Stop it.*"

I ignored my instincts screaming at me to *run*.

He wasn't just a human man anymore.

"You want her for yourself," he said, full of menace. "You're trying to turn her against me."

"Lucas, *stop*." I pushed against him, ignoring the way my hands shook.

He could so easily overpower me.

"You're being unreasonable."

"Am I?" A flash of his new fangs as his lip twisted. "Is it unreasonable to believe that the girl who's never listened to anyone a day in her life would try to wreck my own marriage? You're *spiteful*. You can never be satisfied."

"You *kidnapped* me," I hissed, the words catching in my throat.

"After *you* ran away from your responsibilities." He glared down at me, lowering his voice so as not to allow our argument to bleed through Lucy's door. His hands were on the wall, on either side of my head, so I could not run from him, even if I wanted to. "I won't have you rubbing off on Lucy."

"She's not—" I was powerless; his mind was made up, and I would forever be the enemy in his eyes, no matter what I did. "Where is this coming from? Lucy would never—"

"I think you should leave her be. I don't want you speaking with her alone."

My mouth fell open, gaping in shock. "Do you hear yourself?"

"You're lucky Highsmith has been so patient with you."

A sharp intake of his breath and I flinched, thinking he was going to lunge, to raise his hand, to do *something* to me.

"I don't want to see you in her room again." He pushed off the wall, stepping backward, his eyes never leaving mine. He glanced down at me, eyes trailing over my trembling arms, the way I cowered against the wall, smirking.

Glaring right back at him, I straightened, my hands in tight fists at my sides. "I *hate* you."

He turned away from me, back to Lucy's bedroom door. "Go. Your wedding guests are waiting for you."

ELEVEN

Another agonized cry, a specter leaning down to my ear; cool breath against my cheek, rousing me from my sleep. It rang out throughout the house, a haunting wail, yet as soon as my eyes snapped open, all was silent and I wondered if I had dreamt it.

It was still that dreaming hour, the only light the moon trying to spill beyond the window's drawn curtains. My breath fogged in the air before me.

I lay still, gripping the blankets, my heart racing at being startled awake, listening, staring at the darkness of the ceiling above me. For a few moments, nothing.

Then—

Weeping, low and soft, coming from down the hall.

I slid out of bed, willing my feet to float across the icy floor.

A louder sob, the hitching of breath—

I looked to the door that connected my suite with Wright's. Did he hear it too?

My first thought was of Lucy, but no, her voice was not so low. One of the guests? They'd stayed up drinking and smoking past when I'd retired for the night after hours of my plastered smiles and rehearsed answers to their questions.

The air was frigid, as though it were not summer's eve at all, but the dead of winter. I shivered, reaching for a fur-lined robe. I swore I could see my breath in a cloud before my face. *Hell froze over.*

Silence.

I paused at my bedroom door, pressing my ear against the wood. Surely some servants would have come to the crier's aid. Expecting to hear low voices, the shuffling of footsteps, yet there were none—the hall outside was empty.

I tried the door handle.

Unlocked.

Another sob broke the silence. A woman's voice, the cry muffled by the walls. Each heaving breath was a stab to my heart, each sob another dose of adrenaline, those alarm bells in my head telling me to turn around and get back in bed, to pull the covers over my head and shut my eyes until daybreak.

But the agony in those cries, the misery....

I knew that anguish well.

I slipped from the room, stepping only on my tip-toes to keep from making any noise.

I was gambling with my life, leaving my bedroom. Yet there was a doubt lingering that perhaps these weren't cries of pain at all—maybe I was overreacting, *meddling* when I needed to be wrapped safely in my bedsheets instead.

But at the next sound, I knew.

Would I be interrupting the bloodsport of one of the monsters among us?

Marcel had made it clear he wanted a taste of my blood, and Lucas had no qualms digging his teeth into my flesh, should he want to.

And I knew his restraint was dwindling.

No one came around the corner, not even as I made my way past the entrance to Wright's suite, his door solid and shut. I began to wonder if he stayed in his suite at all.

The sounds became weak, turning into muffled groans which echoed down the hall, the low rumbling of a vengeful ghost sending vibrations throughout the house. One of his wives, come to reap vengeance? He'd done something; everything within me knew that he was to blame. But *how*?

My heart thundered in my ears. Was I still dreaming? My steps were as unsure as in a nightmare, fearing that the floor could give way at any moment, like my limbs were not quite attached, like I was looking through someone else's eyes.

Another moan from the end of the hall, even quieter than before.

A huge, paned window looked out upon the eastern grounds, a large ancient tapestry hanging to its right upon the wall. During the daylight hours, its colors were dull, browned from the passing of time, the image depicting a nude man and woman: Adam and Eve, if I were to guess, within the Garden. I hadn't spared it a second glance in my tour with Lady Whitrow.

And around the corner—

A figure loomed, lit only by the sparse moonlight, a mass of black within the darkness.

Not one figure, but two, barely visible in the alcove.

The whisper of a breathy moan, drawn out, weak and helpless.

My blood ran cold as I gazed upon Lucas with a woman in his arms, his face buried in her neck, and there was red—*so much red*.

Staining the front of her body, her limp arms, her ripped dress. Her head lolled onto his shoulder, her feeble cries, barely more than an exhalation, eaten up by the sound of his low groans.

I slammed a palm over my mouth to keep from crying out.

I watched as my brother drained this woman, her face obscured by the shadows, his hands like claws, clutching hungrily at her nightdress, holding her upright. A deep red snaked down her arm, along her delicate wrist, thin fingers, puddling beneath her, a steady *drip drip drip* until her skin looked like marble.

And when he let go, her corpse crumpled onto the ground.

Her face stared right toward mine.

Anna.

I ground my teeth together to contain any sound that might escape me.

Blood stained Lucas' jaw, his eyes seeming to shine in the pitch dark as he stared down at the body, chest heaving.

"You could not make it five meters to a bedroom?"

Wright Highsmith came into view as I peeked further around the corner. Still dressed in his evening clothes, though dishevelled—his belt missing, his collar unbuttoned, hair a mess. He lit a cigarette, scowling down at the mess.

At Anna's body. Like he had not just witnessed her *murder*.

"We'll have to replace this rug."

"Send me the bill, you know I'm good for it." My brother grinned, wiping his lips with the back of his hand. "Besides, I am not done yet."

And in a moment, his fingers were digging into her chest.

The squelch of her flesh broke through the nighttime quiet.

I was going to be sick.

My limbs would not move, paralyzed.

Lucas paused, his fingers still buried in Anna's sternum, gore coating his skin. Listening, I realized, like the predator he was.

He can hear my heart beating.

My pulse still pounded in my ears, dizzying, the rush of adrenaline finally urging me to *move*.

And then his eyes snapped up, catching sight of me as I ducked behind the corner.

My breath in my throat, I fled like the Devil was on my heels, the sound of my bare feet on the cold floor echoing off the walls. At that moment, I was prey. I was a rabbit and that wolf was right behind me, snapping its maw.

What I had just seen—

He was going to kill me.

My brother—Wright Highsmith—*someone*—was going to kill me.

He'll eat you up.

I didn't have time to look behind me. Didn't have time to *think*.

Because I was suddenly knocked to the floor, a body colliding with mine, just as I passed the threshold to my room. Lucas landed on top of me, pinning me to the ground, all the air wheezing from my lungs as those sharp teeth were bared inches from my face.

My head spun, my skull bouncing off the floor.

"Spying, are we?" Lucas leaned closer. I could smell the metallic iron of his breath. "I told you to behave, Helena."

If I had any air, I would have screamed.

All I could see was Anna's lifeless body before my eyes, her stricken face, her rib cage almost torn open by the monster above me.

White hot pain lacerated my throat and I realized Lucas had sunk his teeth into me.

Lucas *bit* me.

Two sharp knives at my throat, hot needles, sinking deep, cutting through as easily as a hot knife through butter.

My scream died on my lips as his fangs pierced my skin, his movement so quick I had no time to protest. His hold on me tightened, fingers digging into my flesh, wrenching my jaw skyward.

Hot tears already burning at my lashes, I dug my own nails into his arms, his shoulders, anywhere, trying to hurt him just as much, to make his grip falter. I beat at his shoulder, pushing with all my strength. "*Lucas.*"

Now *I* was the poor victim, bleeding out, with no one to save me.

He groaned as he pulled my blood onto his tongue. A hand twisting in my hair to hold me still, the other pinning my wrist to the ground.

Now he really is going to kill me.

My veins burned, each breath singeing my throat. Bright arcs of pain traveled through my skull, my shoulders, every bone crumbling into dust, every muscle trembling.

It was nothing like how Vince drank from me.

There was no pleasure in it, only agony. I couldn't breathe. I swore he was trying to bite through my flesh, to tear through all my sinew and *eat* me.

He pulled away for a second, a dark satisfaction painting his features in the moonlight, leaning in, inhaling deeply. "Your blood..." His tongue laved at my throat, right where my pulse beat against my skin, his fingers bruising at my jaw. "I am so hungry."

I brought my knee up as hard as I could, but it only bounced off his thigh.

His laugh echoed in my ear.

Already, my limbs began to feel heavy, my strength dwindling as I pushed against him in vain. I thought, for a moment, that I wanted him to drink it all—to take every last drop so I couldn't come back, wouldn't have to wake up and endure this torment another day. Wanted him to finally kill me, get this over with.

It was what he wanted all along, wasn't it?

He was going to rip me open and consume me. But the quiet afterwards, the peace—

The room began to spin again, my fingers tingling until they were numb, my hands clumsy as I gripped at Lucas' tattered shirt. With each draw of my blood onto his tongue, he ate away at my strength. Nausea roiled through me, made me dizzy, stars dancing across the pitch-dark ceiling of the room. The shadows along the walls elongated, looming figures stretching over us, grinning, those bride-ghosts watching and turning their noses at me.

Fingers threaded through my hair—but Lucas still had his fist knotted at the back of my nape—another's touch, smoothing errant strands away from my face.

When I opened my eyes again, I felt like I was spinning, disappearing into nothingness.

"Quintrell."

Wright crouched next to me. I hadn't heard him enter, but then again, all I could hear was my fading pulse, a high-pitch ringing. Lucas' groaning.

"Wright." I could only whisper his name through my tears.

Help.

My betrothed stared into my eyes, but there was nothing behind his—no care, no fear, nothing.

Indifference.

Coldness.

This man was to be my husband.

Surely, he would stop Lucas.

"You've gorged yourself enough tonight, have you not?"

My brother pulled away, my blood mixing with Anna's dribbling down his chin, staining his teeth a bright red. He grinned. "Don't you want to join us? Aren't you curious for a little taste?"

Wright's gaze swept the room, taking in the mess Lucas had made of me. "First you interrupt my fuck, now you're killing my wife? Nullifying our deal before it is to begin?"

"No," my brother said.

I clawed at the rug, trying feebly to scramble away; his hold remained fast.

"Wrangling her for you. A wedding present, from me."

Wright sniffed in distaste. "A bit unnecessary, no?" His fingertips grazed my cheek. "She would have learned in time."

I was shivering, adrenaline wearing off, the pain searing, the tears falling and collecting on Wright's finger. He spread the warm drops along my cheek, his touch revoltingly possessive. He brushed hair out of my face, behind my ear, the most gentle he'd ever touched me. The face of the man I met back at our house in New York flickered before me.

"Have your fun, but leave her alive. She must be well enough for tomorrow."

Tomorrow—

The day of the wedding.

A slight growl from my brother. "I am no idiot, Highsmith. Don't you want to see what it's like? It'll be quick—all it will take is a little bite, and you can have her however you want."

I recoiled, the fight in me waning.

I was too late. I hadn't made it out in time.

Wright Highsmith will eat you up.

"I think this is a most advantageous arrangement—you fuck, I feed. We'll find others if we have to. And we'll make millions in the meantime." Lucas' hold on me eased, but I was too weak to crawl away, knowing he'd snatch me right back.

There was nowhere for me to go, nowhere to hide.

Lucas pulled me up to sitting, vise-like hands at my shoulders. Tugging me to my feet.

My knees buckled. I clutched at him, ignoring the fact that I was twisting my fingers in fabric saturated with Anna's lifeblood, holding onto him so tightly, like I could anchor myself in this body if only I didn't let go, in danger of floating away.

The skin of my throat throbbed, fire-hot pokers sinking into my flesh, over and over again.

A warm body behind mine. Hands wandering, a firm chest against my back, his hips level with mine.

"Keep going," Wright said.

My brother lowered his lips to my neck once more, teeth grazing the exact spot he'd already torn into.

I flinched, sucking in air through my teeth; slammed my eyes closed and tried to fall into myself.

The second bite nearly brought me to my knees again. But I was stuck between the two men, and I could not escape.

I thought of Vince. I thought of how his teeth had brought nothing but ecstasy. I thought of how that first time, I'd never wanted anything more in my life but for him to taste my blood, to take that part of me onto his tongue. To be inside him, nourishing. *Festering.*

Wright gripped my hip, the other hand twisting in my hair, angling my head back.

I glared at him through hot tears.

So close, his face inches from mine, he looked down at me like he was utterly enthralled, his sclera webbed with red veins. Intoxicated. Lips parted as he pulled my body flush against his. The stale smell of liquor burned on his breath.

Enjoying this.

No matter how he disparaged the vampires, he watched Lucas with rapt fascination. A sick interest in my brother pinning me in place, killing me slowly.

In one last attempt to fight, I pushed against Lucas. Tried to slip away.

"Be a good wife," Lucas said.

I was suddenly aware of Wright's arousal, his body hard against mine. He grabbed my ass, cementing our bodies together.

If I ever made it out alive, I'd flay my own skin to be rid of this feeling.

His hand traveled from my hip to my chest, suddenly cupping my breast. Lucas' fingers trailed down my arms, encircling my wrists. Squeezing.

I wished the fogginess would overwhelm me quicker. Wished Lucas would tear my artery. Wished he'd get my death over with.

Wright buried his face in my hair, groaned under his breath.

Lucas chuckled. "Perhaps Thornton had the right idea—"

"Perhaps *Thornton* is a mere fool who cannot keep a hold on his possessions."

Marcel.

All gazes whipped to the intruder. Wright let my hair slip through his fingers, taking a casual step back.

Marcel stood in the doorway, arms crossed. His nostrils flared for the briefest second, his eyes dark as the midnight shadows swarming the room. His jaw tightened but he did not move.

I did not have the energy to speak, to beg him to help.

He said he'd protect me. He said he'd hold Wright at bay if I kept him near, if I offered myself to him. At that moment, I did not care what Marcel wanted—my blood, my body—he could have it if he saved me from Lucas' torment.

I would leverage Marcel if I needed to; I would bend him to my will, slowly. Let him think that he *had* me. And then I could run away, run *far* away, maybe even with his help. I knew how he *wanted* me—men looked at me like that all the time, when I showed a little skin and offered them a kiss for a drink.

I would give him anything if he stopped this misery.

"You know I'm right." Lucas all but dropped me against the floor, and I was Anna, falling limp from his arms, forgotten. I slammed to my knees, catching myself on shaking palms.

Marcel's eyes flicked away from me. "Do I?"

"And you know you've wanted to do this. You've wanted Helena. You've wanted to Make Highsmith since I introduced you. You've wanted—"

"What?" Wright took a step back, his confusion darkening as he glanced between the two men.

Cold fury burned in Marcel's eyes. He did not move. "Quintrell is delirious."

The floor seemed to undulate beneath me like I was back on that boat crossing the Atlantic, locked in the small cabin room with only a porthole that wouldn't open to see the sun. I was trembling, an immense pressure building behind my eyes, unable to stop my tears from flooding.

"You're lucky *I* found the mess you made in the hall."

"You know I'm right," Lucas repeated. "What's the harm in doing it now? There is no advantage to waiting."

His fingers tangled in my hair, my scalp burning as he

pulled me up onto my knees again. I clawed at his wrists. Stars danced in my vision, black shadows closing in.

Please.

"Remember yourself," Marcel warned, voice low.

Every word echoed in my head like through a tunnel. My eyelids growing heavy, my movements sluggish.

I don't remember what was said next.

I only remember seeing Lucas' face inches from mine, his lips stained red in a petrifying, devilish grin before darkness washed over me and the pain disappeared with it.

And then I remember another looming form over me. Hours later. Coming-to at the first hint of daybreak. Unable to move. To speak. Was I even breathing?

He leaned down, tender and gentle. His tongue traced each bite, saliva coating every inch of my skin.

I exhaled a sigh as the pain ebbed. Like opium racing through me, calming my nerves, the strongest absinthe.

My eyes shuttered closed, recognizing his dark hair, dark eyes, his scent.

His fangs grazed my skin as he licked at my wounds, making sure that not a drop was wasted. The fire was gone, the burning fading away into a languid coolness, his tongue a soft pressure, each scrape of his teeth a jolt.

It felt so good, and distantly, I hated it, hated myself for not fighting—hated that it felt so good to be within an inch of my life and *letting* him.

"I cannot solve this problem without you, Helena Quintrell."

TWELVE

The wedding would not be delayed, no matter how ill-fated it seemed from the events of the midnight hour. The morning was a blur of maids fussing over me, all under the watchful eye of Lady Whitrow. A young maid—younger than Anna and wide-eyed like a frightened doe—the first to find me, had called her into the room, unsure what to do with me. She directed them to take me to the bathing room, to soak in the tub. She told them I was just succumbing to my nerves.

And perhaps she was right—I was just one more in a long history of girls, weeping before being forced to the altar. Foolish, pitiful things brought to tears once confronted with the responsibility of their sex. What a grave responsibility it was, to hold a man's legacy in your hands and womb. Or was it power?

I let them scrub my skin, didn't flinch when the sponge began to rub me pink and raw. Let them pour the floral water over my hair, let them smooth me with lotions and oils.

My tears had long since dried, and a numbness had settled in, sweeping over me, so that I couldn't even look away from the wretched girl in the mirror.

I couldn't do this.

I was signing myself over to death.

"This is unbecoming, Miss Quintrell," Lady Whitrow scolded me, a scowl twisting her elegant features.

But wasn't I being so good, letting them pluck me clean and pretty? Letting them move my limbs and dress me up like a little porcelain doll?

She had to know what her son was doing. She had to know just what I'd seen.

His piqued interest, letting my brother drain their victims dry. Gratified in watching the deed, pleasure in forcing submission. His sick fascination in observing the last moment of consciousness.

This was the family's secret, the skeleton in the closet. Though, were they really hiding anything?

Anna's murder was committed out in the open, for anyone to witness.

It just so happened to be me.

Were there hidden bloodstains under these rugs? How many other lives had ended at Wright's hands amidst these halls?

The maids pulled the slip over my body, the stockings, the garters. The dress came to my ankles, draping skirts of satin that seemed to shimmer in the sunlight, overlaid with an expensive, spiderweb-dainty lace. A bateau neck, the same satin for the sleeves. They placed a string of pearls around my neck, the Lady whispering that it was a gift from the groom, and shouldn't I be delighted.

From the headpiece, a veil fell all the way to the floor, long enough to trail behind me as I walked. And it did, sweeping down the hall as they steered me toward the lower floors, my slippered feet moving of their own accord, the servants smiling blankly and guiding me with outstretched hands, as though ready to catch me—restrain me—at any second.

Maybe I should have dug my heels in, but I was finding that it never did me any good.

And then there was Lucas, waiting for me outside the large wooden doors, the twinkling of a piano echoing from the other side, the hushed murmurs of the guests within. My hand was slipped into the crook of his arm, his fingers holding me tightly, and he was wonderfully dressed, of course, with a new suit for the occasion. Hair perfect. Even a slight flush to his skin.

I was blind to the faces around me as he led me inside. The family Lady Whitrow had told me of, name by name, but it was just a sea of bodies, all watching expectantly. Between them, the aisle cut the room in half, and at the end: Wright.

His chestnut hair was slicked back, his hands clasped, and to anyone else, it would appear he was holding himself back from me. The groom enamored with his bride.

Only hours ago, he was drenched in my blood.

Only hours ago, he'd witnessed a murder to satisfy that hunger burning in his eyes.

Lucas was leading me right to him.

The family members began whispering amongst each

other, a low murmur echoing off the walls. The chandelier was brightly lit above us, hundreds of candles flickering, casting a low, orange glow on the congregation.

"Go on," Lucas hissed, unsatisfied with my pace.

Was it better to cry and refuse, or to walk to my death with my chin up?

The crowd around us watched with bated breath, as though a real spectacle was about to be put on for them. A bit of midday entertainment. The anticipation was thick in the air.

When I was a young girl, the fairy tales told of heroes pulling the damsel from the clutches of the villain right when disaster seemed imminent. The hero slayed the dragon, climbed the tower, and freed the princess. The hero, to whom she'd give her heart after he saved the day.

I hoped, I *prayed*, that someone would come crashing through the windows to stop it all. That Vince would swoop in, in the nick of time. That he'd be my hero.

We stopped before Wright. The officiant said something, but I didn't hear it. I was swimming in my thoughts, still weak from Lucas' bite, overwhelmed with my hatred.

Wright's stare was unwavering. Unspoken between us was the threat to hand me over to my brother again, if I displeased him. If I so much as spoke a word. He had enjoyed watching Lucas drain me; he'd enjoyed how powerless I'd become.

I couldn't tell anyone. Who would believe me anyway?

Lucas handed me off, and then I was in Wright's gasp, his fingers strong around mine.

His voice was low, but it went right through me, as he made his promises, reciting after the priest. I did the same, but I'm not sure I even knew what vows I'd made. When I faltered, his fingers tightened, pushing me to continue.

The ceremony went on in a haze. I heard the words, the music, at a distance. My fingers had gone numb.

And then Wright was leaning down to kiss me before I could pull away.

I'd felt his lips before, but not on mine. Finally a thread of panic gripped me, my eyes going wide as he closed the distance between us. In front of all these people, he claimed my lips, somehow more intimate than when he'd ground his arousal against me.

I was married to Wright Highsmith, and he was kissing me like I was his lover.

My hands came to his chest, pushing him away, stomach twisting in disgust.

His smile was cruel.

He grabbed me harshly, walking me back down the aisle, his grip owning and familiar, and we walked out amongst the cheers of his guests.

Then, I felt the burn of tears at the backs of my eyes. The blur of my vision that I tried blinking away. I was carted away by my husband off to the banquet, no longer owner of my body and soul, another one of those weeping girls, and I just barely caught Marcel's eyes at the edge of the crowd.

Deep, dark, and perhaps a bit rueful.

A blood-red rosebud was pinned at his chest.

Thirteen

The celebration went on late into the evening. I'd been paraded around to the family on Wright's arm as he greeted them all, introducing me as his wife, the new Mrs Highsmith. I couldn't bring myself to smile, to fake an elation I didn't feel.

No one seemed to notice.

He was clapped on the back, congratulated with sharp smiles, complimented on the beauty of his bride. He kept me close, fingers dug into the flesh of my arm.

In the end, he got what he wanted, and so did Lucas.

There was a dinner, an extravagant feast spread across the table, with Wright at the head. A roast, fruits of every season, any dish I could think of, and a large three-tiered cake at the center. A shame I couldn't enjoy any of it.

Lucas became one of the stars of the evening, drawing a crowd with his charisma. A soon-to-be father soaking up the guests' well-wishes for his wife, bedridden and too unwell to join the party.

Marcel stayed close to his side, sneaking glances at me that I pretended not to notice.

As the night wore on, the formalities began to wear away. Wright abandoned me at the table, as I had not moved the whole evening, in favor of catching up with some old friends across the room.

I followed his every movement. Biding my time. When ten minutes passed and he had not left his spot near the far wall, I stood on shaky feet, brushing my hands down the front of my dress, and made my way to the hall. My steps were slow, unhurried. I forced myself not to wobble on shaky legs. To feign the confidence, the courage I did not possess. Lingering in the hall, I waited, afraid he'd come following.

But it seemed I was forgotten.

I discarded my veil in an alcove, grabbing my skirts so they did not rustle against the floor.

And ran for the front doors.

The night air was jarring, cool and smelling of jasmine, the moon and springtime stars watching over me as I slipped from the house.

Someone must have been foolish enough to leave the keys upon the bench in their car; I only needed to find it and make my escape before anyone heard the churning of an engine. Nevermind that I'd never driven before, I would figure it out if it was the last thing I did.

The sound of crickets greeted me, the music from the party dampened once I was out the door. I flew down the stairs, feet silent, heart in my throat.

The drive was long and lined with cars, but I could make it. I could find *something*.

"Miss?"

Whirling around, I was stopped in my tracks by the male voice a few feet behind me.

A footman, the valet, stood upon the porch. Confusion furrowed his brow when he recognized me. "Mrs Highsmith. Are you alright?"

He was one of the older men on staff. If he'd been my age, I would have somehow convinced him to let me go. But he was not stupid; he eyed me suspiciously, and I had the sudden fear he'd drag me back inside and give me up to Wright, in front of everyone. If I was exposed at the party, embarrassing Wright, proving Lady Whitrow right, I'd find myself locked in a room with the key thrown away.

I would be trapped here. Forever. Or—until Wright decided he was ready to have his way with me.

Cursing under my breath, my fists tightened in my skirts. "Yes, I'm fine."

I wracked my mind for an excuse.

"Just needed some air."

His mouth pressed into a firm line. "Why not come back inside, ma'am?"

Any moment, someone else could come outside.

"It is dangerous to be outside alone at night, ma'am," he said as I passed.

Ruining the skirt with my fists, I didn't respond, retreating back into the house with renewed anger. The doors *boom*ed with finality as he pulled them shut.

My heart could not handle another moment at the party. Luckily, no guests roamed the wings, and I was able to flee to my room without running into anyone else.

I lay my back against the door, catching my breath, chest

heaving with dread and fear and adrenaline, the wood solid beneath my fingertips. I threw the lock with haste. My room before me remained unlit, the moon once again meeting me through open curtains.

There on the rug, just last night, my brother had drank from me.

I paced, still wearing the horrible white dress, the pins in my hair.

Against my will, I thought for a moment about *who* was meant to take the wretched thing off of me.

A sob caught in my raw throat.

This day was not supposed to go like this.

My wedding day was not supposed to be so unhappy. Lucas always bore the responsibility to marry me off, but then Vince had come back into my life. I had thought—I had *hoped* that maybe I could have the dream, the sparkling champagne, all my friends around me, the love that lasted forever, *all* of it.

And did he know? Did he have a sense, a tug at the thread of Fate connecting us, that I had been married off? That I was no longer *free*?

He must have known.

Every cell in my body screamed that this wasn't right.

He was supposed to rescue me. He was supposed to be my knight in shining armor, the hero to sweep me off my feet. He had been, I thought. And yet—

I shrieked in frustration, kicking off a white slipper and throwing it at the wall.

Did it again, but it brought hardly any satisfaction.

Didn't you know that Vince is the one that told Lucas to marry you off?

My lungs ached from sobbing and gasping, then holding my breath until my vision went starry, seeing how long I could hold it within me, seeing if I'd even notice falling unconscious—I hadn't last night—hoping that fainting could be fatal.

I needed to escape. To run away.

You cannot run from it this time.

The wound at my neck smarted; there was nothing but shiny skin, slightly purple under the right light, easily missed. No jagged skin, no punctures left behind. Yet the perpetual lump in my throat stung with every swallow.

Wrenching my wedding dress over my head was a chore, the fabric catching on my hips, my shoulders, constricting, tightening like a boa. I ripped the lace and silk away from my body, not caring if I destroyed the damned thing. It fell in a heap on the floor.

The girl in the mirror was haunted. Dark circles shadowed her eyes. Her hair had grown nearly to her shoulders, dark strands a frizzy mess, the careful style ruined. I wiped at my eyes, smearing the kohl, which would not rub away no matter what I did. The pink lipstick one of the maids applied remained painted on, just as stubborn. Like this house did not want me to forget who I was, what I'd done today.

It was only when I turned to find my dressing gown did I spot the paperknife glinting in the moonlight, beckoning from its place on the little writing desk under the window.

My eyes shot open to the sound of soft scraping. I bolted upright, still seated at the vanity, my spine aching, arms tingling from hours spent folded under my head.

"What are you doing?"

The young girl at my hearth nearly dropped her fire poker. Infant flames were catching on the wooden logs, casting golden light across her features. "Miss! Er, Mrs—"

"*Don't.*"

She went pale, eyes wide.

In my sleep, a fever had settled into my skin, my slip clinging to my damp back and stomach. A glance at the clock told me it was well past midnight. I had slept for hours. My heart was fluttering in a staccato rhythm, the room seeming to shrink and grow around me.

"Apologies, I was just stoking the fire. A chill has come over the house, and I thought—"

"Stop." I winced, my skull pounding. I pressed my fingers to the spot between my brows. "You're Anna's replacement."

The girl nodded, her hands wringing before her. She couldn't have been more than sixteen. A young, pitiful thing. Already terrified. Perhaps she knew what became of her predecessor.

Wright Highsmith will eat you up.

It wouldn't be long before she was next.

"You should leave," I said.

She nodded, and made way for the door.

"No. *Leave.* Get out of Whitrow." My voice trembled, sweat breaking out on my lip. "While you still can."

Her steps faltered, but she inclined her head. "Let me fetch your husband, Mrs. Highsmith."

I was going to be sick.

"You don't understand—"

But she'd already closed the door behind her.

I scrambled onto my feet, head swimming. What a fool I was to waste time. The paperknife gleamed in the firelight, glinting in invitation. I don't know what came over me—it was as though command over my body was not my own.

And the moment my fingers wrapped around the cool metal, the door knob jostled.

No no no.

He stumbled into my room, shutting the door with an unintentional *slam*. His eyes were on me in an instant, dark brown irises almost glowing in the low light, pupils so wide it made his eyes look almost black. His hair was disheveled from before, in nothing but his slacks and dress shirt.

"Wife."

Everything within me curled in disgust at the word.

"Helena *Highsmith*."

Saying nothing, I stepped back, my calf hitting the bed frame.

He moved like he was drunk. The house stark silent, the sounds of the party died away in the time I'd slept. Who knew what he'd been doing, if all his guests had retired to bed.

Found another girl to strangle, to watch life fade from her eyes?

My husband.

Wright Highsmith.

Come to collect his due.

My fingers tightened, hiding the makeshift weapon behind my back.

I didn't care—I'd kill my husband here and now. "What are you doing?" My voice came out small, terror stealing each breath.

He only laughed, slowly making his way across the room, one step at a time. Fingers twitching at his sides, like he itched to sink his fingers into my flesh.

I retreated a step. Knew I had seconds, at best, to find an alternative.

"I have good news."

"Oh?"

"My father is dead." He grinned, not a speck of grief in those eyes. "I am Baron Whitrow. And you, *my wife*, are a Baroness." Each step he took, the dark glint in his eye increased tenfold.

"What did you do?" I whispered.

The hand behind my back trembled, palm damp as I adjusted my grip.

I only knew he'd not become a vampire in our time apart because when he smiled, his teeth were just as blunt as mine.

"Why do you assume I've done anything?" Though he did not seem bothered by my accusation.

"Because you had wives before me. You killed them."

He laughed again, his head tilting heavenward. "You are smarter than your brother gives you credit. More observant."

My leg hit the bedframe. "Tell me," I said. "Did you do it?"

"Yes." Those dark eyes zeroed on mine. "I killed them."

"Why?"

Irritation flashed across his face, a twitch to his lips. "They failed to serve their purpose." He cocked his head.

"It's a betrayal, don't you think, to make vows of subservience, and to never follow through?"

"You think they betrayed you?" I felt as though the ghosts of his wives were huddled around me, breathing down my neck, waiting for his answer. Waiting for the truth.

"I *know* they did, whether intentional or not."

"And your father?" I swallowed around the lump in my throat.

His lips spread, revealing his shiny white teeth. I could smell the liquor on his breath from feet away. "It is kinder to tell you he succumbed to his illness."

"What of your mother?"

"What of her? She'll cope, in time."

"Why?" I shook my head. "Why tonight? Why did you—"

"Because I was tired of waiting," he growled, a sudden anger overtaking him. "Just like I will not wait with *you*."

He reached for me, and by some miracle, I was able to dart around him, thanking my luck that he was drunk and the liquor in his blood had slowed him down.

But it only made him angrier. He grit his teeth, staring at me through lowered eyelids. "Behave, *wife*."

Glancing around the room, to the door—I was still too far, he was still too close.

Don't make me do this.

"I'll go to the police," I said.

He chuckled at my wavering voice. "No one will believe you. Your brother suggested an asylum if you became too much. How uncomfortable that would be—locked in the looney bin. No, I won't allow my heir to be birthed in such filth." He tutted. "I am *trying* to be nice."

A high, frantic laugh of my own. My fingers wrapped so tightly around the paperknife, my hand was beginning to go numb.

Please don't make me do this.

"You can take a lover. Bear me a son, and your obligation to me is fulfilled. Am I not generous, to offer this?" He devolved into something all malice. "You've known what I want from you. No more running, Helena."

He advanced on me, just as something in the corner of the room caught my eye, a flickering.

A true ghost stood in the shadows.

But his face was as clear as a spotlight from the moon shone upon him: I knew his face, every inch of his body, as well as my own.

The curtain fluttered at the window, ajar.

I'd gone mad. All this torture, the blood loss—my mind was fracturing. A trick of my imagination.

I'd *truly* gone mad.

The ghost's eyes met mine, and it was like he looked into my soul, the thread of fate between us pulling taut.

I swore he smiled. Nodded once.

Wright faltered, almost upon me. He noticed the widening of my eyes, staring at something behind him.

"What—?" He did not have time to finish whatever he was going to say.

The paperknife found its home between Wright's ribs.

My first thought was that I had damned myself.

My second was that I couldn't be bothered to care.

Blood spurted from his chest, a crimson river trailing

down my fingers still gripping the weapon. His brow pinched in shock, mouth falling open, firm hands digging into my arms. He looked down at himself. At me. "*You—*"

Viper? Vixen? Whore?

Fuck.

"Wait," I gasped, too little too late.

Wright wheezed, beginning to buckle. There was so much blood. *Too much blood.*

Anna would be laughing.

"What have you done?" my husband groaned.

I shook my head. Said the first thing that came to my mind. "Giving you your due."

I let him fall, my hands eerily steady, watching the man I'd just marry bleed out onto my night slip, onto my bare legs, onto the plush rug. The blade slipped out of him with sickening suction, pulling with it a steady stream of blood, straight from his erratically beating heart.

I'd stabbed him in his *heart.*

Staring down at him, watching the flow weaken, each spurt out of rhythm. In the midnight dark, his blood was a deep crimson, near-black, as viscous as tar and just as opaque. Poisoned with his past deeds, his dead wives getting their revenge. They grinned their vindicated grins around me now.

The knife clattered to the floor. Before me, slender white fingers shining red in the low light, and not an inch of bare skin—I was stained with my sin.

Wright coughed, cursing, writhing on the floor, his lifeblood leaking between his fingers. He could not staunch the flow, couldn't stop what had been set into motion.

A firm hand settled on my hip. The other brushing hair behind my ears.

"It's alright, my darling," the ghost whispered. "Do you not feel powerful?"

I was shaking my head. The illusion had gone on too long. He couldn't be here now, it didn't make sense, I couldn't understand—

A soft kiss to my shoulder. Voice lilting with curiosity. "Shall you show him mercy?"

Wright grunted in pain, gritting his teeth, which began to turn red with blood rushing up his throat; his hate burning for me, for the ghost he seemed able to see. He clutched at his chest, his attempt to stop the bleeding pitifully feeble, and lifted a hand as if to reach for me, to grab me, to—

A shoe crushed the bones of his hands to the floor.

Wright cried out.

The ghost—

Was a living, breathing form.

Vince.

He ground his foot atop Wright's hand. He didn't lift his shoe when he looked at me. Those icy eyes—

"A more merciful killer would make it quick."

He caught me before I realized my knees were giving out, his strong arms coming around me, holding me to him—*our bodies fit together like jigsaw pieces*—his scent overwhelming me, the familiar iron and smoke, the spiced cologne. It was all so utterly him, tears welled up in my eyes.

Vince cradled my face, searching my eyes for something, his concern betrayed by the line between his brows, the slight downward tick of his lips.

I clutched at him. "You're here," I breathed.

Stars danced across my vision.

It's not my fault. I didn't mean to.

"I've been too long without you, darling."

His lips were on mine in an instant. Tongue dipping between my lips, his cool hands on my cheeks. He moved against me hungrily, and I let him: I opened myself to him, meeting him with the same fervor, our teeth colliding. Dizzy with want and adrenaline and maybe this was the bloodlust these vampires whined about, only I had no need to drink it.

Was I any better than the man I just killed?

He brushed his lips against my cheek, tasting my tears, grinding his hips against mine. "You must have known I would come. I cannot stay away from you for long." He captured another of my sighs with his mouth on mine, gazed down at me hungrily, dark eyes flicking to my throat. "I will always find you."

And I believed him. Somehow, he had made his way into my bedroom at Whitrow, much like he had made his way into my room in New York when we were so young. This pull between us, this tether, tangling our fates together.

I felt that truth in my bones: he would always find me. He'd found me twice, now. And I wasn't sure if this was a blessing or a curse.

I'd just killed a man, and yet Vince was pressing his body against mine with a demented urgency, a frenzy that wasn't just bloodlust but his hunger for more. His hands skimmed across my hips, up to my face, and back, as though he needed to touch me, check every inch of me, to ensure I was real.

I was real. He was real.

And I was a murderer—

As I burned for him, I thought that this pain was what I deserved—this rending-in-two, this torture: wanting him and wanting to scorn him. I wished only that we could go back to those few weeks of respite, when I knew him only as my undead lover, when I had no inkling of his schemes. But now, there was a voice whispering at me to turn the sharp edge of the letter opener against his own heart, let him feel every bit of hurt I'd choked down these weeks.

I loved him and I *hated* him.

He pinned my wrists by my head, pressing a kiss to each finger tip—tasting my dying husband's blood, I realized through my foggy, whirling thoughts. And when his nose skimmed my shoulder, racing toward my neck—

He froze.

The scar.

"Who did this?" His eyes flicked to mine, wholly dark and unnerving.

The monster inside him stared back at me and I nearly wept with the relief of it, knowing he was no longer lost to me.

Dazed, I opened my mouth to speak, but nothing came of it.

"Tell me not to kill them all."

"You can't."

"This is a cruel request, when I'm inclined to slaughter anyone that hurts you."

Then slaughter my brother, I thought.

Shame washed over me. I was shaking my head as I held him to me, flattening my hands against the muscular planes of his back, feeling every dip and curve, the steady heartbeat

of his chest pressed to my own. Denying, denying, denying
—*it wasn't my fault.*

I was still afraid that he would disappear, that this was
another dream, or delusion, and I would awaken to the
consequences of a dead husband at sunrise.

I was losing my mind.

Vince groaned again, pressing his face to my chest. His
fingers tightened into fists on the sheets, caging me beneath
him.

I ran my thumb along his cheekbone, his flesh hard and
real beneath me. "Are you stealing me away again?"

He leaned up and kissed me harshly. "You are not theirs
to keep."

No matter that I'd married the Highsmith heir, however
briefly, signing guardianship—*ownership*—of me over to
Wright.

"I am no one's to keep," I said, looking my lover in the
eyes.

Vince's pupils dilated in the darkness. "Indeed. We must
go. Else I'll kill every last soul in this house."

A warm puddle had spread across the carpet when my
feet once more met the ground. Wright did not move, one
hand still covering his chest, but no blood seeped through
his fingers. His head lolled against his chest, slack-jawed, that
crimson trail dripping from his lips.

Vince kicked him over.

Wright's corpse stared at the ceiling with unseeing
eyes.

It was silent; this was the most quiet I'd seen him, the
most peaceful.

For a moment, I pitied him.

I was terrified of what I'd done. Terrified of the consequences.

And then I remembered what he meant to do to me.

Vince—my savior, my lover, my knight in shining armor,
the hero from all those stories I'd read as a girl, the golden
prince. My curse, my affliction. My villain.

He led me toward the open window, the midnight air
curling around my limbs, sending shivers through my flesh
as the breeze brushed against my wet nightslip. He seemed
not to care about the gore, holding my hand, fingers
interlaced.

Just as he pushed the window open further, the lock
busted, the curtains fluttering in the breeze, a realization
came to me: "*Lucy.*"

Still locked away in the house, enduring the ire of my
brother, pulled this way and that at his every whim. I could
not leave her. Once the Highsmiths—my brother—*Marcel*
—found out what I'd done, there was no telling what would
happen to her, innocent and left behind.

Vince paused.

"I must find her," I whispered, with no plan other than
to get her out of this house before its inhabitants tried to
crush her, too.

He nodded once.

"What do we do with him?"

The fury within me sparked as I glanced at the dead
body of my husband. I'd do it over again, I realized; I'd kill
him in every lifetime.

If Vince had not found his way in my room, I still would
have ended Wright's life, because I would not endure the
pain of marriage to a man like him. It was always going to

end up this way, even if Lucas had signed me over to another bachelor. My life or theirs.

"Leave him." Vince stared at the body in disdain.

"But—"

He went to the bedroom door, about to walk out like— like nothing had happened, like he had command of the house and it was his own. Like *he* had assumed the barony in the wake of Wright's death.

My vampire waited with his hand on the doorknob. "What, do you care for him now?"

I shook my head, unable to look away from the corpse. Only hours before, he'd kissed me. Claimed me as his bride. Only yesterday had I found out who he really was—a killer.

So much had changed in the span of a breath.

"No," I said.

Vince held his hand out to me. "Come, Helena."

FOURTEEN

I imagined, as I slipped through the halls, that I looked like one of the specters that haunted Whitrow: white robe flying behind me as I ran on silent feet, the only evidence of my transgression the still-wet blood underneath my fingernails. A wraith, pursued by the monstrous creature that had sworn his fealty; two ghastly figures stalking the halls of the centuries-old manor, silent now as if a blanket of sleep had forced its inhabitants into unconsciousness.

Anna's body long discarded, the rugs had already been rolled away. It was as though nothing had occurred.

I knew the route to Lucy's room by heart, twisting through winding corners, never doubting that Vince was at my back. My dutiful sentinel. I expected servants to appear, a rogue drunk wedding guest slumbering in a corner. Lucas and Marcel could stop us at any second. But the halls were markedly empty.

Apprehension pounded at my skull.

I cursed myself for not grabbing the paperknife—what little good it would do me against the vampires, anyway.

He made me do it.

It's not my fault.

Lucy's door appeared at the end of the hall. We could not waste time, but I hadn't thought about how I would convince her to abandon my brother and slip into the night with us. No matter how my mind was screaming at me to escape now, no matter how the guilt was beginning to creep in, no matter how my blood had turned to liquid dread, knowing *something* was coming. Lucas never let me go easily. To take his wife, I was declaring war against him—that is, if he was not with her this moment.

This could not end well.

I threw open the door, not giving myself time to second-guess my decision, holding my breath, expecting a blow.

What I saw was not the punch to the gut I anticipated.

Lucy—bloody, trembling, standing in the center of the room, weeping, clutching at herself, her stomach.

Her sky blue eyes met mine. In them, the most horrid agony.

"Helena?" Her soft, weak voice.

Blood trailed from her lips, some even in her unbound hair, a dark crimson against her rosy skin. Her long nightgown was stained a deep red and it bloomed from between her legs. *Too much blood.*

My heart cracked. "Lucy?"

Whilst I had been murdering my husband, Lucy had been experiencing horrors of her own.

"What happened to you?" Tentatively I neared, reaching for her.

With one finger she pointed to the water closet across the room.

Wordless. Sobbing.

Her gaze flickered to Vince behind me, fear painting her features, but it was quickly overtaken by another wave of sobs.

"Helena." Vince spoke softly, so as not to frighten the lamb further.

She stood with her hands before her, like she didn't know what to do with them. She only stared at me, her tongue running over her lip, poking at the fangs that sprouted from her gums. A tear ran down her cheek.

Lucy was Made. And she was terrified.

She made no move to jump at me, to give in to the violence of her newly Made body. She only shook like a leaf, glancing from one hand to the other, her face slowly twisting into a mask of anguish. Red drops splattered on the floor at her feet.

"Oh Lucy," I moaned, and I went to her, despite everything.

Her thin arms wound around me, her head falling to my shoulder. I was acutely aware of how close her teeth were to my skin.

I had no misgivings that Lucy's change was anyone's fault but my brother's. And he had forbidden me from seeing her days ago. *When had he done this?*

Vince stepped into the room, shutting the door. His mouth was pressed into a grim line. But he said nothing, only leaning back into the door, as though in anticipation of someone pushing on the other side.

"What happened?" I asked again.

She only shook her head into my neck.

"Can you walk?" I asked. "We must go. Vince and I, we're leaving. Come with me. You have to come with me."

She pulled away, her tear-stained face both pink from her weeping and pale. "You're leaving?"

"We need to." I was not sure how to tell her of the murder. "We're no longer safe here. Are you too hurt?"

Her lip wobbling, she shook her head again.

"Then we must go now," Vince said from behind me. "I fear we are running out of time."

"He's going to come back," Lucy said, unable to do more than whisper. "He's come back every night—"

"Shh." I hushed her softly, not wanting her to relive it, and knowing the more she spoke on it, the more likely I'd be to turn around and find my brother, wherever he may be. Let him feel what Wright felt when I—

I took a deep breath. I could not get Lucy out of here if I succumbed to the madness clawing at my mind.

"Where is he?" I asked.

She shook her head. "I don't know. He doesn't tell me."

"Helena," Vince called again, his gray eyes meeting mine.

"We can't very well go to the front door," I said, glancing around the room as if that would give me my answer.

Vince's gaze flicked to the window. "We can always go the way I came in."

I had no experience scaling buildings, and I doubted Lucy did, either.

"There's a servants staircase at the end of the hall," she rasped.

Vince and I met eyes, and he nodded. It was as good a

plan as any: out of sight, dark, and we were less likely to run into anyone that could stop us.

Guarding our way, Vince followed Lucy and I as we made our escape. The staircase hidden behind a door, the way down was claustrophobic, the walls less than a meter apart. The steps were uneven, and I caught myself from slipping, but Lucy and Vince seemed to have no trouble, all of us descending as quickly as we could.

The landing was eerily quiet, the passageway lit only by the ambient moonlight streaming through the servants' quarters. A hall with doorways in every direction.

After only a moment of hesitation, Lucy took the lead. "This way."

It seemed Lucy had done her own exploring, hiding some secrets of her own.

We crept through the kitchens, the stone floor whispering under our feet.

Any second now, I thought, one of the cooks would walk in. A footman. *Someone.*

And then Lucy was pushing on a set of doors to the outside, miraculously silent on their hinges, and we were running into the night. But not before I glanced back into the house that had felt like a gaudy prison, and swore I saw two eyes in the shadows, reflecting like a cat's.

A car sat just far enough into the tree line that it was undetectable from the house. The moon was bright, illuminating the drive as we made our escape. Whitrow glowed against the starry sky, sitting quiet as though its floors were not stained with the blood of Wright's murderous appetite.

Lucy, sure on her feet, even when she huffed, out of breath.

A figure climbed out of the car as we drew closer.

Surely I was seeing things—because there was Dixon, unharmed, waving at us to hurry.

His eyes widened when he saw the blood staining my nightdress, my skin. Flicking over to Lucy, nostrils flaring. "What happened?"

"Later," I wheezed, helping Lucy into the car.

This was too convenient, too easy—any number of the guests could have peeked out their windows and saw us running down the drive. And where was Marcel? Where was Lucas? It was like we were *allowed* to run. *You cannot run from it this time.*

My maid could enter my room again at any moment and find the evidence of my crime. The whole house would know, my *brother* would know—

Vince grabbed my hand. Pulled me onto the bench just as Dixon slammed shut his door.

"*Drive.*"

"Where am I going?" Dixon's knuckles were white on the steering wheel.

Vince's brow was set in a rigid line as Whitrow shrunk behind us, his fingers tightening around mine, like he was scared I'd float away. "To London."

FIFTEEN

I hadn't thought my first visit to London would ensue running away from the estate of my now-dead husband and two vampires. Even just after sunrise, the city was bustling, people moving about on trams, cars honking, all traveling from one end of the city to the other. My head spun with the cacophony, overwhelmed with both my exhaustion and my emotions, so that I wanted nothing more than to settle into whatever room we rented and sleep until the sun came up the next day.

Dixon pulled up to a rather ritzy looking hotel, and as soon as we all climbed out of the car, a valet was there to take it away and offer to grab our bags, of which we had none. I wrapped my robe tightly around myself, knowing that if anyone saw the blood flaking on my skin, we could expect a policeman at the door in no time. I was already indecent, I didn't need to draw even more attention to myself.

"Three rooms," Vince said to the concierge.

"Of course." The man seemed entirely unfazed by our

appearances: Lucy and I still in our sleepwear, and the men in wrinkled clothing clearly more than a day old. He made a point to avoid looking at us girls, instead glancing at Dixon, perhaps recognizing the viscount. He gathered the room keys and looked at the men expectantly.

Vince reached into his pocket and withdrew some money, counting out the notes. "Lunch and dinner room service. And a week's worth of clothes for all of us to be delivered by tonight."

I'd never seen so much cash in Vince's hands before.

"From Harrods, preferably," Dixon added.

The concierge inclined his head dutifully.

"We'll be gone by lunch tomorrow." Vince looked at the man's name tag, "Mr. Matthews."

"Of course," he repeated, expression a nondescript politeness. A glance toward the viscount once more. "We hope you enjoy your stay, Mr...?"

Vince counted out one more note. "Your discretion is appreciated."

Mr. Matthews gave him a polite smile, then waved over one of the bellhops, ordering him to show us to our rooms. So early in the morning, there were only a few guests lingering in the lobby, still groggy with sleep, or perhaps still awake from the prior evening; only a few spared glances toward our unkempt group, blinking away with bleary eyes, uninterested.

I linked my arm with Lucy's, holding her to me as we followed the bellboy, Vince and Dixon following behind. I was grateful that no one had the energy to scrutinize us this early. Lucy couldn't look up from the floor, her brows pulled in a haunted expression, and already dark circles were growing under her eyes, her cheekbones.

She was thirsty.

Up a flight of stairs, down a hall padded with plush emerald carpets, gilded sconces lighting the way, the bellboy finally stopped at the end, explaining that the suite had two rooms, and the third was separate, across the hall.

Once the door was unlocked and we stepped inside, a weight spilled from my shoulders, the air clearing, and I could finally breathe. I hadn't realized how vulnerable and naked I felt out in the open, exposed for anyone to see—for anyone to report back to Marcel or my brother.

A young woman walking around London, tattered and bloody, matching my description. They'd find us in no time.

"You can have this room," I said, leading Lucy to the bedroom facing the quiet courtyard of the hotel. The curtains were still drawn together, feeble sunshine casting shadows across the cream-colored carpets. At the very least, the sounds of the street did not reach us. "Unless it's too dark, then—"

"No," she whispered, slinking away from my grasp. "It'll do."

"Lucy." My arms felt cold without her in them.

She paused, about to climb into the bed, too weary to face me.

"I'll be back, okay?"

My heart was breaking for her all over again, and as I shut the door softly behind me, the two men watched with grim faces. "She needs to feed."

"I will call someone up," Dixon said.

"What? No."

Lucy would never let herself drink from some poor maid, especially if she'd already refused to drink while at Whitrow. Or had my brother been withholding blood from her? I hadn't realized just how sunken her cheeks had become, how weak she was in my arms. Lucas could've done something about it if he wanted. First he Made her, then he left her to waste away.

"I'll take care of it," I said. "I'll try—"

"Helena." Vince didn't look too keen on the idea.

"I won't let her just starve."

I sighed, my exhaustion pulling at my limbs like gravity. I hadn't slept at all, and I'd been forcing myself to focus on Lucy, so that I couldn't dwell on the feeling of the paperknife sliding through flesh.

I was a killer.

Giving Lucy my blood was the least I could do.

"Let's call for breakfast, then," Vince said. "You need rest and something to eat, too."

"I'll do it. I have a call to make, anyway," Dixon said. "I'll let the front desk know."

Then he was gone and it was just Vince and I, alone in a silent room, the sounds of London below trickling through the glass panes of the window, the sounds all wrong, the way the sunlight streamed through all wrong—everything *all wrong*.

Something had changed between us since he'd climbed in my window and pushed me to slide that letter opener between Wright's ribs like sheathing a sword in a scabbard of sinew. My relief at seeing him again, and the urgency to escape, finally fading away until before me, all I saw was a creature who *looked* like Vince and smelled like him and talked like him, but an invisible wall had erected between us. A distance. Like being apart had torn the threads connecting our hearts.

It was *all* wrong.

He made to step closer, but paused when I fell back a step. Some mixture of concern and hunger tensed his jaw. Though he was windswept and disheveled and a dusting of hair shadowed his jaw, he looked alive as ever, not the least bit exhausted, even though I knew he hadn't slept at all on the drive to London, either, his undead body in need of much less than mine.

He was so beautiful.

I looked at him, and I saw the boy I fell in love with six years ago. I saw the strong brow I'd kissed a million times, the face I'd held in my hands, the young man who was my first love, my first heartbreak. I saw the printer's apprentice. I saw the determined Adam who wanted *more* from this life. Who had fallen in with a rich girl, knowing it was dangerous. The young man who had dreams.

Not the supposed schemer. Not the man who was, according to Marcel, in some capacity responsible for all of this.

I still wasn't sure what was the truth.

What did he see when he looked at me?

Someone who was withering away? The girl who hadn't waited for him? A helpless woman who could not reckon with his new world?

Under his gaze, I was made of glass. Like he could see every crack, every chipped and shattered piece of me.

I turned away from him.

"Helena."

His voice was so soft, that I wanted nothing more than to run to him, to fall into him again. To surrender myself to whatever he wanted from me.

"Let me—"

"I need to be with Lucy." My voice cracked.

But something rooted me to the spot. With fingers tightening into fists at my sides, I waited. I was not sure if I wanted him to stop me, to take me into his arms and murmur that everything would be alright in my ear; I wanted him to lay out the truth—and I wanted Marcel's claims to be lies. I wanted Vince innocent.

I wanted—

Shutting my eyes, I took a shuddering breath.

He didn't come to me. I felt his eyes on my back. He didn't protest again as I made my way into Lucy's room, shutting the door softly behind me.

She was exactly where I left her, only the blankets had been pulled up over her chin, and her stare was pointed out the window. She didn't react when I sat at the foot of her bed.

"Lucy." I was too afraid to do much more than whisper, my voice a booming echo in the small room.

I would kill Lucas for what he did to Lucy.

I would kill him for what he did to Vince.

I would kill him for what he did to *me*.

Wringing my hands in my lap, my fingers trembling with nerves. "I can ring for some tea, if you'd like."

Silence.

"I'm angry, too," I said, voice barely above a whisper. "I'm *angry*. But I'm not sure if anger is good enough of a word. It's something festering in me. Hate, maybe. And I loathe *them* for putting it there. This darkness would not be here inside of me if not for them. I carry this dark cloud, and I suspect now you do too, all because of them."

It'd been brewing into a tempest since Marcel dragged me down to that cellar, weeks ago: a blackness, a *rage*, that terrified me more than the monster living in Vince's blood. This eagerness for calamity, this call for violence, lived within me now, and I hated it. I hated Lucas for planting the seeds in our youth. I hated Marcel for capitalizing on it. I hated Wright for thinking he could tame it.

And Vince—

Your darkness calls to me, I had said not so long ago.

Would he feel the same about me?

"I can't take it away, but how I wish I could. I suppose all there's left to do is stamp it down, or set it free."

Lucy's eyes flicked over to me. But where I expected a monster to stare back, there was only *her*, this young girl, so much softer than I, broken into pieces and thrust into a world she didn't understand. "He's the one you fell for."

I nodded.

"And he's..." She trailed off, thinking—or perhaps resisting the words. "*Like me.*"

"Yes."

"How long have you known?"

Her gaze was accusing, and all my shame came rushing back.

"About Vince? Or—"

"Lucas. How long have you known about Lucas?"

"Since they found me."

She looked away again, towards the window.

"I did not want to get in the way of your happiness," I said, but it was a sorry excuse, and I was burning with remorse as I said it.

"And yet, here I am."

The haunted look returned, the hopelessness that was swallowing her whole. I'd never seen Lucy like this. She was so bright, so *good*, that even my brother's lack of care could never dim her. She was the angel of the house, the perfect wife, everything my mother wanted me to be for *my* husband. But that couldn't save her, and I'd been too caught up in myself that I hadn't saved her, either.

Nothing I could say would make this better. "I'm sorry."

Just like my world had been turned upside down, hers had, too.

I was an idiot to have thought he would not turn on her. He was so quick to threaten me with his bite, and I'd stupidly assumed that she was safe. But I should have known better.

And their baby—

"Let me feed you," I said. Every word was too feeble, too meaningless, against the weight that settled between us.

My blood would be my penance, if she allowed me.

Silent, she turned further away from me, her face obscured, pulling the blanket to her cheek.

I was dismissed, as good as a door slammed closed and locked, the key thrown away.

"What's next, Thornton?" Dixon grumbled as he sat, returned from his errand some time later. He unfolded a newspaper across his lap.

"No luck?" Vince's eyes slid to the viscount over his shoulder. He stood at the window across the room. "She still ignoring you?"

Dixon bristled, but said nothing. I had a feeling I knew who *she* was. How my heart ached to see her again. Especially now, when I wanted nothing more than to be *home*.

I sat at the other window with a steaming cup of Earl Grey, peering out at the crowd in the street. If I tried hard enough, I could convince myself we were still in New York and not on a foreign continent.

Vince leaned an elbow on a window frame. "We return to my coven."

"We're going back home? Will they not just follow? You'll be back to square one."

"No." Vince shook his head. "Not to New York."

I almost laughed—I should have known. "To France?"

"You want to go to Andreas?" Dixon scoffed. "Do you have a death wish?"

I gripped my tea cup tightly.

There was a beat of silence. Then: "That coven is mine. Not anyone else's. Not Andreas', and not Marcel's."

"Tell me what happened the night of the masquerade."

"What happened?" Dixon asked from the center of the room.

Room service had arrived, the spread of pastries and fruits, creams and jams, sausages and roasted vegetables more than four people could hope to finish. The aroma was mouth-watering, but my apricot tart sat untouched next to me, my teacup still full.

I could sense Dixon's tension without seeing him, my back turned. I hadn't forgotten how the night had ended, and I knew he hadn't either.

"You must know I—" Dixon started, then sighed.

"They seemed to have guessed our plan," Vince interrupted. He was only a few feet behind me. Standing, watching out the window too.

I knew we were looking for the same thing.

"Whoever was helping Marcel—they put something in the blood. Incapacitated Veronica, *all* of them, and by the time we'd realized it, they'd cornered Dixon and given him an ultimatum."

"They threatened Flora." Teeth gritted, Dixon repeating the words from that night.

Cars weaved through the throng of people on the cobblestone street. Every person in the crowd moving around each other, men in linen suits, women with children clutching their skirts. Every face shadowed, hidden, obscured —I could not distinguish between them.

"Who were 'they'?" I asked.

Vince came to stand behind my chair. "Men from my old coven. *Andreas'* coven."

I took a sip of my tea, but it was too hot still, burning the tip of my tongue.

Odd, I wondered, how none of these men aided Marcel in dragging me to the tomb.

Not a single one had shown their faces when Marcel found me in the crowd.

"Keep going," I said, shutting my eyes against the world.

"We left that next morning. Before you, it seems," Dixon said. "We had a pretty good idea where they were going to take you, knowing Marcel and knowing your brother, but we didn't realize...."

I didn't hear the rest, my blood running cold.

That night, I hadn't known my brother was involved until I found him waiting underground.

A bitter taste rose in my mouth. I was glad I couldn't see Vince's face, that he couldn't see mine. "My brother?"

Dixon went silent. Perhaps confused, glancing between us. Or maybe he'd been in on it all along, too.

Vince's hand came to rest on the back of my chair. "We knew he'd take you to Whitrow to marry."

Didn't you know Vince *is the one that told Lucas to marry you off?*

"How did you know?"

"How did I know...?"

"That my brother was with Marcel. That they were working together."

The street below me blurred.

He hesitated—for only half a second, but it was hesitation, nonetheless. "Marcel cannot keep his mouth shut. He alluded to their *partnership* during his visit."

I wanted to believe him. I wanted to ignore the doubt splitting my mind in two. I wanted to believe that Marcel's taunts were nothing but that: words to sow distrust between Vince and I. I wanted to accept this explanation. I didn't want to be suspicious of Vince anymore.

Because the alternative was believing he knew *everything*, all along.

He kept things from me before. How could I trust he wasn't keeping the truth from me now?

Marcel's words echoed in my mind: that Vince was responsible, that I didn't really know him. And if Vince was capable of blackmailing my brother, what else was he capable of? Sending me away with his enemies?

I didn't want to believe it.

But I couldn't ignore the voice nagging at me—why else would Vince have known where they were taking me?

The truth was there. Right in front of me.

I would just have to lift the veil, the mask hiding it all, and see for myself.

As dusk blanketed the city, I dressed in one of my new nightgowns from the many trunks procured by the hotel. I'd insisted on privacy for the afternoon, my head pounding, my eyes burning, and every breath more difficult than the last. After a bath and a small dinner brought to me by Dixon, I was pulling back the sheets of the bed when I heard the door slip from its latch.

I froze.

His movements were slow, steps soft, as he shut the door behind himself.

I couldn't see his face in the dark, only the outline of his form silhouetted by the faint street lamps outside.

That mountain of anxieties was building, a sickness wanting to burst from me, words thrumming in my chest.

Accusations. The need to interrogate him, to pin him down and force him to *answer me*.

"Darling."

His voice, so soft, barely even a whisper, as he neared.

And I knew he wanted to touch me, to drag his fingertips across my spine and pull my strings. He was in front of me within seconds, his steps sure, silent.

It came from my lips before I could stop it: "Andreas is dead."

He turned to stone, so still I could see the faint beat of his pulse at his temple.

His fingers tightened, a muscle feathering at his jaw; a shadow encased the two of us, a cocoon of suspicion. A spider's web in which I was so completely tangled, looking the beast right in the eye.

"Yes." The corners of his lips twitched.

I swallowed the lump in my throat. "You knew."

"Yes," he said again. "Rather, I had a feeling."

"When?"

He paused. "In the last weeks. There was a change, somewhere."

Entirely cryptic, a non-answer. It seemed I was doomed to remain oblivious in all things.

He came closer, peering at me, peering *into* me, like the monster inside needed a better look, needed to gaze into my own pupils and read my fears for itself. Dark, wide pupils, so large he could swallow me whole. That monster that had erupted from his skin, taking him over. A veritable *demon* living inside of him.

"Marcel Brancato told you?"

He was so close, and I was torn between cowering and pressing my lips to his, if only to snap him out of it. "Yes."

"What else did he tell you?"

"That he is your coven's chosen leader."

He smiled, dark and so wholly wicked. "Then he is even bigger a fool than I thought."

Sixteen

Six Years Ago

A dam left one hundred and fifteen days ago.
One hundred and eighteen days ago, my brother found us at dinner. One of the nicer dinner clubs we'd attended, we'd had the whole room to ourselves. Multiple courses of oysters and salmon tartare and roast with gravy and potatoes, our dessert of almond cakes about to be brought in, when Lucas announced his presence with a gun to my lover's heart. Cold metal to my own temple, a threat on his lips.

I had tried my damnedest to save Adam from it. Tried to hide him, because I knew how cruel my brother could be.

The first three days I spent in a sort of purgatory, the four walls of my room a prison cell, the wallpaper wavering in a mocking dance, the shadows clustering in the corners tenfold. The daylight through the window was a reminder of the freedom outside, so many people passing by the house, going on with their lives, oblivious to the despair eating me whole. I had no strength to pull myself from my bedsheets.

A hollow pain lingered in my heart, the distant pang of hunger, the shakiness of dehydration.

I spent all my tears the first night.

The second I was too weak to cry, my sadness so consuming that each breath ached.

The third night I became numb.

My mother came to my door once, maybe twice. A gentle knock, her voice muffled by the door; her guilt, perhaps, leading her to wonder about my wellbeing.

But the door remained locked, even when I did not answer.

And as it was locked, I could not leave. Only Lucas had the key—he made sure of it.

That first night I despaired over Adam, wondered what happened to him. Surely my brother was only bluffing? He couldn't really sign another man up for service, could he? And even so, he couldn't ensure Adam really went away?

But, oh, Lucas made sure. In those days he goaded, with a slimy smirk and those dark eyes we shared, telling me every terrible detail: how he found out about us, how long he waited to catch us, the information he gathered about Adam, and his family, and how he'd visited their apartments not long after I had, just to have *words* with his parents. And we'd been none the wiser.

I had thought that Adam was mine. He was mine to love, to hold close to my heart. A secret, yes, but a dream, too. Reality didn't exist when I was with him; Lucas and Mother had no power over me, and I was free to do as I wished. I could make plans with Adam, dream of our future, ignore what I was *supposed* to do, what was expected of me. Because Adam had opened my eyes to the possibilities.

Only, I'd done a terrible job at protecting him from Lucas.

I could take the brunt of the blows. I could handle whatever it was Lucas threw my way, words or otherwise. I could do all of that, to save Adam. Had prepared myself for it, just in case.

But I never thought Adam would be *sent away*. That Lucas' men would show up at his door, before he'd had a good chance to say goodbye, and usher him to the docks, shove him onto the boat and take what little belongings he'd been allowed, some money, his identification. Everything.

Lucas took everything.

And he whispered my worst nightmare in my ears. Wondered aloud how long Adam would last. Smiled that terrible smile as he spoke, each word a lash, until I was a ball sobbing on the floor, no one to save me from that torture. And still he loomed over me, describing the horrors of the fight overseas, and said that that was what Adam was going through. Suffocation. Land mines. That Lucas had sent him to a slow, torturous death. That he might be going mad in those trenches. That Adam would wonder until he died just how much I really loved him, if I hadn't stopped him from getting on that boat.

It was no better when Lucas left, because then I was caged with the roiling thoughts that would not quiet. Like devils taking over my mind, telling me what I should do, how I could make this misery stop. I was on the second floor, after all, and if I fell just right, I wouldn't feel a thing.

The only thing pushing me forward was the minuscule possibility that one day, Adam would show up outside the gate once more, waiting for me, and were I to jump, he would never know what had happened to the girl he once fell in love with and left behind.

After only a few days, Flora came to the front door. I saw her come up the path, heard the knock on the door, the answer from the housemaid, sending her away. She'd walk back to the street, staring up at my window, as though to get a glimpse of me, any sign of life. Lucas was already gone. My bedroom door was once more open. But I could not pull myself out of bed.

How could I go out to luncheon when Adam was fighting a war?

Perhaps it was pity for the girl, but eventually my mother let her in. Let her come to my room. And even though I couldn't speak, wouldn't look at her, Flora would sit with me. She told me about her day. But she never asked what happened. Never asked about Adam. The purple marks peeking out from my sleeves told her enough.

And eventually the weeks began to pass.

A newspaper was brought up to me at my request. Every day. I needed to know if the war ended, needed to know if his was one of the names listed in the paper. I read every word, and learned more about city politics and global goings-on than I ever had before.

Flora tried distracting me with gifts, and eventually, strolls through the garden. After a few months, I agreed to lunch. Put an end to my confinement. Thinking, no bad news had come, and surely it would have by then.

Adam was alright. He had to be alright.

I began going out. Lucas, though he hardly checked on me, had felt some sort of satisfaction at seeing me so wrought with my depression those weeks, and as I grew to enjoy the sun again, his words became harsher, his curfews earlier, his rules stricter.

I took it in stride. Tried to remain hopeful.

This morning was no different, the sun seeming to shine just a little brighter.

And just like every morning, even though I should've known better, I checked the obituaries, because if Adam's name was there—I couldn't go on knowing he may live, he may die, either way doomed to a life without him, a life knowing what he'd been forced to do.

I flipped through the paper, past headlines about the country's involvement in the war, past city news, past the opinion pieces, scanning the columns of fallen soldiers for his name—*Adam Vering*—columns that last the whole length of the page, name after name of boys who would never come home, who died early deaths in a land that wasn't their own—

And screamed.

SEVENTEEN

By mid-morning I grew restless, sitting in one place, feeling like a waiting target for the two vampires to find us, no matter how Vince assured me we were safe.

They would have found Wright by now. His stiff corpse soaking in a pool of his own blood, the murder weapon discarded at his feet. Blank eyes staring at the ceiling, jaw stuck open on a scream that never came.

And his missing bride.

He had never looked so authentically human as he had in death, the mask discarded until he was nothing but a body in that moment. I saw his face as clearly in my mind as though I'd taken a photograph: the dark stubble at his jaw, the unkempt mahogany hair, the small crows feet around his glassy eyes.

I was not sorry that I had done it. In the end, it was my life or his—he had forced me to make that choice. I felt the ease with which the blade had sunk into his flesh, the little resistance as it caught on bone, as vividly as if I were doing it, again and again.

I ate as much as I could, getting my fill for the first time in weeks, each meal more grand than the last: glazed meats over pastries, croquettes, steamed vegetables and roasted potatoes, savory stews, the freshest fruit tarts, and any wine I could ever want, all supplied by the kitchen. There was too much for only myself to eat, but Vince and Dixon helped by plucking a fruit or scone here and there. I made a plate for Lucy, hoping the familiar food would sate her appetite at least a little.

But it was not what she needed. Her body craved a different kind of sustenance.

"Brought you some tea." My voice felt too loud in the space.

A soft murmur from her lips, so low I almost missed it. "I'm not hungry."

"You are," I said as gently as I could.

"I don't want it."

She hadn't moved from before: facing the window, through which the gray morning streamed through. Her blonde hair flat against her skull, skin pale, the dark circles around her eyes purpling. Her liveliness, her light, had been dimmed.

"Are you in any pain?" I asked.

Her eyes flicked to mine. After a long moment, a subtle shake of her head.

She was healed, then, her body wiping away all evidence of her change, of her life *before*.

I saw she still clutched at her stomach, an arm wrapped

protectively around herself, as if to conjure the unborn child taken by my brother's actions.

One day he would reckon with all that he had done.

I sat next to her. It was as though we were in Whitrow again: her, bedridden, and I was keeping her company. The comfortable afternoons we had amidst my impending marriage and her excitement for her child.

Except now her despair was overwhelming, permeating the silence of the room.

She didn't flinch when I reached for her. "Let me run you a bath," I said.

She nodded, gazing off to the window again.

I was not afraid of her—not of her fangs, or her thirst which grew day by day. I was not afraid that she would give in and lunge at me. She would have by now, I realized. But also, I suspected she knew what it was like to have something so completely yours, your *lifeblood*, taken from you.

The washroom had a stately porcelain tub, a gilded mirror and a toilet behind a screen. I helped her into the bath after running the water, making sure it was warm enough to soothe but not scald her skin. She leaned on me, clutching my arm as she lowered herself into the water. Submerging herself, her hair, her face, and erupting a moment later, wiping her blonde tresses from her eyes.

"I'll give you a moment," I said, turning to leave. I could call for more tea, try to get her to eat *something*.

"No." Her small voice echoed. "I don't mind. Stay."

I could not refuse.

Lucy managed to have enough energy to wash the rose-scented suds over her body, washing away any dried flakes of blood under her nails, in her hair. The sheen from the bath oils brought a vitality back to her sallow skin.

She looked at me when she was done, crossing her arms to cover herself. "I'm sorry."

"Sorry? Whatever for?"

She glanced away, sheepish. "Because I have been pushing you away."

"Lucy."

"I am still angry," she said, eyes directed at the shimmering bath water. "But I know that you have not been dealt a hand any better."

"I can't fault you for how you've felt the last couple days." I reached for her, and she gave me her hand. "I just hope you know that I am always on your side, especially when it comes to my brother."

She worried her lip. "I am scared," she whispered. "I was asleep when—"

Her words stumbled, catching in her throat, before she shook her head, squeezing my hand.

"I had no idea that something in him had changed. And when he bit me, I thought—I thought he was *killing* me."

The hatred bubbled up within me, a rage so hot that my face warmed.

"I'm terrified, Helena. I do not know what I am." Tears lined her lashes.

"You're a vampire," I whispered.

She exhaled a sob. "But what happened to me? What am I capable of? Am I going to do the same thing? Am I gonna be like him—"

"No. You will *never* be like Lucas." I knelt next to her, not caring that the cool tile dug into my knees, puddles soaking into my skirt. "You will become whatever you want to be. You will be strong. You will feel whole again."

And as I said it, my own sadness rushed forth, all my ruminations turning to a lump of grief in my throat.

It didn't have to be this way.

"You need to feed," I said, smoothing her wet hair back. "I will not let you hurt me."

Her eyes widened in horror. "I will *not*!"

"Lucy, you must." I held my wrist to her. I didn't think it mattered where she bit me, long as her teeth could sink into my flesh. Her fangs were small, dainty even, hiding behind her rosebud lips.

No matter how she stared at my wrist horrified, a hunger shone through her eyes. She could deny her instincts all she wanted, but it would kill her if she did not feed, and I would not have this on my conscience, either.

"I'll be fine," I whispered. "*You* will be fine."

The moment her teeth bit into my vein, a bright, hot pain needled up my arm. She was hesitant, but she did not pull away when I sucked in a breath at the sting. She gasped when my blood hit her tongue. Both hands locking onto my arm, holding me to her, drinking with gentle pulls, despite the tear that rolled down her cheek.

I was realizing how foolish this could have been, if she could *not* control herself. None of the men were around to help.

But I trusted Lucy.

Her tears did not stop, even when she ripped herself away. She covered her face, drops of my blood falling from her lips and into the bath water, a deep crimson spreading amidst the rosy sheen.

I looked around and found a towel, quickly wrapping it around my wrist. But the flow was already staunching. Perhaps she'd healed me without meaning to.

"I am a *monster*," she sobbed.

"You can't help it," I said gently. "Look, I'm alright."

She rose from the water, which sluiced off her in waves. She wrapped the other plush towel around herself, her golden hair a curtain, hiding her face.

"I'm an *abomination*," she cried, shuddering as her breaths came quicker. "This isn't natural. I—I—"

I held her as she wept; tried to make her see that she had not truly harmed me. The wound was closed, and the pain had been negligible, nothing worse than an accidental cut from a knife when cooking. She hadn't sunk her teeth deep and I doubted it would even scar.

Not like the mark at my neck. Lucas had made sure that the blemish would always remain visible, the skin still shiny and slightly pink under the right light.

I tucked Lucy back into bed after braiding her hair. She was spent, the haunted look returning to her eyes.

Promising to return soon with tea, it wasn't until I shut the door softly behind me that I realized the air of the main living room felt different—and there was a strange person in the room with Vince and Dixon.

A man stood by the door, as though he'd just entered. Dark hair and shockingly familiar gray eyes.

I glanced at Dixon, who sat on the couch, and Vince, standing on the far side of the room with his arms crossed.

"Who is this?"

An immediate gleam of intrigue in the strange man's eyes. Something told me immediately: *vampire*.

"This is Julian," Dixon said, waving a hand. He didn't look particularly pleased. "My brother."

"You have a brother?"

His response was an arched brow.

Julian took one more step forward, a soft smile at his lips, offering me his hand. How dashingly modern. "And your name?" A rich, British accent, the same lilt as Dixon's.

Where Dixon looked severe, if not a little grumpy, his brother was charming, his features a bit softer while still slim and angular.

I slipped my fingers into his. "Helena." Sensing Vince bristle on the other side of the room, I pulled away from Julian quickly. "And can I ask why you're here?"

Surely, this didn't mean Marcel or Lucas were close? My first thought—that we needed another set of hands, or teeth, in case of an attack. We had no idea what my brother or Marcel would do next.

And given how the night of the masquerade had fallen into shambles...

My eyes narrowed on the man. I could not tell his age, but then again, Dixon did not look his true age, either: Dixon, who looked no more than thirty, was in his forties, I'd learned, but still quite young in their world. Born vampires slowed aging once they reached maturity. But if he held the family title of Viscount, then he was the eldest, and Julian was somewhere between Dixon and I in age.

"Pleasure to make your acquaintance," Julian drawled, eyes following me as I made my way across the room to Vince's side. If we'd met at one of the parties Flora and I attended, in another life, I would have fallen for his looks.

Dixon looked weary. He sighed. "I called him last night. Figured if we were to move on, then Lucille..."

"What about Lucy?" My eyes flickered at her door. She could probably hear all of this.

Vince's hand came gently on my shoulder. "It'd be best if she did not come with us."

Julian didn't look particularly happy about the reason he was here, either.

"But she doesn't know him," I said.

"She will be safer far away from where we're going," Vince reasoned.

Dixon threw a glare at Vince. "I offered to take her to Blackwell, my family's home, myself and leave you two to your business."

"But—"

"She will not be harmed," Julian said, looking me straight in the eye. He was just as handsome as his brother. "I swear it."

I scowled. "How can I believe you?"

"Because *I* trust him," Dixon said. "You know I would not call someone I did not trust."

"*She* will not trust him." I lowered my voice, angry. "And you've not told her? She's struggling to come to terms with this, and now you're sending her away with some stranger—?"

"If I may," Julian interjected.

My lips pressed to a line, my glare falling on him again.

"I have experience with these things," he said, voice gentle, like I was some wild animal to keep from angering. "Lloyd prefers to peddle liquor like a self-made human and shy away from our family's brood, but I've dealt with my fair share of Made vampires."

"It's rather a long story," Dixon said, massaging his brow. "The title is enough responsibility as it is, I had no desire to oversee the coven as well. He can protect her, Helena. I would not send her into a lion's den."

And the way he said it made it clear what he thought of Vince's house in New York. He'd said as much to me, once upon a time.

"You know he's right, however it pains me to say so." Vince was solid next to me, his fingers firm and grounding, teasing the hair at my nape. His voice was low, as though only for me. "She will be safer elsewhere, where she can settle into her new life in peace."

I was being stubborn, I realized. Lucy and I had only just reunited after months apart. I could remember the elation on her face when she saw me at Whitrow, that first evening. How excitedly she'd talked in the gardens the next day. How much *life* she had had inside of her. I wanted to protect her, wanted to keep her safe. I'd failed, up to this point. I couldn't keep Lucas' darkness from her. And now—

A Made vampire needed guidance. She was so vulnerable, especially if she would not gather her strength and drink from blood as she should. Each day she refused it, she weakened. The few sips she had today wouldn't last.

And I was only human. I could not usher her into this new life myself. I could not protect her from whatever came next.

I ran a hand down my face. "I need to let her know immediately." I needed to give her the news in such a way that she would not refuse.

Julian's expression softened into something kind, and I didn't think it was a mask at all: something in his eyes told me he *was* someone I could trust. And despite that I was angry with the viscount, I knew on this he told the truth, that he would not send Lucy away to be harmed. He'd spent too long as Flora and I's guard: I liked to think I could read him well.

It was why I could not entirely blame him for what he'd done.

"She will go to my family's house, where she will be guarded by many of our kind. Neither Lucas nor Marcel will be able to reach her, should they venture that far," Dixon said softly.

"I will not allow any harm to come to her," Julian said again.

"You better not. I expect she will be allowed to take my calls." I crossed my arms.

Julian inclined his head. "You have my word."

There was no easy conclusion to this: if I wanted her safe, I had to let her go. We did not yet know what we would be walking into when we ventured to France, and I could be putting her in danger if I brought her along.

"You're taking her now, then?"

Julian said nothing, but the look in his eyes was a *yes*.

"And we must go sooner rather than later," Vince said. "We cannot linger much longer without risking being found."

I knew it was true, and yet—I wished I had more time.

And then, the soft *snick* of a door opening.

Lucy emerged from her room slowly, gaunt and pale as a sheet, yet the grace that straightened her posture hadn't left.

She was elegant in her exhaustion, her movements slow as she centered herself in the door frame, a hand lingering on the wall to steady herself. The little blood I'd given her had lessened the shadows under her eyes only a touch. She needed more.

Her gaze travelled across each of us, lingering on the strange man for a moment longer. Distrust angling her features.

"Am I not to be included in this discussion?"

Though her voice was small, I felt her anger as strongly as if she'd shouted right at us. Dixon had the decency to wince.

"You are welcome to join us, however I believe the topic at hand is settled," Julian said. His hands were clasped behind his back as he observed the young vampire.

"Settled?" Her fingers tightened on the doorframe. "I do not appreciate being talked about as though I am some *child* to be handed off."

"Not a child," Julian said. He took a step towards her. "Your friends here are merely concerned. I am here to help you."

"And who are *you* to help me?"

Julian smiled cruelly at her petulance. "Would you rather rot away in bed? Because that's what will happen if you do not come to terms with yourself." He stepped closer. "And when I say rot, I mean *rot*. You are hardly a step above *dead*. No use mourning what you cannot change."

Lucy's jaw snapped shut.

I'd never seen her so angry and yet so mortified. Her hands clenched at her sides. More tears brimming at her lashes as she stared at the man before her. It came as a whisper from her lips: "Fine."

Julian waved a hand. "Pack whatever you're bringing along. We leave in half an hour."

EIGHTEEN

I stood at the bow of the ferry, the wind whipping my hair, chilling my skin as we floated toward Calais. I refused a sweater. Wanted to feel the bite of the breeze, the sharpness of the air, even if my hands were shaking against the metal railing.

Though he did not deserve it, I wondered if Wright's soul lived on at my side. Was he tethered to me, forced to watch everything his murderous widow did for the rest of her life? Or had his soul faded with every breath as he bled out next to our marital bed?

There'd been no buzz about a murder in London, and none in Dover, either. Perhaps the news had not spread, or perhaps no one cared enough about the sorry man to fan the flames of gossip.

Certainly no one cared to find his lost wife.

I did not feel like a widow; our marriage had only lasted hours. And I did not feel like a killer, either. My hand had slipped, that was it. An act of whatever god made us his play-things. Fate. It wasn't my fault.

Did my mother know? Did she know how I'd stabbed my husband, right through the heart with a paperknife?

Other passengers strolled along the deck, so many different accents, the occasional foreign language, that it became a cloud of noise easy to tune out. The early summer heat had risen in full force that morning, but on the ocean's waves the wind came in frigid bursts. I shut my eyes, let the sun warm my skin.

I felt his eyes on me. Knew it like I knew where the sun sat in the sky above me.

He left me alone for some time. Enough time for my trembling hands to still, for the walls I was building to encircle me and to brush away the tears brimming my eyes.

I was so tired of weeping.

When he came to stand next to me, his presence was gentle, magnetic: the closer we were, the stronger the pull became.

That mountain of words returned, questions and accu-sations and secrets all fighting to come out.

I stared out at the waves skating across the water. "What is your plan?"

His gaze slid over to me, those icy, stormy eyes dark against the midday sun. The wind wend its fingers through his hair when he paused. He hadn't donned a hat today.

He was silent for a few moments.

"The coven will accept me again. There are some who will be angry, a few of Andreas' past... *acquaintances*. But those who are waiting for my return will not turn their backs on me now."

"And then what?" My fingers tightened on the railing.

"We do what we need to do."

It was the grim finality in his voice that told me he'd made up his mind. "You're going to kill them."

He glanced at me. "Is that what you want?"

Was it? Was I destined to bring forth the death of all those near me?

His fingers came to my chin. Turned me to him with a gentle pull. "My plan was always you," he murmured.

I suddenly felt warm all over, despite the chill. I couldn't forget that he was keeping something from me, the truth an unspoken chasm between us. But I'd gone weeks without him and suddenly my body was alight at the touch of his cool fingers.

My face flushed, and I looked away, trying to distract myself by searching the shore along the horizon, growing ever closer. The miniscule forms of buildings peppering the shore, the gulls swooping the air above us.

I swallowed down the rebuttals rising in my throat. Because it was as if I'd been a machine powered off for weeks, and all at once some switches had flipped, a yearning so deep within me catching a flame.

"Do you know this?" he asked, palm cupping my cheek. "That everything I do is for you?"

I bit my lip, unable to answer. Because how could I truly know?

And then I knew I was damned: when I looked at him, this desire burning hot inside of me, it almost didn't even matter that I'd been misled, lied to, pulled this way and that.

I reached up, running my fingers through the rust-colored strands messy from the breeze. Locked my hands behind his neck. Pulled him to me.

His lips met mine softly, hesitantly. Like we were kissing again for the first time.

I melted against him, ignoring my worries and the unease that wanted to seize me, ignoring the memories of the past weeks, instead giving in to the fire burning inside of me.

His other hand came to my hip, his grip gentle. His tongue skated across my lip and I opened for him, craving the taste of him, a hunger I'd ignored for weeks that came back with such an intensity, I couldn't think. When he kissed me, when he touched me, I thought of little else. I became consumed by him, enraptured by his lips on mine, forgetting everything but the feel of him against me.

"Please tell me we'll be alright," I exhaled against his lips.

He hummed, his arm wrapping around my waist, pulling us together. I gasped at the feeling of his arousal against my stomach.

So eager, so quickly.

"We'll be more than fine," he said.

I didn't care how we may have looked to the other passengers, his arms tight around me, our bodies pressed together.

"Tell me you love me," I begged. I needed to hear the sincerity of it, needed to know that *this* wasn't a lie.

He pulled back, just enough to look me in the eyes, to see the darkness there, the wickedness roiling inside. To see how much he wanted me. I could not deny the sincerity in his gaze, the hunger.

"I love you," he said, thumb tracing my cheek bone.

"I've loved you since I met you. I've been *yours* since the moment we ran into each other on that street corner."

He pressed his forehead against mine. At the feeling of being so close, my eyes fell closed, his breath fanning over my lips.

All anger, all fear, was shoved away as *want* took over my mind.

Vince could make me feel good. He knew just how to touch me, how to run his fingers over my skin and conjure my need. He knew how to draw out my pleasure until I was a mess, weeping for him. He could make me forget.

He suddenly whirled me around, and I was trapped between his body and the railing, his arousal pressed against my ass. I gasped, liquid heat deep in my core, my muscles tightening in anticipation. His lips came to my neck. Soft pecks, hands roaming, one arm banded across my chest, pressing our bodies flush.

My knuckles turned white on the railing. I squeezed my thighs together.

"I've gone crazy with wanting you these past weeks," he whispered low, lightly sucking on the skin under my ear.

I stifled a moan, biting my lip so hard I tasted my blood.

"They took you and I went mad. I've thought of only you, every moment. I've thought of how I would destroy them."

He licked my ear, my throat. My head fell back, allowing him all the access he needed, urging him on.

"I thought of what I would do to *you* once I got you back. How I want to kill them and bathe you in their blood, just to lick it all off of you. How I want to spear my cock between those pretty legs while they choke on their own shredded flesh."

I couldn't stop the whimper from escaping my lips.

"I am nothing without you," he whispered.

I exhaled his name, pulling at the hair at the nape of his neck, needing him to kiss me, bite my neck, bite me and drink from me in front of all these people. Wanting him to do whatever he desired. I *wanted* to want that bite.

Because I needed to forget.

He growled under his breath, lips tracing the skin of my neck, my collar bones. "Should we go inside?"

I sighed. "There's no time." The shore was quickly approaching, the buildings growing clearer, the small people moving around at the docks growing into full figures.

Another animalistic sound rumbled from him, low in his chest. He pressed himself against me, harder. "I can make time. I'll pay whatever sum if it means I can get you in one of those rooms. I'll keep the boat docked just to be inside you."

"I thought we needed to *go*," I reminded him, some shred of lucidity coming back to me. "Dixon—"

"*Don't*," he commanded, breathing deeply, as though it was an effort to hold himself back. "Don't say another man's name right now."

"Vince, I—" I turned in his arms, fighting the urge to hitch my leg over his hip, to allow him to shove past my skirt and sink inside of me.

I took a deep breath, steadying myself, placing my hands on his chest.

He held the railing on either side of me, white-knuckled, his pupils expanding—

He shut his eyes, and after a strangled breath, allowed a few inches of space between us.

A few of the other passengers glanced our way, noticing our closeness, before continuing on to their own business. We were about to be in France, after all.

I swallowed down my apprehension. "I can't."

The words felt ridiculous. Because my body was screaming for him, begging for just a moment of respite, every fiber of my being wanting him to *touch me*.

He searched my face for just a moment, before clearing his throat. Taking a step back. "You're right."

Though I was the one to push him away, it hurt.

"I should want to take my time with you," he said.

The commotion on the deck grew, passengers gathering as we neared the docks. And just then, Dixon emerged from the bar, keeping to the other side of the deck, as if he knew we needed privacy. Or perhaps he was tired of our company already.

I ignored the ache between my legs. Now was not the time. "I don't want you to think—"

Vince hushed me with another kiss upon my lips, this one soft and so unlike how he'd devoured me before. "Forgive me, darling. I get carried away."

And though we needed to keep moving, though I knew better than to see it as a dismissal, a rejection, another chip crumbled off my heart, and left me questioning if I'd ever be able to bridge the rift between Vince and I before it was too late.

NINETEEN

Andreas' chateau erupted from the trees like a veritable castle in stark white, sat upon a hill and surrounded by thick forest. Large, arching windows, towers reaching for the dark clouds above; it was built on the side of a cliff, the back end of the house suddenly dropping to the shards of rock below. The dirt road we traveled wound through the trees, peeking in and out of the forest, and as we once more drove under the cover of the branches, shadows encased us.

Entirely abandoned, it seemed, to any traveler making their way closer to the centuries-old chateau. We'd not passed another car or carriage once Reims was behind us.

Dixon stopped the car when the house emerged from the trees before us, something out of a dark fairytale. We idled under the tree line, hundreds of feet away, the engine humming loud enough that any vampire in that house would be able to hear.

They would know they had visitors.

How many eyes were on us now?

He cut the engine, turning to us. "You first, Thornton."

Vince helped me from the car, his grip strong and assured. He laced his fingers through mine—to keep me close, to remind himself that I was by his side, I wasn't sure.

I felt if I spoke, if I made too loud a sound, that I would summon a whole coven of vampires out of the mansion.

I was markedly aware of being the lone mortal. If we were outnumbered and the coven did not accept Vince as he insisted they would....

He could've settled here. Could've had his own crown as Andreas' second, instead of having to make a place for himself in New York. He wouldn't have had to shove his way through the city elites, wouldn't have had to establish a name. He could've just... continued on this ancient legacy.

But instead, he chose *me*.

We climbed up the front steps, directly to the door which sat closed with an air of finality. I held my breath, suppressing the bit of fear that was creeping up my neck, into my veins. As Vince pressed a palm against the door, it gave way, like someone had left it unlocked, unlatched.

Expecting us.

A long, low creak sounded out, echoing through the dark foyer on the other side.

It took a moment for my eyes to adjust. There was hardly any natural light, and there certainly weren't any candles. The only light came from the sun spilling in after us, revealing a foyer two centuries in the past. Patterned stone floors and walls, and a grand staircase leading straight up to the next level. A large Savonnerie carpet underneath our feet, swirling and dampening the sound of our steps.

I gazed around in wonder, almost forgetting why we were there.

The large iron chandelier hung unlit above us. Yet despite the lack of light and the silence, and despite the air of abandonment, there was no layer of dust on the floor, no cobwebs hanging in the corners. It was as though time had stopped within these walls.

Right at the second floor landing, a portrait peered down at us—an older man with light hair, a disapproving stare. His arms were crossed, a sword at his hip, his clothing that of a nobleman, but I wasn't sure from what time.

Instinctively, I knew whose visage stared right at us, positioned to lock eyes with any visitor coming through the doors. His eyes followed in reproach.

A Sire unapproving of his heir.

Until a moment there *was* a person, flesh and bone, standing there at the landing.

The two vampires next to me tensed.

He was younger, dressed fashionably, though casual— slim and tall, his hands in his pockets. Blonde hair, dark eyes. He appeared in a second, moving so quickly I didn't catch it.

I took a step back. But Vince remained in his place, hand wrapped firmly around mine.

The man grinned, the little bit of light shining off his sharp white teeth. He was yet cast in shadow, his form barely visible, though I was sure Vince and Dixon had no issue seeing through the shadows.

"Vince Thornton."

Voice echoing in the quiet, breaking the silence uncomfortably. A slight accent.

"You've returned."

Though we were the intruders, the three of us, a flight of stairs between us and this man, it was as though Vince peered down his nose at the stranger. There was history there, lingering from the time Vince had endured Andreas. An unspoken understanding, only tinged with wariness from so many years passing between them. A familiarity about to snap back into place.

Vince belonged here. And every fiber in his being knew it.

The chateau was welcoming him home.

"Claude."

The man laughed to himself drily, coming down the steps, one by one. Each step echoed off the stone floors.

"And who's this?" The man named Claude was finally at our level, eyeing me up and down, noticing Vince's hold on my hand, completely ignoring the viscount on my other side.

"Helena," I said, forcing my voice not to waver in the face of this vampire. Because if Vince was his superior, then I was untouchable. I would not be afraid. "My name is Helena."

"*Helena*." Claude stopped right before me, taller than me, maybe even taller than Vince.

Was he the next in line behind Marcel? Was he *loyal* to Marcel? But—no, why would Marcel leave his coven entirely behind, if he'd been planning on remaining at Whitrow for some time, with me?

There was a tilt to his lips that betrayed his amusement as he sized me up. "Well, you're easy on the eyes." He threw his hands up immediately by his head as if anticipating Vince's next words. "Don't worry, Thornton, I have no desire to take what's yours. It is one thing to be told you're leaving us to find your beautiful damsel, and another entirely to see her in the flesh."

I glared at the vampire. "You cannot imply I am something to be *owned* and attempt to flatter me in the same breath."

His grin widened. "Oh, I like you."

"As charming as ever, Claude." Vince deadpanned, his hand tightening around mine.

If the vampire was nervous, he hid it well. The thick apprehension from moments before dissipated. I felt I'd passed a test, earning his approval.

"And where are the others?" Vince glanced around, inspecting the foyer. "Or have they sent you ahead to deal with me on your own?"

Claude only made a noise, a hum. After a tense moment, he inclined his head, the mirth giving way to deference. "They're all waiting for you."

He looked over to me again.

"Welcome to Chateau Gaultier."

Part Two

L'Alliance

TWENTY

As though we were descending into the Underworld, we delved further into the chateau that was Andreas' den of monsters, the darkness swallowing me whole, my only tether Vince's fingers tightly enclosed around mine.

The vampires had no need to light the old gas lamps, the candles within the chandelier long melted so that only stalactites of wax remained. In the waning evening light, the clouds outside growing darker by the minute, the chateau was engulfed in shadows.

This darkened opulence, this glimmer into the past, suited Vince more than the sparkling champagne lights of the mansion on Long Island. His unkempt hair from the wind, his sharp angles, the darkness in his eyes—it all belonged here.

I tightened my grip on his hand, afraid I'd never make it out if I let go. I feared these old crumbling walls would make me disappear, fade away, hide me from the light for all eternity.

How many vampires were tracking me through the house, aware of every movement, every heartbeat, waiting to corner me, to find me—

No.

Vince had told me, weeks ago—*They bow to me. And now, to you.*

I summoned the feeling from that night, tried to remember how weightless I felt. He'd taken me in front of all the Made vampires in New York, told me how he ruled them, and now I did too. And I'd believed him. All those people chasing wealth, notoriety, just to end up immortal servants in his mansion, stuck carrying drinks at endless parties, cleaning up after the debauchery. While I sat on the throne, straddling his hips, all of them dying for a taste they'd never get.

These vampires were no different, I tried to tell myself. It was all the same. If Vince was Andreas' heir, they had no choice but to obey—*surely.*

Vince led me with an assuredness He'd walked these halls before. Knew every inch of this house, every room, every person within it.

In these halls, he had changed from the boy I mourned to the man I could never live without. Something monstrous, all mine.

A truth I felt so completely in my soul: I was the only mortal within, the only mortal perhaps for miles.

"They've *been* waiting for you," Claude said. "Your little messenger has had quite the time keeping them patient."

Before I could mull over his words, we were turning a corner into an open doorway, illuminated enough to see a handful of men. Each and every one of them falling silent in a mere moment, all eyes turned toward us.

A chill spread across my skin, whether from the waning daylight, or the stares of these creatures, I wasn't sure. Like the forest going silent at the approach of a predator, a wariness, a reverence, a *terror* commanded the attention of every man in that room. At Vince's arrival, they all went stone-still.

"Light, please." His voice cut through the silence in command.

A moment later, the *snick* of a lighter, and one of the men began lighting the sconces at the walls, old gas lamps with frayed wicks, slowly revealing the inhabitants within. It was no more than a men's smoking room, with emerald-hued wallpaper that turned black in the recessed shadows of the room. A fireplace sat cold, with a marble mantel and a decorative brass screen; a polished mahogany table centered in the room, around which a half dozen men sat. All wide-eyed and hanging on Vince's every breath.

I'd been silly to worry about violence, it seemed: some combination of respect and fear had them stuck in their seats, waiting for him to speak.

Finished lighting the wicks of the lamps, the one man reached into his pocket to pull out a cigarette. As he held the flame near his face, the soft flame lighting his features, I gasped in recognition. "Sinclair?"

He puffed on the smoke. Grinned. "We meet again." Alive and well.

I blinked.

"And *you*."

Amber-colored hair, dark eyes like midnight.

The vampire grinned—I'd met him before, at a top-floor house party, so many months ago. The same night I met Sinclair. The same night Sinclair convinced me to attend Vince's party.

My eyes narrowed.

As if sensing I was about to begin an interrogation, Sinclair nodded to Vince. "How was the journey?"

Vince's eyes slid over to our friend. "As you'd expect."

Claude found a seat, crossing his legs and watching the proceedings with interest, steepling his fingers with a sharp smile. "Yes, we'd love to hear how your extended stay in New York turned out."

The other men were silent, glancing back and forth between the three. Of course I didn't know them, but some memory itched at my mind: a familiar feature here and there, a bad case of déjà vu. Their stares wandered to me before Vince's presence commanded their attention again, but I had the uncanny feeling that I was being watched by more than the dozen gazes in the room, as though even the souls of past spirits looked on with bated breath.

"While I would love to wax on about my time in New York, I believe it more important to see where we stand." Vince's grip tightened on my hand, though his face remained as impassive as stone.

"Where we stand," one of the men spoke out. He had light hair that bordered on red, and deep brown eyes that flickered over to me.

"I made it clear to many of you that I would return. I have not abandoned you. With Andreas' death, the responsibility of the coven falls to me, despite what Marcel Brancato may claim." His eyes skimmed across each man.

"You must know—Marcel killed Andreas," another said in a deep, gruff voice. Arms crossed, hair shorn nearly to his scalp.

Vince did not blink. "I've heard."

"What will you do about this?"

"What is deserved. He must answer for Andreas' death," he paused. "But should you prefer to let this go, I will oblige."

The corner of the man's mouth twitched as though he was fighting a smile. "We trust you'll handle it, then."

The tension in my chest dissipated, the invisible weight lifting from my shoulders. I squeezed Vince's hand.

"You've brought the viscount," another said.

I sensed Dixon bristling next to me. He met my glance, lips pressed into a firm line.

This was not *his* coven. And he was outnumbered here.

"Yes, he's indebted to me. And while he's here, he'll have your respect. At least until this is all over with." He paused. "This brings me to my next point: even if Marcel had not killed our sire, I'd want his head. He has... *overstepped* and I don't take his transgressions lightly."

Though he was vague, I knew every person in the room understood. I held my head high.

Vince turned to Claude. "Where are the others?"

"Defected." A pause. "Or dead."

"For how long?"

Claude's gaze slid to Sinclair. "Since he arrived."

"I told them your terms," Sinclair said simply.

"We are all that's left," one of the other men said. He had dark hair, pale skin. Piercing blue eyes.

In total, there were six of them. The lamps flickered,

casting sneering shadows across their faces. Unfriendly masks revealed in the darkness.

"He won't stay away long," the blue-eyed man said. "After he killed Andreas, he proclaimed himself heir. We played along, but when Mr. Sinclair here announced your return, we realized that Marcel had more *defenders* than we thought. He's been convincing our men of his mission for a while. We fended them off, sent them running, but...."

Vince raised a brow. "You believe he was conspiring?"

Claude opened his palms in agreement. "They did not agree with Andreas' declaration naming you his heir, it seems."

Vince paused, glancing around the room. "He has betrayed us—*me*—in more ways than one, then."

"So what shall we do?"

Vince looked out at his remaining allies, the few that had waited for him all these years. And though they waited for his response, seemingly eager to enact his revenge, a wariness creased their brows. Fatigue. I wondered just what they'd endured together under Andreas' sway. Vince's memories hadn't been fond, that was for certain.

He let go of my hand to pull a seat out for me, the only remaining chair at the table. I sat, tentatively, feeling like I was suddenly the center of everyone's attention, when I should've been the last thing on their minds.

Vince stood behind me, leaning his forearms on the back of the chair. Holding the air of the room in his fist, our breaths stolen.

"I'll say this once," he said, lowering his voice. "You know who I am—*what* I am. And the time for second-guessing your judgment is passed. That you're still here speaks to your decision, but if I find out that even a drop of your blood is sympathetic to Marcel Brancato—"

One of his fingers wound through a strand of my hair as he trailed off.

I felt like I was on that throne again, watching the give and take of bloodletting, knowing that he could command these men to do whatever he wanted. Even Claude, silent, watching through hooded eyes. Sinclair puffing at his cigarette.

"I'll remind you exactly why *I* am Andreas' heir."

TWENTY-ONE

After all the men retired in the early hours of the morning, after Claude and Sinclair and Dixon had retreated to rooms above, and only Vince and I remained in the smoking room, my vampire could look nowhere else but at me.

Tension coiled tightly in his shoulders, his jaw, every muscle rigid after the pressures of the evening.

"Show me to bed," I whispered. My eyes felt heavy, my mind muddled.

We climbed two sets of stairs until we came upon a door with wood stained nearly black. I expected the hinge to screech when he pushed it open, but the door ushered us inside in silence.

The air within faintly stale, the curtains were drawn closed so that the early rays of sun could not breach the windowpanes. I could make out a cerulean wallpaper with filigree, the sheets of the bed a pristine white, and the rest of the furniture the same rich mahogany. Every surface dusted, no cobwebs in sight. It was a gentle opulence, a room fit enough for royalty.

The door fell shut behind Vince.

Alone for the first time in hours, days, weeks, I saw the edges of his mask begin to peel away.

His eyes were already pitch-dark.

"What is it?"

The span of the bedroom was between us, but I could see that none of his tension had abated. He only watched me take in my new room, eyes following my every movement.

I drew near again. Sensed he wanted to speak.

When my fingertips brushed against his chest, he exhaled.

"Is this too much?"

My eyes met his. "Too much?"

"You are the only mortal here. A woman. And you are stained by association with me."

"Is that not a good thing here?"

He frowned.

"I thought—they're loyal to you, are they not?"

"I knew that many would eventually join Marcel. It wasn't a surprise today to see only the few I trusted, but..."

My palm slipped up to his cheek, feeling the bit of stubble along his jaw, the rough angles of his face.

"Every man on his side is another against me. Against *you*."

I swallowed. "How many have you lost?"

"A dozen." His eyes hardened.

And there were only a handful left.

"I should send you back. Have Dixon accompany you home. Lock down the house, so no one comes in and no one leaves. He wouldn't find you, not if he's here, waging this war against me." He gripped my hips, pulling me close. "They won't allow it. He's as good as dead already. If nothing else, I will make sure of it."

In the faint light, I saw the beginnings of the shadowy spiderweb creep across his skin. He was spiraling, turning over every corner in his mind, every possibility, his fingers digging into my waist harsher every second, his words becoming nonsensical.

"Vince."

His eyes snapped back to mine.

I had to believe that Marcel was not lying when he told me how he wanted me. His desire had to be enough. He wouldn't let his men hurt me, would he?

But then I remembered how Marcel had watched as Lucas pierced my throat, his promise to protect extending only to keeping me alive.

"Distract me," I whispered, arching up to meet Vince's lips, because I knew he needed a distraction, too.

He held me still.

"Make it up to me," I said, voice cracking.

Like a knight rushing to his lady, his lips met mine in acquiescence, rough and earnest, with the same ferocity as the night we'd reunited—the night he watched me kill Wright Highsmith.

In a second, my back was to the wall, and I gasped, head spinning at how quickly he moved. He gripped my thighs and I was in the air, arms winding around his neck. I tightened my legs around his waist, needing to feel him, needing everything he would give me, because I did not want to spend another second in my head, didn't want to think about Wright or Lucas or Marcel, didn't want to think about all I'd endured the last two weeks. My memories were turning to rot, morphing into vines that wrapped around each thought, dewdrops of poison slipping into my blood, corroding me from the inside out.

Vince's tongue traced across my lips, demanding entry, until he spread me out on the bed, the sheets bitter and cold. In moments he had me undressed, my breasts peaking, gooseflesh pebbling my skin.

He gazed down greedily. "You'll let me have you?"

"Yes." I uttered the word with no hesitation.

I watched him pull his shirt over his head, unbuckling his trousers, slowly, agonizingly slowly, until he was bare, his cock hard and ready. His eyes never left mine as he palmed himself.

And then my legs were spreading, enticing him to come closer, to bury inside, to make a home of my flesh. "Please," I begged, sitting up on elbows to meet him.

He stopped me with a hand to my chest—which slowly slid up to my throat, my jaw, my cheek, fingers ghosting across my pulse, before he bent and kissed me again.

"I've gone mad not being near you these past weeks. Mad with wanting you, mad with needing to taste you," he mumbled against my lips, his fingers tightening on my jaw. "It is unfair, this hold you have on me. Did you think of me, my darling? Did you imagine what I would do to you once I had you again?"

He gently pushed me back down on the bed, reaching for himself again, running his hands over the head of his cock a few times. I watched him with greedy eyes, nodding, already panting.

"Did you dream of me?" he murmured, kneeling between my legs. He placed a soft kiss to the inside of my thigh and moaned.

"Yes."

"What did you dream, darling?"

"I–" My back arched off the bed, fingers tangling in his hair as his tongue travelled up my thigh, the sensitive flesh shaking, even as he drew further away from where I needed him most. He turned his head, doing the same to my other thigh, placing kisses along my leg, licking the skin, nipping lightly until my flesh was a constellation of pink bruises. His dark eyes met mine—that black shadow taking over, his irises gone, so I knew that monster was close, simmering under his skin—before he delved lower, pressing his lips to my clit.

He paused, hovering over me, dark eyes staring straight into mine.

"I–" My breath caught. "It was you I was marrying. I dreamt that I was no one else's but *yours*."

"And this is what you want?"

"Yes," I sighed.

My thoughts scattered as he began to suck at the bundle of nerves; he loosed a groan when I writhed, his tongue light, teasing, until he found my center. He pressed into me, one of his hands coming to clamp down my thigh as I tensed beneath him.

"So sweet," he murmured against my flesh, his voice rough with desire. Those wicked eyes met mine from below. "Do you ache, Helena?"

I whimpered out my response.

"Do I please you?"

My fingers tugged at his hair. "Yes. *More.*"

"What is it you want?" he asked, pressing another kiss right above my knee.

"I want you inside of me." It came out petulant.

He grinned in satisfaction. "You want my tongue? My hand? My cock?"

"Yes," I repeated, not caring what he did, only that he did *something*. I wanted all of him, wanted him to unleash that monster, wanted every rough edge of his against my skin. Needed him to place me safely in his ribcage, where I could stand sentry to his heart, claim it as mine and *only* mine. To meld together, to become one, to nestle into his bones and marrow and make my home there.

"As you wish."

Two fingers slid into me without any resistance. Biting my lip to keep from crying out too loud, unsure how well the other vampires could hear. And when Vince began fucking me with his fingers, my hips ground against him, chasing that high, wanting nothing more than to shatter.

His tongue found my clit again, his fingers gliding in and out, wringing every bit of pleasure from me. He was wicked with his hands, playing my body like an instrument he'd mastered long ago.

Crying muffled moans into the back of my hand as I shuddered against him, pulling at his hair in a vise grip that only spurred him on. He licked me up, hungrily, coaxing the orgasm from me until I deflated against the bed. He only stopped when I relaxed, panting, my body damp with perspiration, before he rose to his feet, licking his lips.

"I'm not done yet."

His breath fanned across my breasts and he took his

time, placing open-mouthed kisses on my skin, trailing up to my jaw, skating over my neck when I flinched.

I shut my stinging eyes, hating that Lucas tainted this.

And then Vince was brushing his lips on mine, softly, his hips spreading my thighs apart, until his cock was at my center and I was sighing into his mouth at the hard feel of him.

"Is this distraction enough?" he asked.

My fingers dug into the flesh of his back. "*More.*"

We sighed together as he sank in to the hilt.

"Two weeks is too long a time without you," he whispered. "I cannot stand it. I will never allow you out of my sight again."

I grew impatient with his gentleness, hooking my ankles and pulling him closer, deeper. At my restlessness, the greedy way my hips squirmed, he withdrew, sheathing himself again, and again.

"Touch yourself."

Obediently, I reached between us, my fingers brushing against my clit. My pleasure came quickly, and as I grew frantic, nearly whimpering, he kissed me again, swallowing my cries. Eating them up, because everything I was, every drop of my pleasure, was his for the taking.

Something in me gave over to him. If we were two halves to the same soul, then he had command over my very being. I was powerless against his demands. His will was mine, and I wanted nothing more than to surrender, eager to submit, eager to please him.

The ecstasy quickly became overwhelming, and I squirmed beneath him, unable to catch my breath, biting my lip to keep from crying out.

"Bite me," he said, cradling my head. "Let me have your anguish."

And I could think of nothing more than to obey this second command as I shattered again within moments. I sunk my teeth into his shoulder, sure that it brought him pain, the taste of his salty skin on my tongue.

A voice within me whispered, *more, more, more,* as he spilled into me, his moan guttural and nearly a growl. I was so full, both heavy and light, floating and sinking; my vision blurred as my cries turned to sobbing.

Reality was only held at bay for a few minutes. He was still fully seated within me, peppering my face with kisses as his body continued to move, insatiable. It could have been heaven.

"So beautiful, my darling."

But we were in a strange chateau in the mountains of France, hiding from my brother and the vampire who wanted to stake a claim in me, and each blissful second felt like borrowed time.

Vince sensed the shift of my emotions and withdrew, cradling my face. "What is it?"

The urge to let my tears go was overpowering, knowing that despite everything, I would have at least one more day with him. Our future was so uncertain, and I was tired of not knowing what my fate had in store, not knowing what horrible thing came next. I covered my face with my hands, not wanting him to see. How pathetic was I?

"Helena." He pulled my hands away. "Do not hide your-self from me."

"I—"

But I wasn't sure what to say. I had wished for nothing

but to reunite with him the past few weeks, and feeling him now, knowing he was real, that he wasn't some figment of my imagination, was too great a gift. Some debt I would owe the Fates, no doubt: there would be a price for my happiness. But how many times would I have to go through this? How many times would he be taken from me?

His soft touch cradled my face, a thumb swiping away a tear. "Tell me, so I can make it better."

"I am *happy*," I said, staring up at him with watery eyes, at his irises slowly becoming normal again. "I am happy, and that *terrifies* me."

"Have I not told you I'd burn every inch of this earth to find you?" His words should have terrified me, brutal as they were. "What is it you're scared of? That I'd let them take you again?"

"I don't know," I admitted. Something dark hung over us, a scythe waiting to swing and sever our threads.

I wanted so badly to trust Vince. The girl from six years ago did. But I could not until everything was laid bare—*everything*.

It was ripping me apart.

He searched my face once more, his fingers tracing idly against my cheek. And whether he was still hiding things from me, keeping the truth out of reach, that pain in his eyes, that frustration, was real. His features hardened. "Do not worry about those who have wronged you. They will get their due."

TWENTY-TWO

In the midday light, Chateau Gaultier was not nearly as daunting. It was clear that the men within had taken on the upkeep of the house themselves; while from the outside it appeared abandoned, the halls and rooms within were pristine and preserved, as though I'd stepped back into a long-forgotten era. I couldn't help staring at the ornamental door frames, the decorative carvings in stone, marveling how they were older than New York itself.

How many lives had passed within these doors? The past seemed to whisper to me, hiding in the chipped stone walls, as though all I needed to do was press my palm to them to hear their secrets.

Vince had made sure to call for breakfast, and someone had been able to scrounge up some bread and jam, some old tea that had long gone stale. I made do, but Vince frowned in displeasure before readying for the day.

A few hours later, I awoke again to the bright sun, my belly pleasantly full and my mind quiet. It was the first morning in weeks that I had no obligations, no need to put on a face or *run*. Even my thoughts moved at a sluggish pace, and I had half a mind to remain naked in the sheets, like a prized pet waiting for Vince to return.

I only wondered distantly what Vince, Dixon, all the men were up to elsewhere in this house. I took my time selecting from my new wardrobe, pulling a soft lavender dress from the trunk with a low waist and fluttering sleeves.

Stepping out of the grand bedroom, I heard no one as I slipped down the hall, though it was not the imposing silence of our arrival; rather, a cozy quiet, the sunlight warm through the windows.

I did not think anyone else resided in this hall. It was remarkably empty and cold, as though Vince and I had been the first to disturb these rooms in some time. Peeking into a few, I saw nothing but white sheeted forms and drawn curtains in bedroom suites much smaller than the one Vince had chosen. Unused for years, if I had to guess.

Who were all these rooms for?

Traversing the house in my search for Vince, I made a wrong turn somewhere—I came upon a hallway with nothing but windows along one wall, overlooking the ravine below. The drop was steep, and for a moment I became woozy, imagining that should I take one step, I'd plummet to my death on the shards of rock. Beyond, the valley spread into verdant trees of every shade, the village a smudge in the distance.

Each step revealed more of the land, nothing but forest as far as I could see in every direction. If I drew closer to the glass, my nose nearly brushing the windowpane, I could imagine I was a bird flying high above the hills. Free.

I jolted, suddenly shouldering the dead end of the hall, across which a deep velvet curtain was drawn. I hadn't realized I neared the end so quickly, absorbed in the scenery outside and lost in my musings.

Only, the wall seemed to move, rattling as I stepped into it.

Brushing my fingertips along the curtain, I pressed forward, only to feel a slight give again, a soft creaking.

The curtain moved easily as I pulled it aside.

And behind it, a door with iron hinges.

"I wouldn't go in there if I were you."

I whirled around like I was a child caught stealing candy.

Claude stood a few feet away, his smile easy. I scowled.

"Didn't mean to frighten you." He gestured to the door. "Merely an old coat closet, but I imagine a vermin or two who've made it their home would object to the intrusion."

I let the curtain fall, concealing the curious door once more. "I was looking for Vince."

"You'd be hard pressed to find him here. Come, I'll take you to him."

The sunshine seemed to follow the blond vampire as he turned to lead me away.

He must have noticed how I hesitated.

"I'm not going to hurt you."

"I know."

He gave me a smirk that told me he knew *I* knew what advantage I held here. I may yet be human, but I had their heir at my beck and call. One word, and I could have any of these men thrown out. Exiled. Executed.

Of course, not that I would have a reason to do that.

"Tell me: how did you get him so wrapped around your finger?" Claude crossed his arms, leaning against the window, completely blocking my exit.

I walked around him anyway. "Whatever do you mean?"

"You and I both know he kneels at your feet. What'd you do to him, to have him so thoroughly desperate for you? I've never seen Thornton like that."

I shrugged, glancing at him as he came to my side. "I did not *do* anything."

He arched his brow.

"We have a history, that's all."

"Really," he deadpanned. "He hardly mentioned you."

I didn't acknowledge the dig. "And who are *you*? The runt? Last-Made with something to prove?"

He laughed aloud, throwing his head back. "You've got a tongue on you. No wonder."

"Careful."

"I'm a good judge of character." He slowed his steps. "And I think that you *know* what control you hold over him. A human woman who's managed to tame a vampire." His eyes glinted in interest.

"I don't control anyone."

"Semantics." He glanced me up and down. "So shall I now bow to you, *my lady*?"

"Would you deign to bow to a mortal woman?"

His grin widened. "If she were the right woman. Are you up to the task? We can be an unruly bunch."

I thought about Vince last night, unsure if I could handle this new world, if I already struggled to come to terms with his monstrousness, his immortality.

And I thought about how there was nothing left of my

old life, not really: choosing Vince again, running away from my brother and past, had closed the door to my old life for good.

I met Claude's eyes. "My place is here. With him. And should you choose to follow...."

"Gladly, *my lady*."

I spun on him, glaring again. "Stop that. I am not a *lady*."

The teeth he bared were sharp, and for a moment I felt the slightest bit of envy. "Are you so sure?"

My face heated, that shame rearing its head. I'd done my best to tamp it down, to only worry about what came next. To forget the face of the man I'd killed.

Claude's satisfied smirk told me he knew. He continued on down the hall, whether I was going to follow or not. "Yes, I think you'll fit in around here just fine."

In less than a day, the coven had fallen into a comfortable allegiance that it knew by heart, even after years without Vince. Like every man knew his place, knew when to speak. And they looked to Vince for direction.

They told him all Marcel had done in Vince's absence, how the murder of Andreas had come as a surprise; they relayed what they knew of Marcel's plan to bring Andreas' will to fruition. A quiet anger consumed them, a thirst for blood that even *I* could sense, at every reminder of the betrayal.

Because of Marcel, their Sire was dead. Because of Marcel, a number of their brothers were dead.

"This morning I sent messages to our past... *acquaintances* around the continent." Vince leaned back in his seat next to me, crossing an ankle over his knee. "Marcel may have already allied with many of them, if they see his ascension as legitimate."

"But why would they?" Emil asked around a cigarette. "*You* were Andreas' second. And you didn't *murder your sire*."

"Oh, they'll look down upon it, but if you think they won't watch Marcel claim the title just to see what happens, you're an idiot." Claude grabbed the cigarette from between Emil's lips and took a puff.

"We will see who comes." Vince's gaze slid over to me. "I've invited them to the chateau for a banquet. It should be interesting to have so many of them under one roof."

"Or foolish," Claude grumbled.

My eyes widened. "A party?"

"A dinner," Vince clarified.

Sinclair sighed, leaning his chin on his fist, shaking his head. "You're asking for a bloodbath, Thornton."

"If they off each other, so be it." Vince smiled a closed-lip smile that spoke to the malice under his skin.

"Yes, that will help your reputation: all your guests becoming murderous under your watch."

"Less work for us," Claude mumbled.

"I don't have time to speak with each of them individually," Vince reasoned. "Convincing them of my legitimacy as quickly as possible is in our best interest."

"Or else what?" I asked.

Was Marcel really such a threat? He wanted to follow in

Andreas' footsteps, claim the legacy as his own. But could he really turn everyone against Vince so easily?

Clause shook his head when I voiced my thoughts. "Andreas did not have allies. He had enemies, and all others were those biding their time to take a hit out on him," he said. "*That* is what you set to inherit."

You, as if Vince and I were one and the same.

Vince turned to me. "They do not want *another* Andreas. And they'll do what they can to prevent it. To Andreas' enemies, Marcel just did them a massive favor. He took care of their largest threat, and if they agree his claim is legitimate, then they will see to it that I am no longer a danger."

My mouth went dry. "And *are* you a danger to them?"

"Yes." He only said the one word, but with it, the hair raised on the back of my neck, the implied threat low in his voice.

The other men fell away, as if the room got dark and it was only Vince and I left. The intensity in his eyes made me squirm, his attention solely on me, and though his eyes were their normal gray, I knew that the demon was simmering under his skin, that creature that I'd seen him succumb to. It peered out at me often, disguising itself as the darkness within Vince, the anger, the envy.

"So what will you do?" I asked.

He answered as though I were the regent to appease, and he was my commanding general. "Entertain them. Give them what they want. Is that not what I do best?"

In New York, he'd stolen the fortunes of hundreds of men seeking immortality, taking advantage of their fear of fading away into obscurity. Luring them with grand parties, sex, liquor. Their fortunes in exchange for eternity, freely given, though they never released their folly until it was too late.

The vampires he spoke of now had no humanity to bargain. But they could still be swayed if the price was right.

I looked away, breaking the trance Vince had on me. "I'm thirsty. Would anyone like a drink?"

Sinclair stood. "I'll join you."

Across the room sat a drink cart with decanters full of various liquors, bottles of wine brought up from the cellars. Deja vu washed over me as I grabbed the bottle of brandy, wanting to throw my head back and drink it all in one gulp.

I knew that Marcel himself was a threat. I had not known that there were so many others Vince would have to contend with.

"Are you alright?" Sinclair asked, softly. "You look a little pale."

I threw him my best smile. "I'm perfectly fine."

"You do not have to lie to me." He paused. "I heard about what happened. And I am sorry you've gone through that. Should you need anything—"

"Yes. Well." I busied myself with removing the wax. "How is Séra? Veronica?"

Sinclair eased the bottle from my grasp before pouring the liquor for me. "They're alright."

"And you've left them behind?"

Sinclair was silent for a moment. Perhaps debating what to reveal. "He sent me ahead to feel things out."

"But Emil was already here."

"Yes." He handed me the glass. "Emil returned some time ago to be Vince's eyes within the coven while he remained in New York. I was sent to... *warn* the others of his return. Give them a head start to run, I suppose."

"I thought many died."

"And many did." He shrugged a shoulder. "But not all. The few left may be with Marcel, they may be hiding. Who knows. But Vince won't let their betrayal go unpunished."

I bit my lip, the brandy doing nothing to stave off my nerves. This version of Vince... he was ruthless and cruel and vengeful. He spoke of death like it meant nothing. He was so different, even, from the man I'd reunited with only months ago.

But these men didn't bat an eye at the vicious mask he wore. This was the Vince that they knew.

Last night, he'd stepped into his role so effortlessly, it was as though he'd never left. And I was beginning to wonder if the man I'd fallen for all over again had only been another one of his faces, a mask, hiding the monster beneath.

Did they know what lived in his skin?

I downed my drink, reveling in the burn.

"Let's not talk of this," Sinclair motioned for me to follow him back to the table.

"When did he send you?"

I wouldn't meet his eyes, pouring myself another three fingers. Waited, that sinking dread returning. Glanced over at Vince, his back turned to me, and feeling deep in my bones that he knew just what I was thinking.

"I left the morning of the party," Sinclair said, hesitant. "I thought you knew."

Twenty-Three

While every vampire within the chateau was sleeping, I tossed and turned next to a slumbering Vince until it became clear that my thoughts would not let me rest. With only the guidance of moonlight, I slipped from the room on silent feet. Vince did not stir, perhaps as exhausted as I was after our many ordeals.

It was all too easy to creep away; I'd half-expected him to wake at the loss of my presence, but he didn't follow.

The velvet curtain at the end of the hall of windows beckoned to me. I did not believe Claude for a second that all that lay behind was a long-forgotten closet.

A shiver traveled down my spine. A low whisper in my ear, a warning.

The sky was clear tonight, the moon a perfect orb of white amidst the glowing constellations. Bright enough to illuminate the hall, a spotlight on that curtain.

I should've been afraid, wandering a house full of vampires as the only mortal. I should have been afraid to part from Vince. I should have remained at his side, curled up until morning. Should have tamped down all my worries.

I should have trusted him.

And yet, something inside of me knew that whatever was behind this door would put many of my questions to rest.

I swept aside the velvet curtain once more. The wood of the door was worn, unpolished, soft under my fingertips. Cringing at the low creak of the wood, the hinges old and undisturbed for some time, I stepped into the dark within.

I was expecting a long-forgotten study. A hidden staircase to a dungeon littered with skulls. An actual coat closet, even, with tattered, moth-eaten cloaks.

I wasn't expecting to see the remnants of a bedroom locked away behind the curtain.

Once upon a time, the room may have been quite lavish. A small bed was pushed against the far wall, unmade, the blankets thrown hastily. The wall of windows continued on one side of the room, with a perfectly clear view of the ravine and forest below, and the moon illuminated each and every dust mote sparkling in the air.

A perfectly preserved time capsule to the moment the room had last been abandoned.

I let the door swing ajar behind me as I stepped further into the bedroom. I was disturbing something that wanted not to be interrupted, the state of the room a testament to the rage of the last soul to traverse the threshold, this anger seeping from the walls like an invisible mist, noxious and sweet. I could taste it at my lips, could sense the presence as though he were standing inches away.

Books were scattered haphazardly across the floor, sheets

of paper ripped and torn and balled up into piles. Upon a desk sat a stack of novels, an old inkwell that had been tipped over, a black stain spreading across the wooden surface and long dried, the pen snapped in half.

The room was half-destroyed, like someone had stomped through in a rampage, letting loose a bull.

Someone's meager bedroom, separate from the rest, hiding behind a curtain.

A mirror was tarnishing on the wall, and as I passed, the face of a haunted girl stared back. My dark hair was frizzy, long enough to braid again if I wanted; brown eyes shadowy and shining. A thinness to my flesh, like I could see through to my bones, a trick of the light.

I couldn't look at her. When I did, I saw all that she had to endure these past weeks. The hurt there in her eyes; the ghost of a bite at her throat, the phantom blood staining her skin.

And somehow, through it all, she had lived.

So completely *human*.

I didn't belong here. Whatever lurked in this house, whatever legacy Vince was meant to continue, it was not mine. Claude may think that I have some control —and it would be stupid to insist that Vince had no intention of devoting himself to me—but I was not Made by the same Sire as these men. I was an intruder.

A *mortal*.

I ran my fingertips along the books, a few more shelved on a singular bookcase. Some of the titles were printed in golden lettering, other spines nameless: *L'Homme qui rit. Le Rouge et le Noir.*

Dust collected on my skin. No one had entered in a long time.

Righting the inkwell, I noticed more loose papers stacked on the desktop, upon which the ink had splattered, ruining the letters and notes of the previous tenant.

Except—

They were not just letters.

One piece of parchment was dated December 4, 1919,

> *He ordered me to find five more men tonight. There are travelers in the forest looking for work, their villages and farms decimated after the war. It is far too easy to pluck them off the road before their caravan notices. But the towns are beginning to notice. Already a group has taken it upon themselves to investigate the disappearances. They did not find anything. They never will. He let them live, perhaps the only time a visitor has walked away from this house.*

Another from February 14, 1920:

> *Does she remember me?*

> *April 7, 1920. He says I can leave soon, but he will not tell me where he is sending me, nor what I am to do. I have*

begged him to give me direction. Our numbers are well. He says I am not ready.

May 23, 1920. B brought him a woman. An offering. She did not live through the night.

I traced my fingers along the words, a pit sinking in my stomach at each entry. Pages ripped from a diary.

I knew that sloping hand. Sifting through the papers, stiff and brittle, I saw that each and every one came from the same pen.

Then:

November 18, 1920. He says it is time.

I dreaded what the next page would say. Because I *knew* this writing, *knew* the man who'd written it.

So much of his story he wouldn't tell me. And here it was, written out date by date. My eyes raced along the pages, every reference to "him" boiling my blood.

But the next sheet was a list: names in a column, none I recognized, with locations. *Sebastian Heroux, Annecy. Siegmar Wagner, Freiburg.*

And further down the page, *Viscount Blackwell — Percival Dixon.*

Dixon—as in *Lloyd Dixon?*

My hands shook, dropping the papers, sending them fluttering back onto the desk. My heart skipped like I found something I wasn't supposed to, laid eyes on something forbidden.

Each name on the list was some nobleman, the locations peppered all over Europe, some even across the world. A few names crossed out in bold ink.

I took a shuddering breath and rifled through the other pages.

There was a gap in time between the entries, the next coming from later 1921:

> I've only just begun to control it. He says the urges will subside, that it is no different from when I was Made. But he is wrong. He does not know how my mind has been infected. If he knew my thoughts, he would kill me himself. It speaks to me at all hours. We are one and the same.

Then, undated, messy—

> I am not going mad
> I am not going mad
> I am not going mad
> I am not—

Filling out a whole page, cutting off abruptly. The penmanship began tidy, but by the end, the letters were curling, the pen having moved in sharp jerks. Words bleeding into each other.

I am not going mad.

I couldn't look at the pages anymore.

The room was small, growing smaller. Across the room, a door with glass panes leading to a balcony beckoned me. The handle gave, and I rushed outside just as the anxiety racked through me.

The night air was cool, the scent of lilac on the wind.

I sucked in a breath.

Another.

I was beginning to understand. There was so much Vince didn't tell me before, so many secrets and details of his life in this house that he'd kept from me. And I wasn't sure why.

He told me everything was for me.

He told me he *lived* for me.

And yet he'd only revealed half-truths, small details of his past that only left me with more questions. *This* is what he'd been hiding.

Nausea crept up my throat.

He told me he would kill for me. He'd been entirely unphased as I slid that paperknife between Wright's ribs. Threatened it, even, upon the men who declared their loyalty. Death did not scare him.

Because what Andreas had made him do—

I squeezed my eyes shut, bracing myself on the stone balustrade, too tired to hold my body up, too shocked to do anything but attempt to breathe through the noise of my mind. Letting the cool air stretch my lungs, the rough, frigid stone of the railing grounding me through my fingertips.

The earth dropped away before me. The trees below waved in the breeze, a chorus of whispers in the midnight air. Maybe the forest knew his secrets. Maybe he'd spoken aloud out here on the balcony so many years ago, revealing fears and hopes and memories, and the wind carried them to me again tonight, murmuring in my ears.

Maybe once upon a time he felt just as tormented. An iciness had run down my spine hours ago and never left.

And then anger. The *how-dare-you* kind of anger. Pain at being lied to, piercing right through me.

You don't know him, Marcel had said.

And I could no longer deny that he was right.

Marcel was still out there, somewhere.

Shutting my eyes against the darkness, I imagined the world falling away, and we were at another party, and my only worries were to find alcohol and a dance partner. Golden glittering lights, ritzy dresses with reflective beads, liquor that burned less the more you drank it, kisses in alcoves that escalated to more.

Where my only responsibility was to chase happiness until the sun came up.

I exhaled a sigh, ignoring the chill seeping through my dress.

The balcony door creaked. Perhaps the wind.

Or Vince, coming to assure me everything will be alright. He'd kiss me until I forget the ache in my chest, and I'd let him, stay wrapped up in him until the morning, and with the sun I'd remember my demands for the full truth.

A hand slid under my jaw. The warmth of a body behind mine.

My eyes shot open.

"Helena, *dearest*, you make this entirely too easy."

The click of a gun. Cold metal under my chin.

I froze.

"Didn't get very far, did you?" Lucas purred in my ear.

Both his arms around me, one to crane my head back, the other to hold the weapon up to my jugular, pinning me still against his chest.

It wouldn't have mattered—my limbs turned to stone, something sinking inside of me so deep my thoughts were a scrambled mess and I could not *move*.

He was going to kill me.

"It's almost like you *wanted* me to find you, running right where we thought you'd go. Brancato was right: you'll damn yourself for the chance to throw yourself at *his* feet."

I couldn't even scream.

"Don't worry, you can have your fun with Brancato. He'll satisfy you well enough, I think. We'll be long gone by the time Vince Thornton realizes."

"Don't be so sure."

Lucas growled, the sound deep in his throat. Whirling around, dragging me with him, the gun pressing into the soft flesh of my jaw.

"*You*."

And suddenly, I was eighteen again, at the dinner club where everything fell apart. Lucas, tearing me away, spitting vitriol at Adam—aiming the weapon at the heart that didn't belong to him, aiming at *me*, because I never mattered to him, *nothing* mattered except his name and his reputation and his *control*.

He would never let me have anything I wanted. He was always taking and consuming and twisting his fingers into me, spreading his rot until it infected every sinew, every ounce of blood and flesh within me—wrapping his fists around me and crushing me into a mold I could not fit, shattering my bones, my heart, because I did not belong to him.

Except this time, black veins were sprouting from Vince's fingertips, a spiderweb of midnight against the pallor of his skin.

He did not hold the monster at bay.

It all happened in the span of a breath—

Vince rushed towards us, shoving Lucas' hand skyward, the gun going off right next to my ear. The scream erupted from my throat, as I ducked, slamming my eyes shut.

Lucas lunged, and in the commotion, I was thrown against the balustrade, the momentum knocking the air from my lungs. Fingers slipping on the rough stone.

Breathless, unable to shout Vince's name one last time, my eyes snapped open just to see the world tilt on its axis.

The strength of Lucas' throw sending me tumbling over the railing, plummeting down towards my death, hundreds of feet below.

Twenty-Four

I fell, weightless, fingers grasping at air. Reaching for anything, a ledge, a vine, *something* to keep from plunging to my death.

"Helena!"

Strong hands wrapped around my own—stopping my descent so suddenly, my shoulder jerked from its socket, racketing bright pain up into my skull.

Vince hung over the railing, a frantic look in his darkening eyes: fear—*real* fear.

A spatter of blood streaked his cheek.

He quickly pulled me onto solid ground, holding me up when my knees buckled. Cradling my face, he pressed his forehead against mine, while I gasped for air. "You're alright, you're alright."

I could only nod, my heart racing with adrenaline. My hands became claws at his shoulders, but he didn't seem to care as my nails bit into his skin. I was shaking, unable to breathe, my heart *pounding* in my ears, a high pitch ringing drowning out Vince's attempts to calm me.

It took me a moment to realize that my brother was on his knees, cursing and clutching at his shoulder, staring at—

His severed arm lay stiffly beside him. Crimson seeped between his fingers, dripping onto the balcony in a puddle.

Vince quickly cradled my face to his chest, blocking my view. The ringing in my ears was growing louder, incessant, overpowering.

In his arms I trembled, pressing my face against the exact spot his heart beat in his chest, hearing nothing but my own pulse, feeling only his arms encasing me to him. Someone was speaking, but it sounded as though my head was underwater. When Vince responded, the timbre of his voice vibrated against my skull.

Lucas meant to kill me.

I almost died.

"No." Vince's fingers curled in my hair, brushing through the strands. "I got you," he whispered. "I will never allow you to die."

I looked up at him.

Mouth pressed into a firm line, a crease between his brows, he met my gaze, fingers tangling at my nape. The moon cast bluish light across his features. His veins were darkening, his pupils expanding, his fear turning to wrath at having been so close to watching me fall into the ravine. The blood spatter was stark against his skin.

My brother's blood.

Without thinking, I reached up, tracing along one of the dark veins, almost pitch-black like the midnight sky above.

His skin was smooth, the inky spiderweb deep within his flesh, trailing from his chest, up his neck and along his jaw.

He gently grabbed my hand. "You're alright," he said again, a little more insistent.

"Yes," I said, though I wasn't wholly confident.

This vampire. This *monster*.

"You *bastard*," my brother seethed, doubling over. "I ought to *kill* you."

There was commotion in the hall, the men roused at the sound of the shot, calling Vince's name. Claude, Emil, Sinclair—they all stopped in their tracks at the sight of Lucas bleeding out, at the way I shivered in Vince's grasp.

They were staring at Vince, at the darkness about to swallow him whole.

Claude cleared his throat. "We see you have it handled."

"I do," Vince said, his voice hardening into something gruff. His fingers tightened on me once more, and he met my stare, the image of him becoming something blurry, before he bent and grabbed the gun, which had clattered to the ground in the struggle.

He pointed it at my brother.

I couldn't stop the gasp that slipped from my lips, some leftover affection wanting me to shout *No*.

Lucas glared at Vince, recognizing him for who he was— his true identity—and unable to do anything about it now. He gritted his teeth, nothing but hate in his eyes.

Perhaps he was remembering that night six years ago, too.

Emil peered over Claude's shoulder. "Should we—"

"No." Vince jerked the gun. "Get up."

Lucas, for what it's worth, tried, but stumbled back onto a knee.

I almost laughed, feeling like I was losing my mind, at my brother obeying Vince's command. Maybe it was the gun pointed at his chest—Vince did say that a wound to the heart would kill any vampire, no matter how it was inflicted—or maybe it was the monstrousness taking Vince over, but Lucas did not fight, didn't try to lash out or run.

He wasn't moving quick enough.

Vince gripped Lucas' hair with all the brutality of a conqueror and wrenched him to his feet.

Lucas spat another curse, becoming paler by the second.

"Shall we behead him?" Sinclair cocked his head.

Vince only darkened, throwing my brother towards them. "Not yet. He's going to feel it when I tear him limb from limb."

Lucas laughed. "Sure, Vering, go ahead and try."

The only indication that Vince was affected by his old name was the clenching of his jaw. "Lock him away. I'll deal with him later."

The men gave him one last look before dragging my brother away, perhaps too aware of what came when Vince was in this state. The door inside slammed closed, the sound of my brother's shouts echoing off the walls until they faded away into nothing.

And then, we were alone.

Vince stood in the doorway, chest heaving with deep breaths, like he was alive again, hands in clawed fists at his sides. The monster peered out at me. He was transforming into the beast that had appeared the night of the masquerade. This beast that seemed only to come out when he was so close to losing me.

He almost lost me tonight.

I shivered, a numbness beginning to settle into my limbs. "Do you think he was alone?"

To see Lucas like that—I couldn't deny the satisfaction at seeing Lucas *lose*.

Vince was silent for a moment. I turned and found him staring at me from the doorway. Dark inky veins traveling down his arms, up his neck.

Where was the man I met at that party only a few months ago?

He'd turned into this—*thing*.

"If he was not alone, I don't believe we'll be disturbed any time soon," he said.

A gust of wind sent my skirt fluttering, my body shivering almost uncontrollably.

I'd tried to deny what was right in front of me all this time.

"Come inside," he said, voice softer.

I obeyed.

He shut the door to the balcony behind me, locking it with a *click*. Pulled the curtains so we were alone in darkness, only a gas lamp still lit and the single candle. The ghosts of before lingered in the shadows, like the past layered over the present. His old self was in here, too, the newly-Made vampire who'd given himself a new name. Watching from long ago.

Vince looked around, as though he forgot about this place. He set the gun down. "You shouldn't have been in here."

"Why not?"

I realized we were so far apart now, the whole room between us. His gaze caught on the destroyed books, the scattered pages. Staring, reliving some memory. "No one should come in here."

"This was your room. From before."

His eyes flickered to mine in response. In this darkness, the shadows overtook him.

He looked like a *demon*.

Hands nearly pitch dark, each vein a shade of black, eyes no longer their gray hue.

"What happened to you?" I whispered.

Fists flexing at his sides. "I would rather not do this right now."

"I don't think you have much of a choice when you look like *that*." My voice caught.

His black eyes darted between mine. "I was—" Hesitation. "I was created here. Not merely Made into a vampire, but something more."

"What did he do to you? I read these pages," I said. "He hurt you. He made you do *something*."

"I had hoped," his voice strained, "to keep this from you. To make every attempt not to let it take me over. To just be as *human* as I could be with you."

Yet as we spoke, the humanity faded from his eyes.

I had told him his darkness didn't scare me. Told him I wanted all of him. Every last monstrous bit.

But I couldn't deny how frightened I was.

"What are you?"

He took a step closer, tentative. "Andreas found a way to augment the vampirism already inside of me. I have the blood of the ancients running through me. Not just Andreas' blood, but that of the first vampires from thousands of years ago, long enough that we don't truly remember our origins."

He moved like he was afraid I would run.

"Believe me, or don't, but I have a better handle on it than I did a few years ago. And yet..."

"It comes out," I finished for him. "Like it is now."

Black eyes watched for my reaction.

If I thought him a predator before, he looked the part even more so now. There was nothing about him that felt *natural*. Some creature from the underworld overtaking his body and walking amongst the living.

No wonder the men in this house followed his every command. They were here when Andreas made him *this*.

And this was only part of his veiled truths coming to light.

"I am not a good man, Helena," he said. "I've done terrible things. For Andreas. For *myself*."

"For me?" I stared back, crossing my arms to hold myself together.

He must have sensed my anger because he didn't say a word.

"You're going to tell me this was all for me," I said. "You're going to tell me that you've kept these things hidden from me, to *protect* me, aren't you? You're going to tell me that this needed to be done. *All* of this. For what?"

My kidnapping. The pain I'd endured. Having my lifeblood taken from me. Watching the same thing happen to Lucy. *Lucy*, who was god knows *where* with Dixon's brother, Made into something she hadn't even known existed. Watching Anna die by my brother's hand, by *Wright's* hand—and the countless others since he came to New York to fetch me for his bride.

I murdered Wright Highsmith.

"You've not asked me how I feel." I could do little more than whisper.

Vince blinked. "I'm sorry."

"Do you even care how I feel?"

"Of course I care. I just—I know what it's like to be at the mercy of *them*. I did not want to ask you to relive it."

"Them? You are one of them!" All my rage came out at once.

He opened his mouth to speak, but I was not done.

"Do you know what they did to me? Do you know what their plans were for me? They were going to Make me."

"I know."

"Marcel Made my brother, and they wanted to Make Wright Highsmith. My brother—he almost *drained* me."

His lip curled. "I *know*."

"And I was powerless against them. But if you knew? If you knew what was happening why didn't you stop it?" Tears blurred my vision, my heart racing with anger and despair and frustration. My adrenaline crashing, a flurry of emotions building into a typhoon inside of me.

"I could not get to you in time." His voice was low, soft.

"But why let them take me?" I cried. "Why let them take me from the masquerade?"

I thought—I *hoped*—that he would deny this; I hoped everything Marcel said was a lie.

But my heart crumbled when he did not refute me.

"Because I needed Marcel to think he won." Something

in his gaze hardened. Regret there, perhaps. Steely resolve. "I needed a plausible reason to kill him, to get the others on my side." A pause. "You were my bait, after all."

Veronica. She had tricked me.

Vince had tricked me.

"I hate you," I seethed.

His lips pulled in a caustic smile. "I warned you." He stepped closer, crowding me until the desk with all his writings was pressing at the back of my thighs. "I told you I was a monster. And you dared love me anyway."

I raised my hand to strike him, but my fist fell limply against his chest as my tears took over, blurring my vision, my anguish cleaving me in two. Gasping for air, my cheeks instantly stained with my misery.

"How could you?" I whispered.

They had led me to believe it was my idea: to bait Marcel, so they could deal with him then and there.

But Vince let him hand me over to Lucas and Wright, all so Vince could come back to Europe and convince long-sworn enemies that *Marcel* was the real danger.

There, in those writings, was the proof.

Marcel had never lied to me.

Vince was a grand puppet master, pulling at all our strings.

He parted my thighs with a knee, until I was sitting on the edge of the table, clutching at him but wishing to curse him, push him away, *hurt* him.

He stepped between my legs. "It was one of the hardest things I've done," he said, hand winding in my hair.

"Marcel offered himself to me," I said. My voice wobbled. But I put every ounce of my anger in it. All the pain I'd felt for weeks. Had been shoving down the past few days. Made sure he could read it in my eyes. "Protection for a place in my bed."

Vince stilled.

"He watched Lucas drink my blood."

His hand tightened in my hair.

"And then he licked the pain away," I said, glaring through my tears.

My lover glared back with hooded black eyes. The blood smeared on his face a stark red against his skin. The creature inside of him begging for release.

It speaks to me.

We are one and the same.

Wrath burned in his stare, but not at me, I knew. Rage at every moment another man touched me. Rage that the other vampires dared sink their teeth into me.

His fist pulled at my hair, grip iron-strong, claws scraping against my skin. Gasping, I bent to his will, my head wrenching back in his grip. Baring my throat to him.

"Did you enjoy it?" Something rumbled deep in his chest, a beast's warning growl.

"Of course not."

I sighed as he leaned closer, hot breath along my neck, the column of my throat, that sensitive spot he knew how to kiss just right.

"I only ever want you," I admitted. It was the truth, even if it damned me.

Vince's tongue flicked out, licking away a tear.

I'd never had him like this. He'd kept the monster locked away so well, but I was realizing I'd seen glimpses this whole time. His eyes shifting colors, the changes in his demeanor.

But my thighs were shaking around him, already quivering, and he'd hardly touched me. Just the promise of his wickedness left me wanting. Aching. As though I hadn't witnessed him rip my brother's arm clean off for daring to touch me.

"How much do you want me?" he murmured against my skin, breathing deeply, scenting the promise of my blood. "Do you want me now? Like this?"

I nodded, sighing at the feel of him, my hands against his firm chest, his body hard between my legs. He leaned forward, pressing his arousal into the apex of my thighs, drawing a gasp from my lips.

"Even now, when I am the furthest I'll ever be from human?"

I hooked an ankle around the back of his leg. "Show me."

He put only enough distance between us to pull his linen shirt over his head. The darkness began at his heart, skating across the muscular planes of his chest, down his abdomen. Every vein, every artery—*black*, turning his flesh a grayish pallor. It concentrated at his fingertips, which had elongated into sharp points he trailed down my hips, my thighs, like he couldn't help but touch me.

Through hooded eyes, my cheeks still wet, I stared in wonder, entranced by this creature with Vince's name and face.

Andreas may have crafted him, but he was *mine*.

My penance, my ruin.

"Do I frighten you, my love? Am I abhorrent?" He leaned closer. "I am a thing of nightmares, am I not?"

When he grinned, his teeth glinted sharp—*sharper*—in the indigo light.

He was the monster I should've been afraid of all along. He was the villain, waiting to snatch me up in his claws.

I shook my head.

"Tell me." He stepped in between my legs again, gripping my thighs with such strength I couldn't pull away if I wanted. "Tell me that you want me. Tell me that you still love me."

"I want you," I breathed.

A moan slipped from my lips as he neared, ground his cock against me.

"I must erase them from your mind," he growled. "No one else gets to taste you. No one gets to drink this perfect blood but me. No one gets to claim you but me."

"*Yes.*"

I reached up, winding my arms around his neck, and pulled his lips down to meet mine.

Sharp teeth skated across my lip. He didn't hold back, pricking my lips, groaning at the small drops of blood which bloomed. He held me still with the one hand in my hair, able to crush me against him and pull me away at will. His tongue warred with mine, the taste of iron spurring him on. Grinding against me, his cock impossibly hard, only a few layers of fabric separating us.

"Please," I begged, breathless.

"Please what?" He nipped at my jaw, my throat, my shoulder.

"Please fuck me."

He'd never looked so ghastly as when he grinned at me then, the spatter of my brother's blood drying on his face.

He let go, throwing me onto my back against the table, papers scattering and tearing beneath me. In a moment, he reached under my thin night slip and ripped my underthings away, baring me to the cool air. He gazed down at me, my legs spread open for him, my dress around my waist. He groaned, palming himself through his pants as he gazed upon my sex, wet for him—only him.

"You're so pretty," he praised.

And then he was undoing his belt and he was free, hard and long, the blunt head falling against my center. He wrapped his fingers around himself, giving his cock a few jerks. His other hand came to my clit, thumb circling, sending electricity through my thighs, all while moving his hand up and down himself.

It was so wholly erotic—maybe I'd died after all, and this was my demon sent to torment me.

I reached for him, wanting to touch him, going wild with need. Whimpering, begging.

His finger slipped into me, and I cried out. Another finger. Another.

I rolled my hips, trying to find some relief. Heart racing, my thoughts consumed with only want, want, *want*.

He fucked me with his fingers, while he fucked his hand. His black stare never left the spot where his fingers disappeared inside of me. And before I could beg him to put his cock in me, my release came barreling through. I cried out, sighing his name.

"Already?" he murmured, looming over me again to suck at my lips, my throat, nipping at the skin.

And just as the high began to ebb, he pressed the head

against my center, my thighs still quivering from the after-shocks. The rest of me limp.

But the restlessness returned quickly as he worked his way in. Spreading me apart, hooking my knees over his arms. The angle delicious, his cock parting me deeper, until he hit a wall inside me and there was no more room.

I gasped, panting, squirming, trying to buck my hips against him. The pressure was immense, my body trying to accommodate the size of him, the stretch.

He groaned, hands gripping my hips, forcing them to still. His nails bit into my flesh, but I didn't care. The bite of pain, the burn of him stretching me wide, nearly sent me melting into my release again.

"I want to do so many things to you," he said through gritted teeth. "I want to tear you apart. I want to lock you in this room and never let you out." His rigid length twitched inside of me, but he did not move.

"Please," I begged again. Reached for him, but he didn't come closer.

He pressed one hand against my belly. Then his cock slid out, slow, maddening, just to the tip, before he speared himself inside me again.

"Would you let me do whatever I want?" he asked, his thrusts slow. Slow enough I felt every inch, every ridge, the pressure so immense I melted against the table.

I nodded again, unable to form words.

"Ah ah," he chided, sliding in and out again, so slow I was losing my mind. "Be sure before you answer."

"Yes," I repeated, chanting the word. "Yes. *Yes*."

Because I would. I *had*.

Didn't he own me so completely already: mind, body

and soul? He was my past, my present, my future, my *fate* if there was such a thing. We were inextricably tied and I could do nothing to untangle the knot of our lives if I even wanted to.

My thighs were stretched as far as they would go as he brushed his lips against mine, a hand on either side of my head. "I want so badly to make you bleed."

Completely unable to speak, I nodded lazily, head lolling against his shoulder. I was overwhelmed, spent.

I had gone too long without him. No amount of love-making could make up for the time we spent apart. Weeks. *Years.*

I wanted him to make me forget. I *needed* to forget.

Lucas was there, in my mind, waiting to remind me, to whisper again how worthless I was. How I was only good for what I could do for Wright. Every time I shut my eyes, I could see it again: Lucas pinning me to the ground with his teeth sinking into my flesh, that searing agony, and Wright Highsmith watching on in wide-eyed fascination. Marcel— biding his time.

I could not blink without seeing it again. I could not sit in silence, for fear of hearing their taunts again.

And Vince could quiet my mind, chase all this misery away, if but for a moment.

The need to give in to his distraction spurned on my desire, blossoming into a physical sensation deep in my chest, a burning that needed quelling.

"Please," I begged.

I could only see part of his face, pressed against the table as I was. Pure lust had taken him over. He almost shook with the might of it.

I moved my hips, pressing back against him.

"Fuck." He stilled. His fingertips brushed against my clit again. "I've thought about taking you when I'm in this form. I've thought about draining you and Making you mine while deep inside of you."

His breath was hot on my throat, his hips still grinding into mine, his fingers drawing pleasure from me with every move.

"I've thought about doing this in front of everyone. How would that make you feel, darling? To be Made by a monster for all to see? To Make you into one of us while my cock makes you scream?" He said it just as his fingers quickened. Imagining what he said, these filthy words, sent me over the edge.

Then burning pleasure, the heady sensation of his hips moving against me, his free hand tangled in my hair, holding me to him. I didn't even have the strength to keep my eyes open, my body going limp, entirely spent and at his mercy.

Words came from me, I wasn't sure what, but he quickened, our hips slapping together until the desk began to move with each thrust. And then he banded an arm around my hips to keep me still, each thrust brutal, claiming.

"Gonna come," he exhaled. "You'll never be rid of me."

And then he was spilling inside of me, groaning with a thrust, and another, his cum spilling out around his cock, and I hadn't realized I was weeping with pleasure until he stilled. His heart hammered in his chest, the black veins pulsing. My body hummed, each and every nerve ending sizzling. Drunk with an intoxicating dizziness, pressing my face against the cool surface of the table.

After a moment he pulled out. Gathered his cum with his fingers and pushed it back inside of me.

I shouldn't have enjoyed it so much.

But I wanted him to claim me. Take every part of me for his own. Do what he wanted with me.

Make me forget.

And then he kissed my neck, lips trailing along my shoulder, down between the valley of my breasts. Gentle kisses, as if in apology for the mess he made of me.

Damp with perspiration, he brushed my hair away before gathering me in his arms. Carried me to the messy bed, and pulled the flimsy night gown over my head. Set to worshipping me, face between my legs, until I passed out from exhaustion and pleasure, the last thing I remembered a triumphant look in those dark eyes as he claimed me, over and over again.

TWENTY-FIVE

If ever in my life I've come dangerously close to slipping into madness, this night would have been the first time I tripped, stumbling towards that line where sanity crumbled.

Vince's sleeping form glowed in the purple of early dawn. His pale skin was marred only by blood, evidence of the violence hours ago. His chest rose nearly imperceptibly with his slow breaths, impossibly slow, each exhalation a whisper from his parted lips.

How peacefully he slept, how quietly, when all I could do was stare at the ceiling. Morning was almost upon us. I hadn't slept long, only taken under when my body couldn't handle any more. I watched the shadows, elongated across the room, complete their dance, touching every crevice of the walls, darkening each corner, until they were banished by the tangerine sun.

My exhaustion burned, a particular ache at the back of my skull, but it was incomparable to the pain of knowing that it was all because of him.

All of this, because of Vince.

He hadn't moved all night. I'd let him in again, let him take me. I couldn't resist him. He was like the strongest opiate, the most maddening ambrosia, his touches addictive and jarring and pushing away all reason.

He took everything from me.

I slipped out of bed. He didn't stir.

As I came to the window, the valley below was silent, the trees rippling in the midnight wind. Not a sound in the house, a tense silence like something would snap at any second.

Goosebumps pebbled on my skin, the cool evening air, the moonlight, caressing my bare flesh.

Fingertips against the carved wood of the window frame, cool to the touch.

You'll never be rid of me.

I glanced over my shoulder. Vince lay unmoving, his face toward the wall in a serene expression. The column of his pale neck, bared to me; skin I'd kissed and sucked, breathed against him as he entered me once, twice, too many to count.

We hadn't made it out of his old room, the evidence of his life as Andreas' Second scattered all around us.

The gun was somewhere. Under the pile of clothing. A flimsy weapon against a creature such as these. But everything could be killed.

Bad men deserved to be killed.

My lover lay unsuspecting. A monster, a predator, encaged in these walls with me, a human girl.

The sheets rasped as I climbed atop the bed again, on hands and knees, crawling toward him.

How could he?

All of this, *all* of this, because of him.

I thought I knew betrayal. But I hadn't, not until *this*.

They used me as bait. Let Marcel and my brother take me, force my hand in marriage to a man who cared only what I had between my legs.

I straddled my lover's hips.

His hands came sleepily to my waist. Fingers light against my skin, gentle.

How many times had I told him, *I'm yours?*

I lay my palm on his chest. Felt the dull, slow thud of his undead heart. He said this heart beat only for me, that he endured this life only to find me, to reclaim me. Threw parties to attract me, like I was some moth fluttering near flames. And he had fulfilled his purpose. I was here, I was found. I was with him once more. Claimed.

The beast in possession of his maiden.

Running my hands along the planes of his chest, his shoulders, feeling every hard muscle, every bit of him that I craved. It was an addiction. His strong jaw, rough with stubble, his high cheekbones, the unkempt hair like a halo around his head against the white pillow.

Even now, his soul called out to mine. The darkness intoxicating, his wickedness drawing me in.

I leaned down. Pressed my lips to his. Savored the taste of him. The feel of his body against mine, exquisite. Powerful. We fit together, like he was made for me and I for him. Maybe it was true. I always thought we were destined, however star-crossed we seemed.

I pressed the barrel against his chest. Cool metal against ribs.

Vince's eyes opened, hands tightening around my waist.

He was so beautiful.

His gaze washed over me with adoration, eyelids low, lashes fluttering against his cheeks. The haze of sleep still blanketing him, he exhaled like it was the first time he'd laid eyes on me. The inky darkness was gone, the monster tucked away and he was just himself—just Vince.

"What is it, my darling?" Voice barely louder than a breath, husky and low.

Like I wasn't doing anything wrong. Like I wasn't holding his life in my hands.

I steeled myself, adjusting the weight of the weapon.

But he didn't move. Thumbs circling, slowly, idly against my skin.

My eyes slammed shut at the sudden burn behind them, the rush of emotion, like a dam within me had opened up.

"I hate you," I whispered. The words caught in my throat, breaking on the last syllable.

I suppressed a sob. Vince's thumb rubbed my hip bone, fingers tightening just so.

"No you don't."

He saw right through me. Could read me like I was one of the pages he used to print, ink and paper, all my secrets bared to him.

"I want to." I *needed* to. Shaking my head against the truth, wanting to deny every ounce of agony that burned within me. "I love you too much."

Those gray eyes flicked to the gun. Back to me. "Do it."

I shook my head again.

I *couldn't*. Maybe it was weakness—maybe *he* was my weakness. This creature between my legs, who could so easily overpower me, drain me. But he didn't resist, didn't move away at the gun against his chest. He had told me stakes couldn't kill a vampire. That iron did nothing to repel them.

But to the heart?

"*Do it*," Vince insisted. He gripped the barrel, pressing it harder against his chest.

A sob wrenched itself free from me, tears blurring my vision. I was crumbling, folding in on myself, the weapon shaking in my grip.

"Do it," he said again, "because if I am to die, it needs to be by your hand." Voice soft, assured. Unafraid.

He was so unafraid of death.

The tears came harder. "Why?"

He searched my face, looking for *something*, concern only just beginning to crease his brow.

"*Why?*" I demanded, hardly able to speak the words. "Why did you do this?"

His throat slid. Eyes flicking across my face, glancing at my chest, my body.

"It needed to be done." He let go of the gun and reached for my face. Both hands cupping my cheeks, gentle, wiping away the rivers of tears. "I always knew you'd come back to me."

Betrayal, betrayal, he betrayed you.

He knew I would come back—he knew I wouldn't stay away from the masquerade—he knew Marcel would take me —was *waiting* for it to happen—

His fingers became firm against my cheeks. "When I returned," he began, sitting up in the bed, ignoring the metal pressing into his ribs, "I only ever intended to find you. Then we were to leave. I never wanted to stay in New York. I was only waiting to break the subject to you, and already you were struggling with the truth of my new existence."

The words lingered in the air. While I straddled his lap and he held my face, the weapon stayed crushed between our bodies, pointed directly at his monstrous heart. My hand shook, my fingers curled like claws around the handle.

"And then Marcel made his appearance, and I knew I had to deal with him quickly. With Highsmith and your brother." His lip curled at the mention. "We can't be happy with them in the picture. And I knew they would return here, where they *thought* they were safe."

So much scheming, so many lies.

I can't decide if you're safer with me or safer if I send you away, he had said.

My throat ached with all the hurt inside of me. "So you let him take me?"

Vince's eyes flashed. His grip on me tightened. "It was the most difficult thing I've had to do, to let you out of my sight."

"But why?" The cavity of my chest ached. My heart—he'd taken it long ago. Had consumed me, just like I asked, but I didn't know it would hurt so badly. "Why tell Lucas to marry me off?"

"Because I knew if you were faced with two choices: a man that you didn't love and one that you still might, you would choose the latter. You would choose me."

And yet the monster still had the face of *Adam*.

Our mouths were inches apart, breaths mingling in the space between our lips.

I would always choose him. And maybe that's why it hurt so much. His love *hurt*.

"So kill me if you must, because I cannot live without you. I live only *for* you." Vince held my face, like if he let go, I was gone forever.

"I should," I said before I could think better of it.

These weeks with Wright, with Lucas, the scars that I'd borne, the pain he had put me through. It was too much. It was all too much.

"I should kill you."

Vince nodded, his nose just barely brushing against mine. Eyes flicking down to my lips. "I love you. I love this side of you. When you're raw and hurting and bleeding," he whispered, more intense with each word. "I love when you look at me like that."

I hadn't realized I was clenching my jaw so hard, gritting my teeth.

"You're so anguished and I hate myself for it, hate that *I love* how tormented I make you," he rasped. One hand wandered to the nape of my neck, curling in my hair. Bringing me closer, lifting me up, and I realized he was hard underneath me, moving my center closer.

A gasp slipped from my lips as he pressed harder against me, one arm winding around my back, the other tugging on my hair. Baring my throat to him. His breath was hot on the flesh of my neck before he licked the spot above my pulse, sharp teeth grazing my skin.

"If you let me live, you must know this: that I will chase you anywhere. I'll destroy the whole world to get to you. I'll destroy *myself*."

The gun slipped from my grasp, falling into the sheets,

my hands coming to his shoulders as sparks of pleasure bloomed where we met. I shut my eyes, pulling myself back to reason. "You can't keep doing this to me." My voice broke.

He looked up at me through shadowed eyes.

"No more lies. If I am to choose you, I need to know everything." Tears brimmed my lashes.

"I promise," he said, lifting my hips.

My core slickened, my heart beginning to race. He was the drug to which I was addicted

"I promise," he repeated, the words like a prayer, reaching between us and positioning his cock at my entrance.

The breath caught in my throat at the promise of pleasure, a tear trailing down my cheek, my fingers digging into the flesh of his arms.

"I promise," he groaned, palming my hips, pushing me down on him.

I sank down, slowly, ready for him, wet and crazy with need. My need for him as great as my need for air, for sustenance. My muscles protested, sore from his ravishing me all night, but I craved the pain, knowing he was responsible for the ache. Once I was fully seated and he was deep within me, I took a shuddering breath, already overwhelmed at the feel of him. Resisting the urge to tilt my hips, to chase the hurt away.

"I was made for you," he breathed.

And I knew it was true. That he and I were two halves to one whole—inevitable from the moment we met on that street corner.

I slowly arched, and he groaned, burying his face in my

chest. He clung to me, arms wrapped around my middle, pressing his lips to my sternum, to the place above my beating heart. Like if he could, he'd drink directly from the source.

"I promise," he said again. He let me work him, lifting and spearing myself on him, legs shaking around his hips, bracing myself on his thighs.

We fell into that familiar dance, his tongue trailing along the valley of my breasts, before he took one of the peaks into his mouth. His tongue was soft, massaging the flesh. I cried out, my movements faltering, before he slowly took over, his hands guiding. Pushing and pulling my hips against him.

"I promise to make it up to you," he breathed, tracing his teeth along my chest.

I tangled my hands in his hair, urging him to take more. Wanting him to prick my flesh with his teeth.

I must have the said words, because then he was trailing his lips against my throat, and that familiar searing heat shot through me.

Panic, unbridled panic as his teeth sunk into the exact spot Lucas had bit me.

Like he was reclaiming it as his own.

And then heady pleasure, heightening the frantic need in my blood.

He groaned at the first drop, something purely animalistic, before he was piercing every inch along my shoulder, down my chest, taking the peak of my breast into his mouth and biting down.

My head fell back, breaths coming in quick gasps each time I fell upon his lap. In no time, I was chasing my release, moving my hips quicker, tugging at his hair, grinding against him, opening my legs further so he could touch me deeper. On top of him, I set the pace, I had the control, and he let me take it, let me fuck him the way I needed to.

He watched in rapt fascination, looking up at me with glazed eyes, my blood staining his lip. My chest was a mess of purple and red bruises, each wound already smoothed over, but the evidence still lingered at the corners of his mouth.

"That's it," he said, fingers digging into my waist, restraining himself. "Use me. *Please use me*."

I pulled his hair, feeling the tell-tale static in my limbs, my fingers, and shoved him back on the bed. Lust burned in his hooded eyes, his tongue running over his fangs, removing his hands from me, gripping the sheets. My fingers fell to his throat, feeling the quickening pulse, claiming him as *mine*. Sitting up and circling my hips, sighing at the new angle. "I—"

"Use me," he bit out, "I'm *yours*."

"You're mine," I sighed, and then I was coming, melting against him, fucking him into the aftershocks of my orgasm. My breath escaped me, all my thoughts wiped away except that I had never felt so perfect. My body seized around him. Knowing that I could command him if I wanted, could order him not to come, could demand he pull away and use his mouth on me, that wicked mouth.

He gave me only a moment before he snapped, thrusting upwards. The groan in his chest was guttural as he spilled into me, holding me in place with dagger-like fingers, cock twitching deep inside me. I swallowed his moan, tightening my fingers around his throat, feeling the vibrations of his voice, feeling the erratic pulse beneath his skin.

And when he was done, and my body began to ache, I

buried my face in his shoulder. Caught my breath. I couldn't help but move my hips, grinding against his spent cock, every inch of my skin buzzing.

"You are everything to me," he whispered. "Do not forget."

"Prove it."

"As Andreas' Second, I was his sword. After I was Made and the change was complete, he used me as a weapon. Trained me to follow his orders. At first, I was only to help build the coven. Find men from the battlefield and add them to our numbers. Marcel was the first."

It was midday, the sun peeking through the curtains. Vince had ordered someone to bring up food again, and made sure I ate my fill of the fruit and cheeses that were procured. We lay in bed, and I lazily traced my fingers through his, staring in wonder at the veins which looked so normal now under his skin. My hunger sated, my body used and tired, I'd dragged him back under the sheets with me, pulled his arms around me, and demanded he talk. He could not deny me now.

"Once I proved my usefulness, my sire sent me to neighboring covens—to make good on his promises. I made use of the daylight hours to spring my arrival on unsuspecting men. Rarely ever was I met with warm welcomes. It seemed they knew who I was before I'd introduced myself as the enactor of his will. I was given clear instructions: secure their obeisance and have them recognize Andreas as sovereign, or death."

Vince paused. Was quiet for a while.

"My reputation was tainted before he even decided to change me further. He brought me to his study one day and explained his plan: told me what he had found in one of his ancestor's books, writings in a margin that detailed instructions for creating a spawn of Hell. There were indications it had been done once before, but if it was successful, it was never recorded. I thought it was some joke. At first."

His hand began circling my hip, fingers moving in patterns. Something to distract himself. I was stone-still, enrapt by his words, afraid if I spoke he wouldn't tell it all.

"I wasn't... *asked* for my opinion or permission, though I shouldn't have been surprised. His mind was made up. At that point I was a dedicated pupil. Lost in my new existence, pessimistic that my fate led in any other direction. I didn't see much choice. He already owned me.

"He did it that night. I remember the look on his face—the fascination, like testing a new chemical reaction in an experiment for the first time. Discovering a new species. He didn't hear me when I begged, didn't aid me when I screamed, didn't stop even when I thought I would die."

His hand stilled. "I thought I would die, for good this time.

"The blood—it was so old, not even Andreas knew for sure its origin. But he was a collector of rarities and antiquities. His collection contained many artifacts he claimed were cursed, or divine. I had asked him one day why he bothered to hoard such items. I was backhanded so hard I couldn't breathe. He told me if I did not understand the importance, then my new existence was wasted on me.

"When I was first Made, it was as though I'd been given

an entirely new existence, new body, new everything. Life was not as I knew it before. I struggled—immensely—with my new instincts, my new *hunger*. I've told you this before. I'd been pulled from the battlefield, already good as dead, and thrust into the life of a killer.

"But after I drank from that vial, it was as though I was finally becoming what I was always *supposed* to be. All my life there'd been a veil over my eyes, and it was finally lifted. It came full-force—a poison rushing through my body, a monster erupting from me at the same instant I swallowed. I became—*this*."

He gestured to himself, though his skin was pale, clear, his irises their normal icy gray.

I bit my lip, my hand resting right over his heart. "Can you call it forward at will?"

"Yes," he said, his hand stilling on my waist. "It is easier to fall into that form than it is to keep it away. I thought I had better control. I thought *I* was in control. Until *you*. Once you came into my life again, it became apparent that the beast wanted you, too. Especially when you were taken away from me again."

I lay my head on his chest, feeling the fine dusting of hair, hearing the faint pulse, wondering if the monster lived in his heart, and if it could hear me, too.

He pulled me closer. "Make no mistake that I am the monster, darling. Existence as a vampire is already nightmarish, especially to those of us who do not wish to kill. But I have no such qualms when it comes to you."

He tucked a finger under my chin, forcing our eyes to meet. "I am sorry I did not tell you sooner. But how could I expect you to love a creature like me? To be unafraid?"

That was why his mask hadn't slipped until Marcel was dragging me away. He'd been trying so very hard to keep this secret, this half of his existence, tucked away. How long would he have waited to tell me?

"I am not afraid," I said.

He shook his head, like he didn't believe me. "I fear you will change your mind."

"Don't give me a reason to."

A muscle feathered in his jaw. I looked down at him, at the concern lingering in his eyes, at the way his auburn hair spread across the pillow, the way his chest rose with each breath. I looked at him and I saw Adam. I looked at him and I saw my fate. If there was no him, there wasn't *anyone*. And I told him as much.

"I must confess one more thing."

I stilled.

He swallowed, thumb skating across my cheek. His gaze falling to my lips, like he wanted nothing more than to devour me again.

"While I did not behead my sire, I am at least partially responsible for his death."

"Marcel did it." I blinked. "He admitted it."

"Yes." His eyes met mine again, a finger trailing behind my ear, tucking away a strand of my hair, his caress gentle, even when he talked of murder. "But I put the idea into his head. I would have done it myself, but Marcel was always a sycophnt. All it took was a little push."

"Does anyone know?"

He shook his head. "I'm not sure Marcel even knew."

"How?" I asked.

"My initial intention was to leave, and in my absence,

Marcel would feel *compelled* to kill Andreas. Do the dirty work for me. I could not have patricide on my conscience, when already the world thought me a monster. All it took was a few comments here and there to plant the idea in his mind."

"You never wanted to return to New York," I realized. "You only came back for me."

His lips twitched into a small smile. "Can't deny that I enjoyed my time there. And I will return again. *We* will return."

"But this is your home."

And with Andreas gone, there was no one Vince was beholden to—he was in charge, completely, with a reputation that preceded him and loyal vampires on two continents.

"After everything, I refuse to be chased away from all that I am to inherit. I *deserve* Andreas' wealth, his name, his notoriety. He did not Make me, just so I could squander it and let someone like Brancato take it."

"Do you regret it?" I leaned closer. "Do you regret killing your sire?"

"Not for a second."

And I couldn't blame him, not after everything he'd told me.

"Who was Andreas? Why do so many fear him?" *Why do so many fear* you?

"Besides being one of the oldest of our kind left, he had a reputation for not taking 'no' for an answer."

"Seems like a lot of you are averse to the word 'no.'" I said it without realizing the weight of it, my mind drifting to the many nights I'd spent at Whitrow.

"You aren't wrong." Vince sobered a little, his hand stilling at my cheek. "It is why I felt I needed to put an end to Andreas' control. Not because of how many he has hurt in his time—no, I'd be a hypocrite to kill him just for that—but because I did not want to endure him anymore."

It scared me how similarly I felt, knowing that somewhere below, my brother awaited his sentence.

He lifted my chin, looking deep into my eyes. "I feel I don't deserve you."

And perhaps it was true. The young girl I'd been, corrupted by this young boy, our fates forever intertwined. We'd fallen into each other so fast, it was as though my destiny was always to be debauched by the man below me. My life certainly would've been different if we'd never met. I would've become the woman my mother wanted me to be, prim and proper and married off to a man exactly like Wright.

I glanced at the door, as though he would barge through any minute.

"Who knows of this?" I murmured, tracing my fingers along the center of his chest, the toxin in his blood waiting to erupt at his command.

He paused. "Only a few of what I am. The men here. Dixon."

"And you are the only one?" I asked. "Andreas didn't do the same to the rest? To Marcel?"

"I am alone."

That we know of, I thought.

His grip on me tightened, my body cradled against his. "To see me as the monster was a death sentence to those who would not bow down. My sire made it clear that none of his enemies were to know, else I'd be hunted. Executed. I wasn't to let myself free, unless we were met with resistance."

My breath caught in my throat. I sat up, clutching at him, the bedsheets. "But Marcel and the others... they know, right? What if they tell those you're trying to ally with?"

"Rumors were already spreading well before I ran to New York," he said, something grim flashing across his face. "Andreas' heir a true monster. An abomination. A *demon*."

"Then prove them correct." I looked down at my lover against the pillows, the midday sun casting a glow to his flesh.

His fingers twitched against my waist.

"Let them come. Let them see what you are. Perhaps then we'll be left alone. Or," I swallowed. "We do what we must."

He sat up then, so we were face to face, and a wickedness glimmered in the dark center of his eyes. "Thirsting for blood, my love?"

"Who's to say Marcel hasn't already turned them all against you? They may arrive in a few days, and if they know what you are, if they decide you're too much a threat..."

Was it better to reveal the truth, and hope they feared him? Or hide it, and convince them he was no threat at all?

"Indeed," he murmured, his gaze flicking to my lips. "What would you like me to do to them?"

I blinked. "What do you mean?"

"I mean that anyone who sides with Marcel will answer for what he has done to you. Have you considered what we shall do?"

"You don't—" Pain resurfaced, everything I'd been pushing down swarming in my mind. I slammed my eyes shut, refused to drown in the reminders, the anxieties, the ache, again.

"How do you feel?" His thumb traced my cheekbone.

When I opened my eyes, he gazed upon me patiently, knowing the tumult in my heart.

"Angry," I whispered, holding back a sob.

Another swipe of his thumb, his touch gentle. Soft when I wanted it, hard when I needed it. And innately he knew which to choose, how to touch me, whether I was about to crumble or if I was as unwavering as iron.

"Frightened."

"What else?" he coaxed.

"There is not a word for it."

Since my kidnapping, a blackness had roiled in me, a storm that grew and grew until the clouds were pitch-dark and stormy, moments from ripping open, flooding, drowning. And like Vince's monster, I struggled to keep this—this *despair*—at bay. If I gave it a spark, it would become an inferno and bury me in flames.

I told him about the moment I realized Lucas wasn't human. I told him about my husband's dead wives, the secrets shrouding Whitrow. I told him about my brother's interest, Marcel's; the wedding, Lucy. The evening Lucas drank from me while Wright watched. I told him about the dead girl, and how she haunted me every time I shut my eyes.

I told him about Lucas' appetite for hearts.

Vince became still as stone. But the set of his jaw, the way his fingers tightened around me—I knew he used every bit of his resolve not to fly down to the cellar and murder my brother then and there. Eyes glazed over, fighting for control.

And a wicked part of me was enthralled by his reaction, loved knowing how vengeful he was for me. That he'd do something so terrible. For *me*.

I couldn't help it. A small laugh slipped from my lips. Maybe I really was mad. "Am I terrible for wanting to make them hurt?"

Vince returned to the moment, dark eyes landing on me. And he grinned.

Twenty-Six
Six Years Ago

"What'd you think about Anthony?" Flora looped her arm through mine as we walked out onto the street.

"He was nice enough."

"What about Freddie?"

"Talked too much about golf." I scrunched my nose.

"Peter?"

I led her around the street corner, shaking my head. "Not him. He asked me to kiss him in the hallway."

"His family is well-off. Lucas would have approved."

"Then I like him even less."

Flora sighed. "You're hopeless."

The dance hall a ways behind us, fatigue was beginning to catch up with me. After hours of dancing with whichever boy asked for a turn, hours of plastering on a smile, entertaining small talk, I was growing weary. It was almost nine in the evening, but we were not done yet.

"I'm not hopeless," I countered. "I just—have boys

always been this dull? I had the same conversation at least five times tonight."

"You've never noticed?" She laughed. "It has always been this way. And then once they decide you nod your head prettily enough, they'll start talking about marriage and children."

I grimaced at the same moment I made eye contact with a young man walking in the opposite direction. He looked away quickly. He would have been cute, if only he had the face of another.

"Maybe I've run out of boys to speak with. There are no more interesting ones left."

Flora gave me a look. "We're in New York. That's not possible."

"I'm not good at this," I said.

"You've *never* been good at this. That's why I was so surprised when—"

Her eyes widened at what she was about to say. She gave me a sheepish smile, the apology clear in her eyes.

"Oh, I mean, boys like that kind of thing. You can be quiet sometimes, and they like having to work for it. You *should* make them work for your attention."

I forced myself to smile back at her. "Maybe you're right."

She didn't know how I saw him at night. How he floated in my room, watching me sleep, waiting for me to notice him. She didn't know how I saw him even when I shut my eyes. Awake, or dreaming, it didn't matter. He was always there.

Some nights, I convinced myself that I truly could see his spirit. Some nights, I convinced myself that it was his hand between my legs. That the words whispered into the dark were his. I convinced myself that he'd crossed the veil, lingering in the world of the living, waiting to usher me into the other side. Whole. Unharmed. Young for the rest of his days.

She didn't know how Lucas found the same name in the paper. How he cut out the column and slipped it under my door the next day. How he circled his name in red link. How he—

Another group of young men passed us on the sidewalk. Laughter faltering as they took the opportunity to look, leering, staring through us.

One of them stopped in his tracks. "Where are you two headed?"

Flora rolled her eyes. "You're not invited."

The group snickered at the boy who was rejected, and they continued on.

We made it to the apartments not long after. The sky above was a deep blue, nearly black, the stars speckled through like a woven blanket covered the city.

"Who's party is this?" I asked. She'd told me before, but recently, I found I was forgetting everything.

"My cousin is back in town, remember?" She grinned again. "He has some friends that, if I remember correctly, are going off to Columbia in the fall."

"How interesting," I said, letting her lead me through the building's doors.

The party was on the third floor. We didn't need to knock, because the door was left open and the noise of chatter coming from inside made it clear where we were headed.

She was positively delighted as we crossed the threshold. In crowds, Flora bloomed. There had to be only a dozen people or so, but the windows were open to let out the heat. The walls were hardly decorated, the paper peeling along its seams, and the furniture didn't match, but there was a neatness to the room, like whoever lived here tried to keep it tidy.

Someone called her name, before a young man pushed his way through the throng. All eyes on us.

I wanted to shrink.

"Helena, this is my cousin, Michael. Michael, Helena."

He had dark hair, dark eyes, and his youth still stuck to him like ink on skin. "Pleasure to meet you," he said.

I nodded, forcing myself to smile. Again.

"Here, let me get you a drink." He led us to another room, the kitchen, where refreshments were laid out on the table. He handed me a glass, and another to Flora, before he introduced us to the group of his friends crowding the room.

I didn't hear any of the names. Hardly noticed their faces, the sound of their voices.

I was trying so hard for Flora, *so hard*, to be normal again. I'd been trying for weeks to return to the girl I'd been before, to enjoy the parties and the dinners and the boys and the drinks and the gossip. I wanted so badly to be myself again.

But I couldn't breathe. I couldn't look at another man without seeing his face. I couldn't hear what they were saying, because *I did not care*.

Mumbling something about needing air, I handed Flora my glass and returned the way we came. At the end of the hall, a door opened up to a small balcony, only large enough for one person, two if you were familiar. The laughter faded away.

I almost expected Flora to follow, to ask me what's wrong, to insist that it's alright if we went home, she could visit again later.

Once I was outside, a heaviness lifted.

"Oh."

I whirled around.

Another boy stood there in the doorway. Blond, hazel eyes. Not much taller than myself.

"Sorry. I didn't see you."

"Or maybe you followed me." I sighed, looking out on the street below. This late, the traffic had long died down, and only the random pedestrian lingered, men leaving their shifts late, drunkards. I was tired of putting on a mask. I had no energy for it left.

"Follow you?" he asked, and I could hear the confusion in his voice. "Why would I do that? I saw the door open, and thought—"

I didn't say anything, peeking at him over my shoulder.

"I'll leave you alone. Sorry," he repeated.

"Wait."

I leaned against the railing, tightening my fingers around the cool metal, feeling the painted iron flake under my nails.

"Are you one of the boys going to Columbia?"

He nodded. "In three weeks."

"What are you studying?"

"Mathematics." He cocked his head, like I baffled him.

Something came over me. I wondered what it would be like to kiss him. His lips looked soft. He wasn't unattractive.

And he hadn't glanced down at my chest once. I sensed an earnestness in him, and I wondered what it would be like— to have that innocence in my hand and take it, to press my mouth against his and see what sound he'd make. I wondered what he would say if I kissed him, what he'd promise me for another, and another.

Maybe there was something to this. Flora had them wrapped around her finger, always. She said what she wanted, she got what she wanted, and they all loved her for it. Maybe they could love me, too. Maybe if I tried harder, I could forget.

"Do I know you?" he asked, brows furrowing.

I stared back at him through my lashes, taking one step closer. "Not yet."

Twenty-Seven

"I thought that perhaps tonight would be an opportune time to partake from the finest Bordeaux in our cellars." Claude popped the cork from a deep emerald bottle.

A handful of us—Claude, Emil, Sinclair, Dixon, Vince and I—had congregated in the smoking room after sundown. Someone prepared our dinner, which the men picked at like birds, favoring the blood in their gilded cups. Where they had harvested the blood, I did not ask.

He poured the half-dozen of us each a glass of the rich wine, and lifted his in the air. "A toast."

"To?" Dixon raised a brow. I was surprised that he hadn't left. He did not pretend to enjoy Vince's company, and this coven was not his; he could've returned to New York at any moment. Returned to Flora.

And yet, he stayed.

His eyes flickered over to me for a moment, as if he felt my staring.

"To our returned heir, our leader," Claude declared. "And his bride."

"Oh." My eyes widened. "I'm not—"

Sinclair lifted his glass in agreement, smiling with an amused lilt. "Hear, hear."

"And to our eternal camaraderie. To the Sire who Made us." Claude paused. "And to his everlasting death."

Next to me, Vince lifted his glass of wine as well, the rest of them following suit, before they downed it all in one gulp. Dixon watched, frowning, looking entirely uncomfortable.

Sinclair reclined in his seat, crossing an ankle over his knee. "I have to say, Vince, I much prefer these men over those on Long Island. I've slept better here than I ever had in New York. No parties, no loiterers."

"Yes, New Yorkers are a bit too frenetic for my taste." Dixon took a sip from his glass.

"Not frenetic," Vince argued, running a finger over the rim of his glass. "Just—*opportunistic*. You must remember your family is older than my city."

"Which is why men like you jump at the opportunity to drain them dry." Dixon directed his stare at Vince.

"I must visit sometime," Claude said. His eyes slid to me. "Perhaps one day you can give me a tour of your home?"

If *we ever returned*, I thought. "Sure. But there's more fun to be had, I think, finding your own trouble in the city. Looking for underground bars, hidden doors, illegal jazz clubs."

"Ah, yes, I'd nearly forgotten. How fun that must be. A city of criminals." Claude grinned.

A slam echoed from the hall.

My first thought: that Marcel had returned to wreak

havoc, to get his revenge. I flinched at the shock of noise, meeting Dixon's concerned eyes across from me, the interruption clearly unexpected.

I was on my feet in a second, but the men were quicker. Only Vince lingered, his hand at the small of my back as I rushed to follow. Since our arrival, the sconces across the house were lit until dawn, lighting our way to the foyer, from which the distinctly *feminine* voice rang.

Two women were being dragged into the main hall, each subdued by a man with her hands behind her backs. The evening dark spilled in from the open entrance, a cool wind whipping through the room as tumultuous as the cursing of —*Séra*.

My anger flared red hot as I came to a halt, recognizing the dark curls, and the blonde next to her.

"Found these two making their way up the road." One of the men, Rogier, had his hands on a silent Flora. Her blue eyes were widened in shock, streaks of dirt on her knees, her cheek.

Séra was calling Matthias every name in the book, struggling to wrench herself from his grasp. "You bastard. What a way to handle a lady. You think you're tough, huh?"

Beside me, Sinclair sighed and pressed the spot between his brows.

"Intruders. We were just patrolling the drive, watching for villagers." Rogier looked to Vince, perhaps for approval, but *he had his hands on my friend*.

"Let *go* of them." Even I was surprised how my voice carried in the foyer.

A beat of silence.

"Now."

Flora nearly fell to her knees when she was released, rubbing at her wrists and looking every bit like a doe about to flee.

"*Flora.*" Dixon came to her side immediately, glaring at Rogier as he gathered her in his arms. "What are you doing?"

Matthias cleared his throat, addressing Vince, who was silent at my side. "They were halfway up the mountain—"

"And so you shoved them around like brutes?" I interrupted.

Matthias and Rogier grew uncertain, eyes sliding between Vince and I, like they couldn't decide who to appease.

I wanted to growl. "She's human."

"With all due respect," Matthias said, his arms crossed. "Human or not, they could still very well be sent from Marcel, or any number of the vampires that are headed our way. They could be spying—"

"They're *not.*"

"I can attest to this." Dixon bared his teeth.

But Matthias ignored him, waiting for Vince's answer. His short hair, the scar at his brow, almost, *almost* hid his unease. Of all of them, Matthias appeared the most accustomed to fighting, to getting his hands dirty. Yet when Vince turned to him, I saw that toughness falter, that guise of confidence cracking.

Rogier inclined his head, eyes wide. "Our mistake."

"Any harm that comes to her will be repaid, Thornton." Dixon warned.

Vince rolled his eyes. "You can stop with the dramatics anytime, Dixon. I wouldn't allow such a thing."

"Well." Séra dusted off her skirt, beaming at everyone

like she hadn't just been dragged into a chateau full of strange vampires.

At the sight of her, at the sight of Flora, both of them unharmed and *alive*, something surged in my chest, a warmth I'd been missing for weeks. They were here—together—and however foolish it had been to travel here, I couldn't deny how my heart burst with happiness.

I threw my arms around them, pulling them close.

Séra laughed. "Hey, stranger."

"You two are *crazy*." I couldn't help laughing, too. Remembering we had an audience, I pulled them away from the men. "Follow me."

Dixon protested, but Flora turned a scathing look onto him, stopping him in his tracks.

A whisper traveled about the room. Claude stepped closer to Vince, his voice low, but I could hear pieces of it all the same: "Is it wise to let human women reside under this roof? Perhaps for their safety..."

Flora shuffled after me, still stunned into silence. She looked around at the stone walls, at the chandelier, at the men doing their best not to stare, lest they have Dixon to contend with. I led my friends to the hall, looking for a quiet and secluded place to talk, away from the superhuman ears of the vampires.

Séra couldn't hide the hungry glance she cast Sinclair's way, and his eyes followed her until we were out of sight.

I pushed them into a parlor once we were far enough from the foyer. One of the lesser-used rooms, it smelled of lingering smoke and dust, the curtains drawn, the hearth cold. But it would do.

The door fell shut behind us. I whirled on my friends, both relieved and afraid. "You were in the forest *alone*?"

"Well how else would we get to the house?" Séra seemed entirely unconcerned.

"How did you...?"

"Sinclair does not hide anything well." Séra rolled her eyes. "After he left, I found a note from Vince in his room. We really must talk with them about leaving evidence for their plans around for anyone to read."

I blinked.

"They're vampires." Flora had never looked so serious.

"Yes, I told you," Séra said. "*I* am a vampire."

"But, *you* were honest about it from the start." Anger narrowed Flora's eyes. "Dixon is a liar. Vince, too. Are you...?" She eyed me warily.

"No."

"Good." She *humph*ed. "I'd feel left out. I have to admit I'm surprised you didn't tell me."

"Would you have believed me?"

"Touché. I guess I would've assumed you'd had too much of a bad batch of gin." Flora grinned. And then her arms were around me again, a hint of that lavender perfume still lingering on her clothes, and for a moment, I felt like I was at home again.

I pulled away, glancing between the two. "Why did you come? It's not safe here."

"We came because *you* are here." Séra smiled. "And because we couldn't let the men have all the fun, could we?"

"That night you snuck out? Dixon snuck into my room like some *criminal*, sporting a pretty good black eye. He was

frantic. I thought he was going to wake up my parents."
Flora shook her head, exasperated. "Saying how he was gonna
be gone for a few weeks, if not months, and that I should go
to Vince's house if I felt afraid. Afraid from *what*?"

"Marcel Brancato. My brother." A dry laugh slipped
from my lips. "If I told you everything, we'd be here all
night."

Something glimmered in Séra's eyes. "We have the time,"
she said.

I opened my mouth to speak, but the words died in my
throat. How to put into words everything that had
happened the last few weeks? How would I tell them about
Marcel's plan to turn my husband and use his name? How
would I tell them about Vince's scheme? How would I tell
them that my brother was locked away, somewhere below us,
in this very house?

Flora's sunshine smile, Séra's spirit, they did not belong
here.

I worried the darkness of this house, the darkness that
also lingered inside of *me*, was a rot that could spread, infec-
tious, until all that remained was rage and sorrow. But I was
glad, at least, that out of the three of us, *I* was the one that
had faced such misfortune.

Séra's hand came to my shoulder. "Tomorrow, then. We
can talk about it later. Tonight, we have plans to make."
Something mischievous glimmered in her eyes. "I heard
we're throwing a party soon?"

Twenty-Eight

"Are you angry?"

I sat upon an old desk that used to belong to Andreas, papers scattered across the surface as Vince rifled through, looking for—something.

The tension had eased with the rising sun and some much-needed rest. Though no one would speak it aloud, we were all uncertain, wary of what came next.

All of us, it seemed, except for Vince.

He paused. "Angry?"

"That Flora and Séra have come," I said. "I know it's not what you've planned."

He exhaled a laugh under his breath. "There is much that has not gone the way I've planned."

"That leaves only Veronica to guard your house."

"Veronica is more than capable of running things on her own."

I leaned over onto an elbow, obscuring half the desk and covering the papers. His eyes flicked up to mine.

"You said she was the first one you Made."

"In New York, yes." Vince let the papers fall from his hands. "What is it you really want to ask me?"

I shrugged, suddenly feeling uncomfortable by his stare.

With a finger under my chin, he brought my eyes back to his. "Helena."

"I am wondering why you never took the chance to Make me," I said. "I'm thinking of all the time you had in New York, bringing others into your life, before I even knew you were *alive*—Séra, Sinclair, Veronica. I'm wondering why they got to have you, and I couldn't."

He was silent for a moment, his gaze searching, a muscle ticking in his cheek. "You're asking me why you are still human."

I glanced away again, though I was held in place by his fingers. "I am asking why there were so many in your world before I came into it."

"You've always been a part of my world."

"And yet, I found you living amongst other vampires within an hour from the city."

He sighed. "I thought we talked about this already."

Frustration coursed through me, because I couldn't find the words—and I didn't know why these feelings were coming forth, either.

"Are you jealous, my love?" Something sparkled in his eyes. "You can't possibly be jealous of them."

"I don't *want* to be," I said.

He leaned closer, his lips inches from mine. "Have I told you how they came to my house?"

I shook my head.

"Finding Veronica was entirely by chance. She was being

followed down the street by a few men at midnight and she didn't even know it. I caught on only moments before one tried to drag her into an alleyway. And she put up a good fight. One of the men was bloody before I even got there. She defended herself—but not before they stuck a knife through her leg."

"I can't deny I was drawn to the scent of her blood when I offered immortality to her. I was in a new city, and I'd tried my best not to take from anyone unwilling, though my control over my hunger was reaching a tenuous point—you can imagine how difficult that is. And when she accepted readily, knowing she was about to bleed out, I gladly took what she offered."

I looked away, ashamed at how I wished no one else knew him as I did. It was a ridiculous wish, especially when I'd flirted with dozens of men in the years we were apart. But it burned in me, the jealousy that he'd given others his blood.

His fingers came gently to my chin, forcing me to look him in the eyes. "Let's not talk about this."

"No," I said, "I still..."

He waited patiently.

"We've only had a few weeks together, all in all. I don't want there to be anything hidden between us."

Gazing at me intently, he only went on after I said, "Please."

"Séra arrived not long after the first blood party I ever threw. Back then, I did not invite many to the manor, because I hadn't yet realized what a boon there was to be had in drunken rich men with nothing to lose. Only the vampires of the island, and a few from the city, would convene in my manor and find themselves giving over to their baser urges. I provided a service, of sorts, a place for them to do this. And it was all very hush-hush, because I still was not sure if Andreas or the others had followed me, and the vampires who did spend their nights in my manor did not want word getting out—as though it was something to be ashamed of, enjoying drinking blood and fucking.

"A month, perhaps two, after these parties began, a young girl showed up on my stoop. Séraphine Dupont, she said her name was. And of course I allowed her in. She was shaking like a leaf and clearly scared and I knew—" He paused. "I knew that if she needed protection, I was the best she'd get. I could make her disappear, if she wanted. And she did."

He looked at me, a small gleam in his eye. "Did you know she tried to kiss me?"

I blinked in shock. "No."

"Yes, she did." He laughed. "That first night. Maybe out of some sense of gratitude. But I did not let her. Told her to find someone else at the party to kiss. She didn't take it well. But I hadn't kissed anyone—since *you*—and I would not allow myself to."

While he had waited for me all six years, had spent every second surviving in the hopes of finding me, I'd been running around the city with whomever struck my fancy any particular night, drinking, dancing, doing my best, and failing, to forget *him*.

"She never left, even if she was cross from my rejection. And I found I didn't mind. She and Veronica hated each other, at first. But they learned to coexist.

"And eventually some humans began showing up at my

house, the liquor-hungry sort who were under the impression that my parties were bacchanals of that nature. I allowed it once—just to see. Would they run? Would they join in?

"Veronica and I never partook. She had no interest in *anyone* it seemed, and I was too stuck on you. Séra had no such qualms. She grew livelier with the new guests, enchanting them, taking a sip here and there, and many of them awoke out on the lawn, with nothing but foggy dreams about women or men biting their necks. But there was no evidence. Until Sinclair." His lips quirked in amusement. "He told you, I presume?"

I nodded.

"Sinclair was Made by accident, and rather than thrust him out into the city to acclimate to his new life on his own, I welcomed him to stay.

"After this, we locked the gates to all humans. The house was 'abandoned' for some time, when really it was just the four of us and the other vampires of Long Island cavorting amongst ourselves."

It made sense, then, why I had not heard much about the enigmatic Vince Thornton and his parties until they were the talk of the city.

"But it was not enough," I guessed.

His eyes gleamed, gaze catching on my lips. He leaned closer. "No. It was not.

"It became clear after a year that my sire and the rest of my coven were not going to appear. At least, not yet. But after a year locked up in that manor, roaming the city on occasion, only conversing with those I trusted with my name, I grew bored. Hungry. Tired of waiting for you."

He shifted in his seat—Andreas' old seat. Settled into

well, like this had been his study for the past centuries, and not his sire's. That these were his notes, his letters. He took up space like this room, this chateau, had always been his.

Like the moment Andreas drained Vince of his humanity, he'd signed his own death warrant.

And maybe he had.

"What did they do with him?" I wondered aloud.

"Andreas?" His eyes flickered to my lips. He paused for a moment. "His body was burned. One of the only ways to guarantee a corpse stays dead—destroy it. I've been told Marcel took the head. Where, I do not know."

His hand cupped my face, and he was all I could see—those gray eyes trained on me, his dark red hair combed back with pomade today, face clean shaven. He looked at me like he wanted to wholly consume me. He looked at me like I was the last drop of water in a desert, like I was the last crumb during a famine. Like I was a statue for his altar, like he'd get on his knees before me, whisper his hopes and his wishes, kiss my feet and *worship* me.

His intensity terrified me, because I couldn't deny what he was any longer.

And I was terrified of myself, because I knew I'd never be able to say no.

Halting only an inch away, his soft breath fanning my lips, he sensed my hesitation. Ran his thumb over my cheek once more, before pulling away. The trance broken.

"In all honesty," he said, clearing his throat. He shuffled a few more papers around, resuming his search. "I don't care what they've done with the body, long as it's gone. It's harder to venerate a man when there is no gravestone to visit."

I took a deep breath, unnerved. "You worry they still mourn him?"

"Worry, no." Vince frowned at the various sheets of parchment. Flipped one over to read the scrawled writing on the back. "He was their—*our*—sire, and there will always be some sense of loyalty to him, even if he is dead. But if they are smart, they will look to me now. It's what he would have wanted, after all."

His eyes flicked to mine again. "No, I rather think I'll erase his memory altogether."

I stood from the desk, to give myself something to do other than feel pinned down by his stare. My face heated.

"Flustered, my love?" There was a cynical lilt to his voice.

"Don't be so cruel," I whispered. I was suddenly aware of how small the room really was, full of bookshelves and old wooden cabinets and only one small arched window. Suddenly aware of his eyes skimming along my figure. Suddenly aware of the unrest low in my belly.

There was a shuffling sound, the papers falling to the desk, the chair moving. "Let me show you something."

He went to a chest under the window, the hinges creaking as he pushed it open, a plume of dust scattering in the air. Within, a tome was locked away. Its cover was gilded, the pages wrinkled and browning with age. He held it out to me.

The little voice in my mind told me not to take it, not to read it. But my curiosity was piqued.

I didn't meet his eyes.

The pages protested, stiff and dry, the spine cracking.

Drawings of animals, anatomical skeletons and muscles

and sinew and blood, the ink a deep rust-color. Plants with diagrams, a bisected human eye, a scrawled map of some coastline. I couldn't decipher the handwriting, which stretched across the pages in a looping, severe script. I knew, without a doubt, that this was his Sire's notebook, the language so foreign to me I couldn't recognize it.

But I wasn't sure why Vince was giving this to me.

"What's in here?" I asked. Afraid of the answer.

"It is proof of all of his crimes. Against *me*, against everyone he ever Made, against everyone he ever encountered."

That was when I flipped the page, to see a portrait in charcoal. A young man, eyes shut, face serene. The artist had taken care to sketch the angle of his nose, the mess of curls atop his head, the bow to his lips. He appeared to be sleeping, whoever this man was. Or—

"He was meticulous about keeping records," Vince said.

The next page, a list. I thought they were names, but I could not be sure.

Another portrait, another page filled with hastily scribbled writing, dates at the corner of every page, starting—my eyes widened—over two hundred years ago.

I flipped to the end. Drawing after drawing of young men, the faces unmistakable, even in charcoal and ink. From the most recent to—

The book nearly slipped from my grasp. I slammed it shut.

Because inside, *Adam*'s portrait looked back at me.

It was the closest I'd ever come to being there on the battlefield with him.

Vince darkened, something akin to disgust twisting the corners of his mouth as he glanced at the book.

"That's—"

"This coven was an experiment, of sorts," he went on. "He stalked the fields every night, found the ones he liked, and..."

A fury colder than ice doused my veins.

"It seemed like an addiction, the way he watched us come back to life. Forcing his blood down our throats so our bodies reanimated. And this was when... this was when he found out how far you could push a fledgling's body before it went mad with thirst. This was when he found if you torture a man enough, he'll tell you anything."

His throat bobbed when he looked away, his dark hair falling messily over his face.

"Andreas was so feared because of his knowledge. He knew *everything* about *everyone*. Knew how to coax someone's more valuable secret from their mouths, knew how to wield them like a sword. He was infamous for his might many centuries ago, but as he aged, he picked up a blade less and turned to words. He tired of getting his hands dirty."

The vagrant trades in information. Lucas' words echoed in my mind.

"He knew the acute appetites of his contemporaries. Their pastimes. How they deepened their coffers."

"Acute appetites?"

He was silent for a moment, his expression damning. "Your brother would fit in perfectly well with the vampires who are in this list."

The image of Lucas' fingers digging into Anna's sternum, gore staining his fingertips, the carved-out heart of the corpse under the tomb, they burned into my retinas, taunting me even when I tried to blink it away.

I thought Vince would stop there, but he continued, to my horror. "Many who have found... *unique* ways to quench their thirst. Blood slaves. The trafficking of children. Infant's blood, a delicacy. I could go on."

"And you want these people to come *here*? You want to ally with *them*?" A bitter taste spread on my tongue.

"No, I want to finish what I've started."

Draining them of their worth. Taking *everything*. Just like he did with those foolish enough to cross his path in New York.

I could only stare at him, stunned, only realizing I'd been holding my breath when my chest burned.

Vince nodded his head toward the book in my hands. "I am giving this to you. Burn it, and I can no longer hold it over the heads of my enemies. They may be frightened of a monster, but they are more afraid of losing everything. Their standing in society, their fortunes, *everything*."

"Aren't you afraid I'll hand it over to someone else?"

"No," he said, like it was simple. His hands turned to fists at his sides, like he was resisting coming closer, reaching for me. "I want you to trust me."

"I could ruin everything."

"You won't," he whispered. "And if you do, then I'll deserve it."

I turned away again, unsure what to feel, what to think, wanting to hurl this book away from me, wanting to write a paper and have it printed. Wouldn't that be fitting—Vince brought down to nothing with a newspaper?

"Helena."

The uncompromising trust in his eyes was even more terrifying than the lust that usually burned there.

And on my way out of the room, my gaze caught on a still life hanging from the wall, the name of a Dutch artist inscribed underneath, the colors fading, the glaze taking on a yellowish hue; I faltered in my steps when I realized that since Whitrow, not a single rose had been left behind on my pillow for me to find.

TWENTY-NINE

When I visited my brother in the cellar for the first time, three days had passed since he had thrown me from the balcony in his attempt to kidnap me once more.

As the sun fell beyond the horizon, cloaking the house in shadows, I went underground, a lamp in hand to light my way. I'd told Vince to wait for me in bed after dinner, forcing myself to do it now before I lost my nerve.

My steps echoed as I descended the stone stairs. For a brief moment, I was back in the tomb—forced down the stairs to Lucas and Wright, waiting in the underground chamber. Terror seizing my heart.

I paused. Took a breath and squared my shoulders.

I wouldn't let him have this hold on me any longer.

And then I continued on.

He was not far from the landing. The cellar stunk of rotting wood, something acidic like vinegar. Iron. There were no lights, just barrels and cases and broken bottles scattered about.

And him.

"There you are." He grinned.

Never had I seen him in such a sorry state. He deserved it, of course he did. But I could not ignore who he was to me, no matter how I wanted to.

He was tethered to the wall by an iron collar around his neck, his one arm locked in a shackle with a short chain in the ground. He wouldn't be able to stand without great difficulty. Dried blood flaking at his mouth, his eye; wounds that weren't there before he'd been dragged into the cellar. He'd been thoroughly beaten. And the wound where his arm had been ripped away—the flesh was dried, tattered in ribbons and the color of rust. Not healing, but not festering either.

I avoided looking at it, ignored the tang of metal in the air.

"I was wondering when you would come visit me," he said.

How strange, to see my brother so helpless. Locked away. Powerless.

I peered down at him, only a few feet away. Unreachable.

"Here to taunt me?" The haughty air he usually carried with him was tangible, that smug look remaining even when there was iron around his throat.

"No."

"To gloat? Come, make your idle threats," he almost purred, glaring at me through narrowed eyes.

"No."

"What is your plan for me then? To keep me locked up down here until your lover decides to kill me?"

"Who said *he* will kill you?"

He barked out a laugh. "You, then?"

I was surprised that the inkling of fear that arose when I entered had already passed. In its place, a sense of calm had settled into my bones, my veins, as though I'd downed a whole bottle of gin; calm—and anger.

Resentment.

Rage.

My brother, who had taken from me more times than I could count.

And now, he could do nothing to me. He was weak, trapped. No different than any other man, now.

Those fangs would never touch me again.

He would never touch me again.

I didn't answer his question. My silence only spurred him on.

"Is this the life you want? To fuck a cad and be his blood bag?" He shook his head, his brown eyes almost black in the wavering light. "If immortality is what you wanted, I could have given that to you. I *wanted* to give it to you, sister. I wanted nothing but the best for you. But you couldn't help whoring yourself out to the highest bidder."

"Where is Marcel?" I asked.

He only bared his teeth in a sharp smile. "Brancato wanted you, too, you know. *Everybody* wants Miss Helena Quintrell. I'm starting to wonder just what's between your legs that's got the men going crazy for you. Did you give Wright a taste before you slaughtered him? Did he fuck you and put an heir in you?" He laughed again, high and echoing in the small chamber. "Imagine that, the bastard Highsmith heir the son of a *printer*."

I counted my every inhale, every exhale.

"Do you actually believe that he loves you? He's just using you. Vince Thornton has been using you for *years*. What was his name?" He laughed again. "*Adam Vering*. How very like someone of his class to try and hide amongst people like us. He'll always be low-born scum. But I guess that's the kind of cock you like, isn't it?"

Don't react. Do not react.

"You *like* being used."

He wouldn't shut up. *He wouldn't shut up.*

"Did you tell him how many men you fucked after he left? Does he know that you couldn't even be bothered to wait for him?"

The high-pitched ringing started up again in my ears.

"And did *Adam* tell you how he and I met?"

I blinked.

Lucas was grinning, ear to ear. "He didn't! How rich." Cocking his head, he sneered up at me, the malice burning in his eyes. Leaning closer, as far as the chain would allow. "Maybe you should ask him. Poor bounders like him have no reason to loiter outside houses like our's. I warned him, I gave him a chance. But he didn't listen. See? I *try* to be kind, Helena."

The ringing grew louder. When I spoke, the voice wasn't mine, my hands weren't mine, the bite of pain from finger-nails piercing my palm dulled to a mere pinch. "Tell me where Marcel is."

"Why, leaving *Vince* so soon?" His lip curled. "I don't know where he is."

I flexed my fingers at my sides. "Then you came alone?"

"I have a question for *you*, dear sister: where is my wife?"

I knew if the chains were not holding him back, if he had not been injured and captured, the ruthless hunger in him would be wholly directed at *me*. He would strangle it out of me, and when I gave him what he wanted, he would kill me for good this time.

"A trade in answers: you tell me where Lucy is, I'll tell you where Marcel may be."

I straightened, ignoring the ice down my spine, my hair on end. I was still yet in the presence of a predator, and the mortality in me knew it. A lion was still a lion, even in a cage.

"Do you regret it?" I asked, willing my voice not to break. "Do you regret harming her?"

"I only mourn that I do not have a son," he sneered.

I did not listen to whatever else he had to say. The ringing in my ears grew cacophonous, almost too loud to bear. He would not give me answers; I'd wasted my time on vitriol and lies, and I should have known better.

Giving Lucas one last look, I turned. Made the slow climb up the stairs. Tried to quell the tempest brewing within my blood.

There was a wickedness whispering in my ear, the words unintelligible, but poisonous all the same. Thoughts intruding from elsewhere, as if they weren't my own.

Sinclair waited for me at the landing. I called his name as I emerged from the dark.

He raised a dark brow.

"Do any of the men have experience in pulling teeth?"

THIRTY

Vince lay amidst strewn sheets when I came through the door, not caring if it slammed behind me. He hardly looked up from his book, reclined against the feather pillows, his chest bare, the blanket low at his waist.

"I received messages from a few of our *guests*," he said. "A handful have accepted the invitation. A few will arrive within the week."

I went to the wardrobe, ripping my dress over my shoulders. Throwing the fabric into a heap. Nearly growling in frustration when I couldn't decide what to change into.

"How is he doing down there?" Vince asked, and I could tell I had a little more of his attention, could feel his eyes on my naked back.

Breathing in deep, counting to ten. My thoughts were moving at light speed, so quickly I could not reach out and grab them, slow them down. Couldn't tame how they squeezed around my heart like a fist. Could get my brother's taunts *out of my head*.

"What did he say? You know he's just trying to upset you."

Even so, it felt like a paperknife had been thrust through my heart.

His footsteps neared. But he did not touch me. "What is it?"

"Lucas—" I shut my eyes, tears burning in my lashes. All of it, rushing out of me at once: "You knew who he was. Back then. You'd met him before."

Silence.

Fingertips hovering over me, the ghost of warmth at my back.

I whirled around. "Lucas saw you outside our house. He *knew* about us. He told me you were *using* me."

"And you believe him."

"I don't know *what* to believe."

"You keep doing this," he murmured, shaking his head so subtly, a crease forming between his brows.

"Doing what?"

"Blaming me then wanting me. Pushing me away and then coming to my bed. Back and forth."

"I don't feel like I know you," I whispered. Tears brimmed at my eyes, and I quickly wiped them away. Angry. So *tired* of crying. "Like I *truly* know you."

He threw out a hand. "What more do you want? I've told you. And you held a *gun* to my heart."

"Did you not think I would find out?"

"No, I—" He pinched the bridge of his nose. "Yes, perhaps, but everything would come to rights in the end and it wouldn't matter—"

"Did you expect me to come out of this unscathed?"

"Of course, I—"

"You've *used* me." My voice broke. "I was just—just—*a pawn* for you to get what you wanted."

"*You* are what I want," he said, rushing over to me. "None of this matters without you."

"Then why did you send me away?" Sobs were stalling in my throat, great gasping breaths that shuddered through me. My misery and anger and rage were so intertwined I couldn't distinguish between them. "Why tangle me up in this?"

"I—it could not be helped."

"Yes, it could have! You could have prevented all of this—"

"*No.*" The word came out as a shout. He nearly trembled with the force of it. "No, I couldn't. This is what it means to be my muse, my lover, my other half. This is what loving me entails. I am a monster, and I do not know how to act any differently. The very blood within me has changed. I thought maybe you understood."

I was shaking my head, my vision blurred with tears. "Understand what?"

"*I am not Adam.*" His voice hardened.

"I know."

"Do you? Because what humanity I had is long dead, and yet I have the feeling you still expect it—that old me that doesn't exist."

My mouth opened but the words stalled on my tongue.

"When I awoke from death, in that cellar with my Sire, I swore never to utter that name again. *Adam*," he spit the name like it was poison, "died the moment I stepped foot on that ship. *This* is me, Helena, the monster born from that wretched soil, forced to live on in his place. Forced to forever reckon with the man you had before."

"The man you were before would never have handed me over so easily."

"Are you so sure?" Something dark twisted his features. A cruel smile curled his lips. "I walked away that night, didn't I?"

When Lucas threatened him—us—Adam had not put up much of a fight. But Lucas had a gun. He'd held it to my head and threatened Adam with death. How could anyone fight against that?

"You had no choice."

"Yes I did. I could have taken him over, easily." He laughed. "Your brother cannot fight. But then where would that have left us?"

"So you gave up on us? On me?"

He laughed bitterly. "I never gave up on you. How many times must I prove it?"

"Repeatedly, it seems," I threw at him. "When your actions scream nothing of love."

"It's *obsession*, Helena." He gripped me, pulling me closer, his fingers digging into my flesh, as though he could cement himself into my veins. "You take up my every waking thought. I cannot drink, speak, *breathe* without thinking of you. I'm entirely lost to you. Mad for you."

I shook my head.

"I was Made into a monster. You cannot fault me for acting like one."

"You've hurt me," I whispered. "I was hurt because of you."

"Then I will spend the rest of my meager life making it up to you. I will lash myself for you. I will starve myself. I will do whatever you wish. Just do not forsake me."

"How?" I shut my eyes. "How could I not?"

"Please," he begged. I felt the brush of his lips against mine, the insistent kiss, the almost desperate way he crushed me to him. "Please don't leave me."

It had not truly crossed my mind to leave—where would I go? If I returned to Mother in New York, Lucas would snatch me up again. She might be angry enough to cast me out of our house. I could not stay with Flora and her family, couldn't risk what creatures would follow. And I couldn't much travel by myself without any money. I had nothing. There was nowhere to go.

And were I honest with myself, I didn't want to leave.

Being with Vince was inevitable. A pull forever drawing me to him, no matter if it was for my own good or not. Something magnetic lingered between us. Something incessant and *hungry*.

I felt it in the way he tasted my lips, pressing them to mine over and over, as though to make sure I didn't fade away and disappear between his kisses. I couldn't leave him behind. He'd remain with me forever anyways. His ghost would haunt me, follow me to the ends of the earth. I'd never outrun him, never outrun the memories of him.

He and I were doomed to each other, for better or worse.

"Please," he said again. "I will do anything."

"Anything?" My lips brushed his as I spoke.

He searched my eyes. Nodded.

A hot tear traced down my cheek. "How did we meet?"

His fingers tightened, just a fraction, a simple twitch, but enough.

"You know how we met."

Shutting my eyes, shaking my head, because I could not keep from crumbling if I saw the look in his. "The truth."

The silence was saturated with his hesitation. "I—"

"*The truth.*"

A sound of frustration, the words spoken so harshly, the thing he'd been hiding all along: "I sought you out."

And though I'd wondered, mulled over the serendipity of running into him, of accepting his offer to walk me home, hearing the words sent a microscopic fissure through me, a tremor through each and every bone, a fault so fundamental I could never be put back together as I was five minutes ago.

"I sought you out," he repeated. Shaking my shoulders once, to cement the truth between us.

My eyes snapped open.

"It's no secret I knew of your family before we met. It wouldn't be out of the realm of possibility, what with how often your family's name popped up in the papers *I* printed. Your father, and Lucas, used every opportunity to brag. And I..."

His throat slid, exhaling a nervous laugh. He was *nervous.*

"You know how I felt, back then, about that kind of man. And now, how I—"

My throat ached. Marcel's claims became truer every day, and I hated him for sowing these seeds of doubt. Ignorance was bliss. How much happier would I have been not knowing?

"I sought you out to get information. I meant to get

close to you, to have access to your father. Your brother. Whatever information they had. To blackmail them, at first. Find some dirt. I could've easily put something in print that they wouldn't want brought to light. I knew, even then, that all those men had secrets. Companies don't grow without some dark, back alley agreements. Loop holes. Fraud.

"*You* were never supposed to happen." He clenched his jaw, trying and failing to compose his features. Eyes darkening. Fingers tightening.

Andreas' heir, indeed.

He let go of me suddenly, wrenching himself away. His hands hovered in the air like touching me had burned him.

"*Goddamn it*, Helena. But I would do it again. I was never lying about how I felt. The *only* lie was that I didn't know who you were when we met."

The more he spoke, the more spilled out of him. Hands in the air by his head like I was aiming the gun at him again.

"I waited for you. I learned your route. And I hadn't planned to, initially. But you fell into my lap so prettily, and how could I refuse the opportunity? I learned your name one afternoon on my way home, walking not too far behind two girls, one chattering away, loud enough for the whole street to hear. She must have said your name a dozen times— *Helena*—but it clicked when she said *Quintrell*."

I was numb, freezing from the inside out.

"I put myself in your way, on that street corner. Knew you'd be alone that day and waited for you to appear. Jumped in front of you just in time. After that first day, I knew I had to have you. That's when it began." He stopped. Muscles straining in his neck, fingers flexing at his sides, like he was in pain. "*Say something.*"

But I couldn't. My mouth opened, but my tongue had dried up, my voice missing.

It made sense, what he was confessing to. Why he was so insistent, despite the risk, to continue seeing me. Why he never heeded my warnings about Lucas.

"You stalked me."

He stepped closer, cradling my face again, pressing our foreheads together. His sigh was warm against my lips. "Yes."

"You used me."

Echoing Lucas.

A sharp intake of breath. "Yes."

He was right.

"And you love me now?"

"Yes." He pulled away, only an inch. "Are you really so surprised, Helena? Have I not made my devotion to you crystal clear?"

Marcel was right. Marcel was right all along.

"I love you. I need you. Let's run away, like we wanted to before. We can go wherever you want. I'll make it happen." He kissed my cheeks, my nose, my brow, each brush of his lips singeing my skin. "Let's get away from all of this. It doesn't matter anymore. Only you. *You* are my everything."

"Vince."

He looked me in the eyes. "What do you want?" he asked. "Tell me, and I will give it to you."

"Don't make another promise you can't keep," I warned.

His fingers tightened around me.

"Make me," I said. "I want to be strong. I don't want to be human anymore."

I couldn't help but think that if only I'd been a vampire,

I would have been able to fend Marcel off. I could have defended myself against Lucas.

The rebuttal was already forming on his lips. I wanted to *scream.*

"*Why* are you so against this?" I cried.

Pain, real pain, in his eyes. "Because once it is done, you cannot go back."

"You think I don't know that?"

I had asked him so many times, and each time he brushed me off. Each time he told me *no, not yet.*

I was tired of waiting.

He shut his eyes, pressing his forehead against mine again. Warmth radiated from him, and when I glanced down, his arousal strained against his pants.

My lips ghosted over his. "Please, Vince." My fingers curling in the hair at his nape, holding him to me, my other hand running up his chest, settling over his heart. The faint thud against my palm, the coolness of his skin giving way to warmth.

And then like he'd come to his senses, he pulled away from me, a groan rumbling deep in his throat. "I cannot deny you. But—"

"Would you prefer I grow old without you? You said that you would do it, because you cannot bear to live without me."

"I also said I wanted to take my time with you." He set his jaw.

Pressing my body against his, I wrapped my arms around his neck. I wore nothing but my bandeau and tap pants, the silk the only barrier between us. His arousal pressed into my stomach, and I thought that if I got on my knees, then maybe I could work him into a frenzy and find his teeth in my flesh, anyway.

His hands encircled my waist, holding me still. "Give me one more night."

I thought it was a promise as good as any. So I drew his lips to mine and showed him my gratitude.

THIRTY-ONE

While the house was being readied for its dozens of guests, Séra and Flora took it upon themselves to brighten the decor where they could, much to the chagrin of the men: curtains dusted off from storage, refreshed portraits, new candles in the chandelier. The vampires gave the girls a wide berth whenever they weren't directly employed in a task, perhaps fearing what Sinclair or Dixon would do if they stepped too close. I noticed that they did the same to me, averting their eyes, stopping themselves from speaking when I was in the room. Like they were afraid of me.

Claude had no such qualms.

"They have not had the company of women in a while," he said, when I asked why they acted so strangely. "Trysts here and there, but no woman has stayed in the chateau for more than a fuck in a quite some time."

I glanced at him. "But we don't make *you* nervous."

He shrugged. "I'm not intimidated by either sex." He

grinned. "The last time I fell into bed with a woman... it must have been the last party Andreas threw. *Years*, now."

And I found it hard to believe he'd abstained since.

"Andreas threw parties? He doesn't seem like the type to enjoy company."

We were on the second story of the ballroom, looking out over the main floor as Séra directed Emil and Matthias, rearranging the furniture to allow room for dancing.

"He didn't throw parties because he enjoyed them." Claude's eyes fell to the men below, carrying a large mahogany table between the two. "He threw parties because when you crowd so many people in one room, lips loosen and inhibitions disappear."

I hummed. "Vince told me..."

He turned to me, raising a brow when I did not go on.

I remembered everything Vince had said. The book was still in my possession, hiding in one of my trunks, as I didn't know what to do with it. But I knew it was too great a leverage to throw away.

Claude seemed to know what I was about to say. "Andreas was..." he trailed off, looking out at the ballroom below. He scrubbed at his jaw with one hand, mulling over his answer.

"A monster," I supplied. "The *true* monster?"

He glanced at me. "Perhaps at some point in his life, yes. He was very old. Toward the end..."

I blinked, confused. "What do you mean?"

"He was terrible, yes. He forced us—all of us—into a life of blood-theft. Eternal life, in theory. He ripped us away from our humanity. Though, was it a kindness, if we were to die from suffocating on mustard gas, anyway?"

I was reminded how close to death Vince—Adam—had been. How close I'd been to losing him forever.

The portrait in the book—

"But?" I pressed.

Claude sighed. "*But*, I can't help feeling somewhat sympathetic for him. For his end, anyway. He was my sire, after all."

"Marcel killed him."

"Yes."

"This is why you've thrown him out?"

"Marcel committed patricide before convincing half the men here to join him. He insisted, upon Andreas' death, that he was the heir. But he didn't know that Vince planned to come back. There was *much* he didn't know."

"You were waiting for Vince."

Claude looked at me directly. "He was always going to return. Before he left for New York, he told us he'd be back in three years' time. What he didn't say was what he was looking for."

A flush heated my face. "Well, I had no clue he was coming," I said, voice soft. I wasn't sure why I was comfortable enough to lower my guard with Claude. "I thought he was dead."

Claude was silent for a moment. "I always knew there was someone. No young man has that look in his eye unless he's determined to return to *something*. Unfinished business. I'm sure you know what I mean."

"You said that Andreas was not quite so bad in the end. Why?"

He hesitated. "Because your lover became something so much worse."

My heart stumbled a beat. "I don't understand."

"The most terrible man I've ever met Made your lover first. Andreas—he was pure malice at the start. By the time I'd come along, Vince was well on his way."

The hairs on the back of my neck stood. "Well on his way to what?"

Claude turned to me. "Are you a fan of literature?"

"When the mood strikes."

He smiled, and a fang poked out from his lips, nearly startling me, as I'd forgotten for just a moment that Claude was inhuman.

"I just finished a novel, though I cannot remember the title. A work of horror. Man playing God and lamenting the consequences." He looked at me again. "It seems a lesson that man—and vampire alike—are doomed to repeat."

I rolled my eyes. "Let me guess, you're going to tell me that Vince is dangerous and I must stay away."

Claude laughed. "Oh, no. He is not dangerous to *you*. Even I can see he'd prostrate himself before he were to hurt you. No, you are in the prime seat of all: you can give the command and watch as he obeys. *You* are most dangerous."

I wondered if his opinion of me would change, were I a vampire?

There was a slam from below, and then some bickering, the table dropped between them. Emil and Matthias, butting heads, their voices carrying all the way to the second floor.

Séra glanced up at me and grinned, like she enjoyed every second of it.

"You keep saying that," I murmured, realizing that the vampires below could very well be eavesdropping.

"And you keep denying it." He leaned on the wooden railing, his eyes returning to the scene below. "Every man in this room had an occupation before we were forced to join the war: Emil, a painter; Matthias fought underground, but he'll deny it if you ask; Vince, a printer; and I was working at my father's law firm, though I wasn't very good at it. We lost that. And most of us, with immortality, lose our faith. In God, in humanity, in goodness, take your pick. But Vince..."

He looked directly at me again.

"There's a reason he was our Sire's Second. Not only because he was Made first, but because he wouldn't crack. Andreas couldn't—" He stopped himself, shaking his head. "The only thing Vince had to lose was you, and I've never seen a man hold onto something so tightly, even if it would kill him."

THIRTY-TWO

My humanity felt like shackles at my ankles. A burden, now.

Early in the morning, the inhabitants of the house still drowsy from the night, if they were awake at all; the perfect time to slip away. At the front doorstep, the rising sun shone down on me with rays broken by the forest, warming my skin, and I closed my eyes, enjoyed the sensation, because I did not know what life was like on the other side of immortality.

Letting my feet carry me forward, I took a deep breath, the sweet air settling into my lungs. Wanted to just be *alone.* Because if I went back inside, if I returned to the house, I was forever in ear-shot of a vampire. My thoughts were beginning to feel like they weren't solely my own.

The soft soil of the forest gave beneath my feet, a deep brown, littered with fallen leaves and twigs. Amongst the trees, the air was sweet; I tasted each honeysuckle inhalation, letting it cleanse my lungs, my mind. A few birds chirped, fluttering their wings up high in the branches. The treetops formed a canopy, shielding those at the forest floor from the sun.

In only a few steps, the chateau was hidden from my view. I was a dryad, wandering her domain, aware of each insect, each wildflower, aware of the wind, calling it forth. Made of the same dirt and dew as the flora growing towards the sky. Detached from civilization, wary of wanderers within.

The further into the trees I walked, the more I felt I was being watched.

Of course I was.

But I took a deep breath, let the fresh air wash away whatever lingered in my heart, until all my thoughts were gone.

A butterfly fluttered across my path, twirling around my head before disappearing amongst the brush. A squirrel clambered up a tree, stopping when it saw me, before completing its climb. Flowers reached for me, vines wound along the ground.

In a moment, a stream erupted between the trees. The water was crystal-clear, bubbling against some stones, moving at a languid pace. The air was warm, summer slowly slipping into the late-spring afternoon.

Without thought, I lifted my dress over my head. My slip followed, my shoes, my stockings, all thrown into a pile. I stood bare, basking in the sun on my skin, relaxing into the silence. Feeling perfectly, foolishly alone. Exposed.

Any number of vampires could be hiding in the trees, waiting to spring on me; any of Marcel's sympathizers, or even Marcel himself.

I had thought surely he would taunt me by now. I thought he would follow soon after my brother and show up on the balcony, hiding behind a curtain until I was within grasp. I thought he would've made another attempt to steal me away. Claim me.

And yet.

I toed the water—I'd been expecting ice, but it was only slightly cooler than the breeze—before stepping in, the water rising to my knees, then my hips. My breasts pebbled as the waterline rose to my chest.

Sucking in a breath, I submerged myself in the stream. Felt the currents pushing against me, ushering me further downstream. Burst from the surface when my chest began to ache. Ran my fingers through my hair, wiping off the bit of sweat that dampened my brow.

Like a baptism, the water washed it all away.

The ghost of a bite at my throat.

Memories of rough hands, iron fists.

The remnants of weeks away from my home.

I closed my eyes. The wind caressed my cheek. I could not hold on to the anguish any longer. Somehow, I knew it would kill me, drag me down. I let go of the roiling storm within me, let go of the terrible, tar-like misery that festered —all but a drop. I couldn't forget. They would haunt me no longer. But I wouldn't forget.

The silence was heavy, the only sounds the flow of the water along the rocks, the whispering of the leaves.

"You can come out now," I called out to the forest. The water bobbed along my chin.

I wasn't sure who I was expecting, knowing that he could have sent any of his men to watch out for me, but I should have known. He was always there, always following, never far. Obsessed. And as he stepped out into the light, my heart gave a little kick, echoing in my head the word: *mine*.

Vince stood alone against the bank. His eyes were unreadable, a firm set to his jaw. He watched me for a moment. Then, "Come here."

The water sluiced from my body as I rose, each step revealing another inch of my skin to him. His eyes darkened, lingering on the juncture of my thighs before I stopped upon the shore.

His hand came to cup my cheek, and I shivered at the contact. "I worried someone took you."

I saw then the fear in his eyes, subsiding now, but the monster was near, waiting to be unleashed.

His hands came to settle on my waist. The gentle touch alone brought a flare of desire between my legs. I saw it in his eyes, too, the moment his maleness became attuned to me, my bare body. He shook his head. "You are a reckless woman."

"Isn't this our land?"

"Any manner of creature could prowl these woods. Still —" His grip became rough, a hand sliding to my ass, palming it roughly. "You offer yourself up, naked."

"I thought the chateau had a reputation? No one will come wandering through these woods."

"Maybe not a villager. But I certainly have half a mind to ravish you here." His lips skimmed my throat, and suddenly he was lifting me up, thighs wrapped around his hips. He groaned as our centers met. He was long and hard beneath his trousers, aching with need.

My toes curled at the contact. "You cannot wait to take

me to bed?" The words came out breathy, as he was peppering my throat with kisses, nipping at the skin.

"No," he growled. "You tempt me like this, you cannot expect me to let you get away unscathed." He held me close, grinding himself against me.

"You're insatiable," I breathed.

"My desire for you never sleeps. It's a feat that I pull myself away from you. You've ensnared me, completely."

"Then take me," I dared.

In a moment he was lowering us to the ground, his body between my thighs. Still clothed, he managed only to loosen his belt and pull himself free before he was sinking into me.

I cried out at the sudden pressure, my body drawing him in. Nails biting into his shoulder, gasping with each thrust, overtaken with the feeling that I was his prey; that something purely animalistic had him rutting into me, frenzied and rough, like our sole purpose was to mate, over and over again.

After only a minute, my thighs were shaking with the pleasure of it, my core clenching around him. He made a satisfied sound, before he was spilling into me with a final, brutal thrust. Once. Twice.

Our breaths mixed in the space between us as we calmed our hearts. He pulled away and rolled next to me in the soft dirt.

We hadn't even laid a blanket down. I laughed at the ridiculousness of it, my chest light, the rest of me addled with the aftershocks of pleasure.

He grinned as he propped himself up on an elbow. Looked at me intently. "You have not laughed in a while."

A small smile pulled at my lips. "No, I suppose I haven't."

"I want you always this happy," he murmured. He ran the outside of his finger along my cheek.

I shivered, the flush of my body giving way to the chill of the air again.

And then he said the words, "Marry me." Like a thought unwittingly said aloud.

They stalled in the air, waiting for one of us to catch them.

I hadn't expected it from him. Not yet, at least. We'd only just reunited, and even then, I'd only spent a handful of weeks with him in New York. I'd only *just* broken his barriers and learned the truth. And there was still the matter of my brother, locked away in our cellar, and Marcel, and all the others—

I was lost for words, staring up at Vince, tousled and powerful above me.

His hand came to cover my mouth. "You do not have to answer yet. But I want you to know my intentions: it's you, Helena. It's always been you. Despite everything, we find our way to each other. I'll be damned if the universe takes you away from me again."

I stared at him, stunned. "Marriage?"

He nodded, and I saw something in him darken. "I want to call you my wife."

My soul floated above me, watching him caress my cheek, watching the water from the stream lapping at my feet. Lightheaded, I lay back, staring up at the leaves swaying in the breeze.

"Marry me," he murmured, lowering his lips to my neck,

the ghost of his breath skating along my flesh. The touch sent me spinning.

I clutched at his shoulders. "Not—I can't." The words coming between gasping breaths as he kissed my throat, trailed along my collarbone, my shoulder, dipping towards the top of my breasts. Sending every nerve ending into haywire. "Not yet."

"Whenever you want," he breathed. A hand coming to cup my breast, pinching lightly at my nipple.

"I—I just—" It did not take long for him to have me squirming on the ground. "*Wait.*"

He pulled back only an inch, looking up at me through hooded eyes. But he waited.

I placed my palms on his cheeks. "I won't do it. Not until I'm Made," I said.

His stillness was preternatural.

Then he slid up my body so he hovered over me, an arm braced on either side of my head. He was already aroused again, heavy against my leg.

Before he could say anything, I rushed the words out. "I am so defenseless. I'm tired of relying on you, of needing you to protect me. And how can I exist in your world when we are so opposed? You are a predator who sustains himself off of human blood. You are *my* predator. How can I remain as I am and be safe? I don't want to be so *helpless.*"

"You are not helpless," he said, voice firm. "You wield power over me, and thus all these men, and those in New York, too. Don't you understand?"

"But I can't possibly guard myself against a vampire. I don't have the strength."

"Does a queen fight her own wars?"

"No." I sighed.

"Selfishly, I admit I want to do all of this for you," he said, his features softening. "I want to be your protector. I want to keep you safe, so you are not burdened with these thoughts." He pressed his forehead against mine, caging me against the ground, but the comfort of his body around mine had all tension in my limbs fading away. "I want to shield you from the harm of the world."

"I don't want you to," I whispered.

He pulled away again, those grey eyes looking through me, brows furrowed.

And there, next to the stream, deep in the forest, with my vampire lover above me, something shifted: as subtle as the change in direction of the wind, I knew the version of me that Lucy had said goodbye to was not the same Helena she'd greet again.

Vince seemed to sense it, too. Eyes widening, he looked around, and for a moment, I thought someone would come from the trees, interrupting us. But when his gaze returned to me, I could see through him, too. His soul on display, as innate to me as my own.

It was of little consequence if Vince and I were fated or not, I realized.

He would always choose me, and I would always choose him, even if our threads pulled us in opposite directions.

His throat slid. "This is your one condition?"

I nodded. "I want to be your equal."

He exhaled a tired laugh. "You *are*, my darling, if not my better."

"I don't want to grow old without you," I said, pulling

his face to mine. "I don't want to be taken from you, ever again."

He hushed me with a kiss, his lips soft but demanding, sending all my attention to the taste of him, the feel of his strong body against mine, the steely length of him against my leg, inching closer to my hips. "Don't worry about these things," he said, lips skimming my jaw. "Put them from your mind."

With his last bit of restraint, he looked me again in the eyes. "When would you have me do it?"

"Now," I said on an exhale, clutching at him, hands skimming his chest, feeling the muscles of his back flexing as he held himself back. I didn't listen to the fear trying to ease its way into my veins, the self-preservation telling me to stop him.

He hummed. "I can hardly do it in the dirt, darling."

"*Please.*"

My thoughts intrusively turned to Wright, and our wedding, the way he presented me to the crowd of his family, as if to show off his virility and control, the ritual of snaring a bride and soiling her for his own gain.

With Vince, I needed it to be messy. Just the two of us.

"It will take time for you to control your thirst," he said.

It had been his excuse before.

"It took me months. It took each one of these men at least a few weeks to wrangle themselves into control. And that thirst—it is maddening."

But I remembered Lucy, newly Made, confused and frightened, and not the least bit tempted to rip into my flesh.

"What better time to do it than now, when I can use that violence to our advantage?"

He warred with himself, consumed by his lust for me, but I saw the gleam in his eye at my words.

My nails dug into his back, desperate. I hooked an ankle around his hip, drawing him closer. "*Please,*" I begged.

His darkness was returning, his restraint waning. Lust winning the battle. The monster, eager to surface. "How can I say no to you?" he said, voice strained.

His mouth came to that sensitive spot under my ear. Sucking harshly, he broke the skin, drawing my blood onto his tongue. The thrill of it sent desire straight to my center.

I welcomed the pain. Wanted it to hurt. I wanted him to set every bit of me on fire. I wanted to die in his arms, heady from the pleasure.

I wanted him to take me—*all* of me.

He was Made, and came out even more powerful on the other side. He died, and came back, immortal. And in his arms, I knew he'd catch me. He was my angel, protecting me from that dark eternity.

But he only drank a little, his tongue trailing down to the valley of my breasts. His hair brushed along my chest, a thousand soft touches, as his lips closed around my nipple with a moan.

I arched into him, fingers winding into his hair, his tongue massaging the bud, sucking, pulling, drawing a cry from me. He kissed along my skin to the other. My hips bucked against him, already overwhelmed and needy. His tongue circling, his rough hands, his body pinning me down —I needed *more*.

He kissed his way down my chest, my navel, biting into the flesh of my hip. Crimson trailed down my breast, the same crimson staining his lips, and every time he looked up at me with those pitch-black eyes, I melted, my desire pooling between my legs.

"You are so sweet, Helena."

His fangs skimmed my thighs, his fingers wandering, caressing. Spreading me apart for him, his tongue brushed that spot at the apex of my thighs. Sharp teeth scraping the sensitive flesh, fingers finding my entrance and lightly teasing. Anticipation curled in my belly.

He took his time drawing pleasure out of me, pressing one finger inside as he bit down on my thigh. Instinctively, my legs began to close.

Growling, he glanced up at me, throwing my legs over his shoulders so I couldn't escape him and his bite.

I threw an arm over my face, gasping for breath.

He knew just how to unravel me. He knew how to tease with that mouth until I was begging him, my core squeezing his fingers, writhing for release. He played me like a puppet, my body wholly overtaken by his control.

He bit me again, and again, teeth sinking into the soft flesh of my thighs, drawing pain forth, instantly soothing it with his tongue. The skin between my legs became a constellation of red marks, his teeth bruising, sucking, draining me, while at the same time he forced a climax out of me, his fingers pressing in and out. Slick with my arousal, he sat up.

He shed his clothes, throwing them in the pile with mine. In a moment, he was bare above me, all godly musculature, an ancient statue of marble.

I realized my thoughts became fuzzy, my limbs feeling heavy, the familiar lightheadedness of giving him my lifeblood. Not the panic from my brother's bite, but the potent intoxication from the night at the altar.

He pulled me onto his lap, holding me up so I was straddling him. I wrapped my weak arms around him, fingers tugging at his auburn hair.

Deliciously disheveled, lust burning in his eyes, he pulled away enough to catch his breath. "How are you, my darling?"

"Keep going," I whispered.

The veins of his neck were darkening, the inky blackness spreading from the center of his chest. He kissed me roughly, guiding my hips, thrusting upward to meet me in the middle. I took him in greedily, stretching around him, pleasure curling my toes, and he slid in easily, the remnants of our earlier lovemaking slickening his intrusion. In moments he was fully seated.

He held me there, his chest expanding with real breaths, as if he were alive. Every fiber of my being tingled with the heady pleasure of his body against mine. He had said he could call forth the monster at will; the transformation took only seconds, as though he lost his control over it, veins spreading, eyes dark, teeth growing ever sharper, his nails digging into the soft flesh of my hips. But he didn't move, just let me adjust to his size, already delirious and floating.

"Look at us," he said, holding on to the nape of my neck. He stared at where we joined, glistening with his seed and my arousal, transfixed at the image of my body taking his cock. "So perfect."

I felt like I was going to explode, every nerve humming.

"You're going to wake up, and I'm going to be inside you. The first thing you'll know is how much I love you," he said, lifting me up and lowering me down onto him, sounding breathless himself.

I savored the glide of our bodies. I was too drowsy to move, too spent to arch myself into him. But he didn't mind, moving me like his own plaything.

His teeth returned to my throat.

"Are you ready?" he murmured against my skin.

This was the moment of no return.

I gave him a weak nod.

And then gently, his teeth sliced through my flesh. Burrowed deep into my neck, he took long, hard pulls, drawing my blood into himself.

It was unlike every other time he'd bitten me.

He moved beneath me, chasing that high, guiding my hips against his, while he drained the life from me. We fit together so perfectly, my body craving his. He was Death, this monster grinding his cock into me. Sinful.

If anyone were to walk up on us, what a sight we'd be— him, looking nothing other than a demon's spawn, and I the bloodied maiden, sighing at each thrust.

I always knew Vince would kill me.

Cradling me close, he shouted into the flesh of my neck. His cock twitched within me, each thrust a jolt of ecstasy. His thumb brushed my clit and I was clenching around him, the last beats of my pleasure stealing my breath and I saw stars, weakly grasping at him, another release taking me over.

He bit me again, the sharpness digging into the artery,

pricking me like a knife, tearing deep into sinew and muscle. It hurt.

It hurt.

My vision didn't clear, the black shadows at the edges coming closer.

Heart racing, breaths shallow, my body clinging to the last dregs of life I held.

An instinctual panic seized me. I couldn't feel my limbs.

My thoughts scattered.

"Shh," he whispered, breath hot against my throat. "I got you."

It was the last thing I heard before my mind gave out, and mortality grasped me with its cold fingers, pulling me under.

I dreamt I was falling. Red ribbons trailing behind me, lacerations at my back burning, stinging, like a wound doused in alcohol. My wings—

All my screams stalled in my throat.

The same nightmare, over and over again.

I knew how this played out.

Lucas, emerging from the mist, looming over me, only now his soul was black; he was biting at me, chewing, shredding my flesh to whet his appetite, chipping away at me until I was breaking, crumbling in his hands.

Except this time I latched onto him, and he came careening with me, snarling in outrage.

We fell towards a ground that we would never again meet. Weightless.

My wings were gone.
But Lucas could never fly, anyway.
And then—
I hit the ground—
And I opened my eyes.

PART THREE

HONEYMOON

THIRTY-THREE

My life began again with a sweet taste at my lips, a burn between my thighs, and the overwhelming sensation of hunger. Thirst seared my throat even as a nectar was pouring into me, the most exquisite ambrosia, like molten gold on my tongue.

"That's it," a male voice whispered in my ear.

I knew him, distantly.

But I couldn't focus, couldn't think of anything but the nectar trickling down my throat. I needed it like air, each drop on my tongue making me crave more, more, *more*.

A hiss of pain that turned into a groan. "*Easy.*"

I began to feel—a cool breeze along my spine, eyes stinging from the sunlight, the sound of flowing water.

A hand trailing along my leg.

And then like a veil lifted, I saw him.

Vince.

I was still in his lap. He was still inside of me, achingly hard. He looked at me with such intensity, my first instinct was to cower. Black veins spider-webbing across his skin, that heart beating slowly in his chest.

I could hear it. His heart.

Thump. Thump. Thump.

It was his wrist he held to my lips. His blood on my tongue.

"Hello, my love," he said, the timbre of his voice rumbling through me. It was silky, a caress even smoother than his touch.

I gasped.

Every movement a shock, every gentle beat in his chest echoed by the organ in my own, I was engulfed in sensation. Could see every pore in his skin. Could taste my own blood running through him. Could sense the shifting of the trees around me. All of it, immense and heady. The feel of his thumb on my skin was addictive, spurring me into a frenzy.

And then I was grinding against him, circling my hips, every beat of pleasure heightened tenfold.

He was beautiful, he was so beautiful, and he was all *mine*.

His sharp teeth glinted in the sun, the depths of his eyes reading triumphant. He pressed my face towards his neck.

"Drink," he commanded.

I couldn't refuse, even if I wanted to.

My teeth were sharp against my lips, foreign and unwieldy, but I bit into his flesh like I'd done it a million times before. This intake of his breath, and the twitch of his cock, were the only indications that he'd felt it. The intoxicating taste of him bloomed on my tongue again, the fervor going straight to my head.

I moved with renewed vigor, energy thrumming

through my limbs. It was almost too much, overwhelming, like I'd been plugged into an electrical socket, each of my nerves a live wire. Latching my teeth onto his throat, I braced myself on his legs, moving myself up and down the length of him. Moaning into his veins as pleasure shuddered through me.

I understood the parties. Understood why so many of them chased this high, feeding on each other until the sun rose. Giving and taking like it was my duty.

He clenched his teeth, falling back onto his elbows, letting me take care of him, letting me take what I needed. When my thirst was sated, I pulled away, only to capture his lips in a kiss. At the taste of himself on my tongue, he gripped my hips, pulling me closer, *harder*.

No one had bitten him since Andreas.

Every bit of hurt in him caused by his Sire, I'd chase away. I'd make him forget. The pain of our youth, all the terrible things since—I'd replace with this moment, taking him into me, my heart offered to him on a gilded platter.

Only when he trembled against me did I slow. Hands roaming his chest, I felt every miniscule flex of his muscles, could feel the blood rushing under his skin.

He exhaled a shaky laugh, grinning dangerously at me, sharp teeth on display. "Done yet, little vixen?"

And then, as the sun began to set, we did it all over again.

It was me, this evening, who was insatiable. My new body craved him, thirsted for him, frenzied thoughts thinking only of him, his blood, and the intoxicating way he moved within me.

Only as the sun set did I separate myself from him, slipping into the water. Tried to regain my mind, shock it into submission with the icy stream. We could not stay out in the forest forever.

"Do you see now why I cannot resist you?" he said, smoothing the wet hair away from my face.

I quelled the urge to climb atop him again, instead moving away to retrieve my clothes. "Maybe we should sleep in separate rooms tonight."

He scoffed. "Not a chance."

The silky slip felt like the softest flower petals as I pulled it over my head. The movement nearly sent me falling to the ground, still unsteady on my feet.

Vince stared at me, that hunger still blazing in his eyes.

"I should have done this sooner," he said.

I pulled my stockings up my legs, the material so thin, I could see every bruise and bite through it. The marks would be gone by morning, most likely, but I preened, feeling deliciously dirty every time I looked at them. When we returned to the house, there would be no doubt what we'd been up to.

"Are you sure?" I gazed at him through my lashes. Even in the moonlight, he shone, clear as day. "I cannot stop wanting your blood every few minutes."

"You can drain me dry, if you want."

"Then who will terrorize all these bad vampires, if I kill you by accident?" I slipped my feet into my shoes.

His stare was piercing. "You."

The walk back to the chateau was through a scene from

the fairytales I read as a young girl. Each insect's legs whispering against flower petals, the rustle of birds' wings, the groaning of the trees' trunks as they grew; I heard it all, the forest coming vibrantly alive. I took it all in, slowing our progress, because each sound, each breeze, opened up a whole new world, and I couldn't miss one second of it.

I didn't think I could ever leave the forest—how could the drafty halls of the house even compare?

My fingers were laced through Vince's. I caught him staring, with the most wonderfully boyish smile, reminding me of the young man I fell in love with over six years ago. How young we seemed then, how naive.

"What happens next?" I asked him, brushing my fingers against a bunch of daffodils waving in the breeze.

"Bed," he said. "You'll wake hungry. It will be this way for some time. My first inclination is to keep you hidden away in the rooms until I know you have control."

"You don't think the men will have an issue with me?"

Nevermind that I didn't think my *control* would become a problem.

"No," he said, pulling me to a stop. "They would never touch you. It's *you* who is a threat to them."

I laughed, though I knew a part of him was serious.

It was just after midnight when we stepped through the front doors. A whole lifetime had passed since the morning. The darkness of the foyer and the halls had given way to a gentle sea of shadows, my sight acute enough to cut through as though it were daytime.

Vince tensed beside me.

Sinclair was stopped at the foot of the stairs, and in his arms, Séra, carried like a bride. She giggled at whatever he had said, before they both realized they were no longer alone.

Eyes widening the moment their gazes caught on me. Sensing—

I was one of them.

After a moment, Séra grinned. "*Finally.*"

THIRTY-FOUR

"Now you've done it." My brother was laughing, the whites of his eyes more prominent than before, as I emerged from the stairwell into the cellar.

The scent of rot intensified, along with it the odor of piss, and vomit, and that smoky iron of blood.

There was a manic gleam to his eyes, pupils completely dilated, his teeth bared. His gums were almost white. The wound at his shoulder was beginning to fester, the shredded flesh looking anything but like skin. Decaying, oozing. The touch of death spreading from the ravaged flesh, across his chest, his neck.

His pulse was erratic, like a hummingbird's wings echoing throughout the chamber.

"You just couldn't wait, could you?" he taunted. "Or did he force you to become one of us?"

I stayed far enough away, worried if I got any closer, I'd get sick myself from the stench.

He pulled at his chains, testing the boundaries with his one good arm. "You'll be sorry, Helena."

"For what?"

This enraged him. "*Stupid* girl—"

"You can call me whatever name you want," I said, not bothering to raise my voice.

"Didn't you listen to a word I said last time? I guess I shouldn't be surprised. You *like* that he uses you."

He leaned closer, and I knew if the chains had not stopped him, he would've stepped into my space, face inches from mine. He would have pinned me to the wall. He would have bit me, just to prove he could.

"Will he share you with his little followers? Will he watch as they line up to *use* you? Or have they already?"

I crossed my arms, if only to hide how my hands shook. Even now, when he couldn't hurt me. "It bothers you that I was Made."

"It *bothers* me that you are so insubordinate."

"It bothers you, because you were not the one to do it."

His eyes narrowed then. He wanted so badly to touch me. I could see it there, in his eyes, how he coveted my blood. How he itched to sink his fingers into my flesh, pull my ribs apart, one by one, and consume my heart—consume *me*. He wanted to pull the tendons from my bones, just to see what would happen, just to hear how I'd scream.

And when I laughed, his eyes widened, stunned.

"What are you going to do, Lucas?" I shook my head. "You are chained up and I'm not. You are *thirsty* and I'm not. You have *nothing*. No one is coming to save you."

This was how I felt on the boat across the Atlantic. This was how I felt when he locked me in my room, taunting me with Adam's death. This was how I felt every time his fist connected with my skin.

I cocked my head. "What are you going to do?" I repeated.

Pure venom stared back at me.

And I took a demented sort of glee in it: seeing his body decay while his immortality kept him alive, watching him realize he was losing his control on me, on his life, on his world.

If I were kinder, I'd strike a killing blow.

He was silent for the first time in his life. So I let him have it.

I recounted every time he wronged me: every insult, every instance he tried to humiliate me, every moment I wished for his death. I asked him if he remembered the first time he hit me. I asked him if he remembered how we used to be friends as children, and I asked him if he thought Father would be proud, how he beat down the women in his life. I told him how I found Lucy, bloodied and afraid. I told him how I knew Wright was a villain all along.

I could not forget, so I would make sure that he couldn't, either, even if it was his last coherent thought.

By the time I was done, he was seething in anger, almost shaking with it in the chains. "That's alright," he muttered. "You might get away. You might kill me. You can have everything that you want now, huh? But I'll follow along, everywhere. I'll always be there, Helena."

He came as close as he could in the chains, staring me straight in the eyes.

"I will always own you."

THIRTY-FIVE

The guests began to arrive the day before the banquet. Vince wanted to greet them personally, his charade beginning the moment they stepped foot on the property, so I did not see him much at all. Emil, Claude, Matthias, Rogier, all of them occupied.

Dixon, at least, had no obligation to make appearances.

"I have to say I'm jealous." Flora pouted, glaring at me over her cup of coffee that morning, though there was no real malice in it. "I'm the odd one out."

I nudged her with my arm. "Sorry." A little white lie.

"You'll just have to join us." Séra smiled, showing off her teeth.

"And you." Flora turned to Dixon. "I am still angry with you."

"You can be as angry with me as you'd like," he said, sipping his own tea. "I was only trying to keep you safe."

She rolled her eyes. "I have half a mind to leave you, Dixon."

"You wouldn't dare." His eyes flickered up to her, in a look so intense, her cheeks turned pink. Her heart fluttered.

It was odd, the sensations that I could now pick up on: a quickening pulse, almost as though I could sense emotions. The shift of air in the room at someone's entrance. And each person had their own scent—Vince's was something sweet, musky, like toasted caramel.

Séra leaned a little closer. "Do you *want* to be Made, Flora?"

My friend looked unsure, flustered from Dixon's gaze. "I could be convinced, I think."

We readied for the party together, Séra, Flora, and I, picking out each other's dresses, applying rouge and kohl in the dying sunlight. The wardrobes were stocked full, every fabric we could think of in any color we wanted.

I chose a short red dress that exposed my thighs through its beading. When I spun, the skirt flew out around my hips, exposing enough to cause a scandal in polite society. Flora curled my hair before rooting around in the wardrobe for a matching pair of shoes.

She smelled like lavender and sugar and my favorite street-side cinnamon buns from home.

Spending the hours with them, laughing over our men and memories from the months prior, listening to their stories from their journey to the chateau, mended a crack in my heart that I hadn't known was there. As though none of this was happening, and we were just three girls enjoying each other's company, readying for a night out in the city.

But beneath it all, I could not ignore the dark feeling in my gut, my shame, reminding me they did not know about my darkest parts. They did not know what I've done. They did not know what I planned to do.

We linked arms once dusk began to settle across the mountain, deciding to brave the night together. The hallway was quiet, though the music from below was a soft siren's serenade, leading our way.

"Do you think Dixon will dance with me?" Flora wondered aloud.

"I think he will, if he sees you approach another man," I said. "He wouldn't let another man—or vampire—touch you."

She sighed, almost dreamily. "He *is* protective, isn't he?"

My name was called from the opposite end of the hall. When I whirled around, I saw Vince—dressed in a fine evening suit, a midnight black, his silk tie striped with red. His auburn hair was slicked back, a single stray curl falling boyish over his face. His hands in his pockets, leaning his shoulder against the wall, a leg bent casually.

If I didn't know any better, I would have thought he was born into this world of money, it suited him so well.

"Go on," I said. "I'll catch up."

Flora and Séra gave each other knowing looks before they ducked around the corner.

Vince watched my every move as I came closer. His heart was steady, slower than any normal man's, but just as strong. A cologne, deep and rich, purely masculine. Leather and iron. Mixing with the smell of *him*.

My mouth watered.

His eyes raked across my body, catching on the frilled

edge of my dress, my exposed legs—no stockings. Pupils dilating. Perhaps having the same thoughts I was.

"Are you ready?" he asked.

I nodded, stopping only a foot before him.

"The vampires you are about to meet are not like those in New York," he said, with an edge of caution. "And I cannot be by your side all evening."

"You worry too much."

"Because I know you." His eyes glimmered. "I know you have a penchant for getting into trouble."

Something had changed between us.

It scared me, this clarity. I looked at him and I saw— Vince. Not Adam, not this enigma that I couldn't crack, not this ruthless vampire. Just Vince. If he wore a mask anymore, I saw right through it. And I hadn't cared to don my own.

"I have something for you."

Another velvet box. This time, the edges were worn, the case a deep emerald. He handed it to me, watching for my reaction.

Inside: a ruby red necklace, the gem in the shape of a teardrop. Blood red, glinting deliciously in the low light.

I gasped, recognizing the cut.

"A shame, the earrings are back in New York," he said. "But if I'd grabbed everything before I left a few years ago, I wouldn't have this to give you now."

From Andreas' coffers.

He'd told me once that his mansion in New York, and the money that funded it, came from his wealthy Sire. Coffers that were now his. And I was delighted at the idea of discovering what else Andreas had been collecting.

"Help me put it on."

His fingers brushing mine, even now, were electric. Priming me with anticipation for whatever was to come. As I turned in his arms, my desire flooded my senses, and I wanted nothing more than for him to press my front against the wall and find his way under my skirt.

"If we had no obligations..." he purred, knowing exactly where my thoughts had gone.

The ruby was heavy against my chest, inlaid in a polished gold. As it touched my skin, I felt the weight of its years against my breasts. Like the gem had watched empires rise and fall.

"This belonged to Andreas' lover," he said as I turned back around.

I balked. "His lover?"

Vince only laughed. "Centuries ago. I don't remember her name. But neither of them will be needing it now."

He stole my breath when he pressed his lips to mine. Rough and bruising. Desire pooled in my center. I almost whimpered with it, and I didn't care that we were expected downstairs.

But he pulled away, smoothing his hair back.

I used my thumb to wipe the lipstick off his mouth, peering up at him through my lashes, though I was half-tempted to let him walk into the party like that. Claimed. *Mine*.

"Later," he promised.

I had not been expecting a party exactly like the ones thrown on Long Island, but I hadn't anticipated just how dull the vampires of Europe were.

Séra had done her job, turning the ballroom from dated and moth-eaten into an elegant space fit for a royal ball. Golden threaded curtains layered with gossamer, the floor shining like glass. The paneled walls were lined with mirrors, giving the illusion that the ballroom was much larger. Plush sapphire couches pushed against the wall, and mahogany tables lined up in the center of the room to make one long feast.

We stood off to the side, near the doors, observing as the crowd came in one by one. Flora watched in rapt fascination, though she stuck close to Séra and I, for fear of rogue teeth. Dixon had yet to appear.

There was no one to announce names, though it seemed the vampires all knew each other, anyway.

I spotted Vince across the room, caught up in conversation with a group of men I did not know. As though he could feel my stare, his eyes met mine, and I had the most uncanny deja vu.

A ghost, spotting me across a room of hundreds.

Blushing, I averted my eyes.

"Where is Sinclair?" I asked Séra.

"He's been put on 'guard duty,'" she said, pointing to the balcony. He was leaning against a marble column, eyes scanning the crowd below. I knew that in a room full of so many creatures, fights were bound to happen. But I had the distinct feeling that Sinclair was watching out for a specific set of party crashers, should they arrive.

It was not lost on me how similar this all was to the last

masquerade. And just like that night, the air was tense and thick with anticipation.

Only, this time I was not bait—and even if I were, I had the fangs to bite back.

A stream of soft music came from the other side of the room, musicians hired from Paris on top dollar. I caught more than a few eyes lingering on the mortals, though no one made to snatch the players.

"How much do you think they'll take to play something else?" Séra whispered.

"I kind of like it," Flora said. "This is fancier than anything we've attended at home."

"Maybe we should start throwing balls instead of bacchanals."

Flora shook her head. "Nobody would come."

And there was probably some truth in that.

"Are we supposed to *waltz*? I don't know how to waltz."

I grinned, grabbing both of my friends' hands. "Doesn't mean we can't try."

We attracted every pair of eyes as we glided to the dance-floor, laughing amongst ourselves in an otherwise subdued room. The three of us, holding hands as we twirled. Other couples danced in circles, hands at their chests, something too slow for my tastes. A hesitation subdued our movements —the fear of ridicule—but after a few songs, I found I didn't care anymore, and slowly the ice melted from around our limbs.

And the musicians were grinning, watching us spin.

As we traversed the floor, I swore I saw Claude's shock of blond hair at the edge of the floor, and next to him, a blushing Emil. Claude grinning, sliding a hand across Emil's shoulders.

"And this is your bride, Vince?"

I stopped my dancing so quickly, my feet skidding against the polished floor, that I almost toppled over. Smile faltering, hearing the derision in the stranger's voice.

I'd lost my friends—Flora and Séra were already on the other side of the dancefloor.

The man had short black hair, slicked back with pomade, though it curled around his ears, deep green eyes that seemed to shine like emeralds, and an eastern accent.

Vince was smiling, despite the disdain of the man. "Indeed."

"Michal Popov." The man outstretched his hand, bending at the waist.

"Helena," I replied, slipping my fingers into his grasp. There was a touch of hate in his stare, and I wondered if he was in Andreas' book—and if so, did he deserve the sentence Vince would eventually deliver?

"I've heard of your parties in New York." Michal turned to Vince, though his eyes lingered on me. "Can we expect a little taste tonight?"

At that moment, he noticed the ruby around my neck, glinting under the candle light. Something crossed over his features, a slight widening of his eyes. Sweat on his palms. *Nervousness.*

"Not tonight." Vince bared his teeth in a smile, clapping a hand on Michal's shoulder. "Though I'm sure you'll find yourself sufficiently entertained."

Thirty-Six

"Why have you called us here? This dispute with Marcel Brancato—you do not need our permission to kill your rival."

Hours later, the banquet long over, the guests of honor were assembled at the enormous table at Vince's request. The party had been a formality, I realized; an excuse to host this meeting, not just a show of good will.

It was nearly dawn, if I had to guess, and my eyes were growing tired, my throat slowly becoming dry. But I sat at Vince's side, doing my best to appear like I belonged amongst them.

Vince's smile did not reach his eyes, as he responded to the portly man's question. "I want to settle a few rumors for good. Make peace."

A laugh, from a woman a few seats away. Her hair was a fiery red, long and braided down her back. "And why should we even hear you out?"

"It would've been a waste of time to make the journey and not hear me out."

Michal waved his hand for Vince to go on.

"I won't act like an alliance between us is a possibility. And I won't apologize for my past, for what I was *made* to do," he said, as though he was reminding them of this fact.

There was some disgruntled murmuring, but Vince ignored it.

"I want to assure you that Andreas' cause was his own."

"To continue his *legacy*, no?" Michal sneered. "Did not your Sire want to establish a royal line? This would make *you* a king, should you succeed in subduing us all."

"No, I do not want to make myself some sort of king," Vince said, eyes landing on every person in the room. "You forget I ran *away* from Andreas."

Though I was too afraid to speak as it was, I was stunned at how Vince spoke to them: familiar, like he'd encountered them many times in the six years we'd been apart. They knew him, were wary of his reputation; they may have even known his secret.

And I was sure he knew all of theirs.

"You want us to believe that after years as his errand boy and his heir, you are washing your hands of it?"

"Yes, I was his heir, but I have no desire to make every vampire on the continent answer to me. It'd be a nightmare."

The red-headed woman rolled her eyes.

"Then we're in agreement."

If these vampires backed down, and truly believed that Vince was not going to continue the bloodshed Andreas had begun in his attempt to create a throne, then they would leave us be. They would turn Marcel away

"A council, then, if not a monarchy," Claude said with splayed hands. He sat on Vince's other side, silent thus far.

"A council? How original."

"And who would make up this council?"

Claude gestured to the room. "I think we have a fine sampling here in this room."

"This does not feel very democratic," the red-haired woman said.

Another vampire hummed. "I believe we can all agree that we'd rather be left to ourselves and our covens without the threat of adversaries."

"We must agree to keep the peace, but defend when necessary."

"Defend from whom?" Michal's eyes slid to Vince.

Vince titled his head, his stare wholly calculating, and I was glad I was not on the receiving end of it. "Marcel Brancato. If you fear a tyrant, *he* is the threat you're looking for."

A few more scoffs.

"It is your word against his."

"Proof? You want proof?"

There was a hesitant silence.

Vince motioned with a finger. "An offering, then."

The doors burst open, and between Emil and Matthias, three men were dragged across the floor, hands knotted behind their backs. Lean, bones jutting against their skin.

Vince grabbed the grimy hair of the first man, skinny and covered in dirt. "Lidia—this one was the newest of our bunch. Barely eighteen before the war started. Condemned by his family for his *fondness* for a young cousin."

"For you, Michal," he said, gesturing to a well-muscled man, who stared at the seated vampires in desperate hunger, his sharp teeth jutting from his lips. "The keeper of an illegal and cruel blood brothel."

The last, an older man, who fell to his knees almost immediately. "And his crime, the simple fact that he was an ally of Andreas."

The seated vampires were stunned into silence. But they couldn't hide how they coveted the blood of the three trapped men.

And I knew Vince had them.

Entertain them. Give them what they want. Is that not what I do best?

"Take this gift," Vince said, "and in return, all I ask is that next time Marcel Brancato steps foot upon your land, he meets his death."

No one said a word.

But it was acceptance enough.

Vince turned to me, and when I slipped my hand in his, we put the banquet, the ballroom, and all the vampires within far behind us.

THIRTY-SEVEN

"Where will we go now?"

I lay with Vince, naked in his bed, my chest pressed against his, trailing my fingers along his throat. I was fascinated by his slow heart beat, mesmerized by the faint pulse underneath his skin.

Since the last guest from the banquet had left, I remained in the bedroom, wanting to pass the time caught up in Vince's embrace, distracted by his taste, his touch, the feel of him inside of me. I hadn't wanted to think about anything but *him*. That evening I'd lured him to bed, and he had gladly obliged. I hadn't let him out of my grasp since.

It was three days later, and we were only beginning to come up for air. None of the other men had bothered us, and I suspected they were spending their time similarly—for the first time in a long time, they had no imminent foes.

The tension that had permeated the chateau since our arrival dissipated. An unfamiliar lightness had taken the weight from my shoulders, a burden I hadn't known I was carrying, because it had been there my entire life. So ingrained, and now that it was gone, I almost didn't recognize the way my body moved.

But I also knew—we were not entirely done. Knowing the vindictive nature of these vampires, we were never wholly free of our adversaries.

Vince relaxed with his eyes closed, a sheen of sweat along his brow. "We can go back to New York, if you'd like."

"You don't wish to stay here?" I asked. Sitting up, my weight tilted into my hips, which straddled his waist.

He cracked open an eyelid, one of his hands gripping me. "I only wish to be wherever you are."

"Hmm." I thought on it, splaying my palms against his chest. I had fed only a few hours ago, but looking down at him, I had the urge to bite, a literal tingling in my new teeth. "Do you remember how we used to dream about traveling the Mediterranean?"

A small smile pulled at his lips. "Of course."

"We never got to run away," I said, looming over him.

"No, we didn't. But there is no running away now," he said, his grip possessive on my hips. "There's only doing what we want, when we want, *wherever* we want."

"And what is it that you want?" I leaned down to kiss him, our hearts beating together through our rib cages.

"You," he murmured against my lips.

"You," he exhaled, breath hot, his strong hand guiding my mouth to his throat.

"You," he groaned as I bit into his flesh.

His blood bloomed on my tongue, and I knew I was hopelessly obsessed with the taste of him. With just one drop, the impulse to suck the delicate skin of his neck between my teeth drove me wild. I wanted to make a mess of him, wanted to drink him until he and I were made of the same stuff, like a star split into two, the halves forever in each other's orbit. I wanted to claw my way into him, under his skin. I wanted to *eat him whole.*

Fingers tangling in my hair, he only pulled my mouth away when the dizziness turned to lust in his eyes. And then I knew I was in trouble.

I grinned a bloodstained grin and splayed myself open for him, eager to let him have his way with me for the rest of the night.

When the time came, I followed Dixon and Flora out to the car, which sat idling, waiting for the journey back to England. He nearly had to drag her out of the house, an arm around her shoulders.

"Must we go?" she said, teary-eyed. She slid from his arms and fell into mine. Over a breakfast of tea and buttered rolls, she had remained optimistic, grilling Dixon more about his family and their estate. But once outside, the facade fell.

I hugged her tightly, basking in her lavender scent, in the familiar feel of her in my arms. If I had my way, we'd remain together, forever.

She sniffed, pulling away. "When will I see you again?"

"I'm not sure," I admitted. "But soon."

Nodding shakily, she caressed my face pressing a kiss to my forehead.

"I need you to do something for me," I said, once Dixon had stepped away to pack their trunks.

Next to me, a small suitcase waited. Locked, I'd made sure of it. The book inside hidden in a blanket, should someone find their way inside. It wasn't fool-proof, but I trusted her. I lifted it by the handle, offering it to her.

"What is it?"

"Something very important. A secret."

She didn't ask another question, nodding, the look in her eyes telling me she understood.

I'd find my way back to it, eventually. I just didn't know when.

Vince and I had some unfinished business to take care of first.

Dixon came around and held the car door open for her. "Come," he said, gently. His usually hard exterior had cracked a little for her. He would take care of her, I knew; he would put his life before hers, if it came to it.

She kissed my cheek, one of her tears falling to my skin. I held it there, watching her climb in the car, missing her instantly. "Take care of Lucy for me," I said.

She nodded. "You know we will."

Dixon shut the door behind himself, putting the car into gear. Flora held back a sob, chin wobbling. He met my eyes, unspoken promises and well-wishes lingering there.

"I'll send word," I called as the car eased forward.

And then they were off, down the winding path through the forest, away from the chateau and away from the uncertainty of what came next. The engine rattled into the distance, fading into a hum, and then finally dissipating into the whispers of the trees.

THIRTY-EIGHT

It did not take long for the effects of hunger to eat away at Lucas. Such a young vampire could not go long without drink, and yet, he did.

He was crazy with bloodlust. Snapped at the chains each time I entered, choking off his own air in an attempt to break the iron, to lunge across the room at me.

He sputtered obscenities, his mouth more foul than I'd ever heard it before. He spit promises at me I pretended not to hear, curses that turned into mad rambling, his saliva foaming at the corners of his mouth.

Mostly, I felt pity for him.

He was wasting away, the flesh of his limbs seeming to evaporate, until he was all skin and bones. His clothes hung on him loosely, like he was a gruesome sort of scarecrow. Every day, he looked less like the boy I'd grown up with.

We'd been friends once. Had experienced that childhood joy together.

And then something had changed him.

I wanted to see him one last time, before the bricks and cement sealed him inside. The damp, pitch-dark cellar seemed a fine enough tomb for me.

One last time, I stood before him. Blood coated his front, his eyes the rabid white of an animal, pupils mere pinpricks. He was losing his fight, hanging limply from the chains, the iron collar at his neck digging into his throat, his jaw. But his stare followed me, his lips pulled back in a silent snarl. Those sharp teeth missing.

I would never tell my mother what had happened to her son. Maybe wouldn't ever see her again myself—I wasn't sure I wanted to.

I didn't feel particularly bad for the creature he'd become. He had sealed his own fate.

In fact, I hoped the thirst consumed him. I hoped he felt every agonizing second of his death.

I wondered if this was how Andreas felt, starving his fledglings, to see how long they could last? This sick curiosity only grew with each passing day.

Lucy, wherever she was, had lost a husband, even if he was of the worst kind. She had tried so hard to please him; she'd done everything right and still, what had she gotten out of it? I mourned for her humanity, for her lost child. I'd do everything I could to see her happy.

And my mother lost her son. Her darling child, her favorite, her greatest achievement—though that said enough about the kind of woman she was.

I'd lost my brother long ago. I didn't have much to grieve any longer.

"Goodbye, Lucas."

I climbed the stairs out of the cellar, and ordered the workers to seal it shut.

Thirty-Nine

After two weeks in Paris, I grew impatient. My lust for blood could not be quenched—Vince had been right about that—but I could quell the constant ache in my teeth if I bit into his vein every morning. He gave it to me, gladly, finding his own satisfaction in sustaining me, letting me drain from his strength, his power.

And after the events of the last weeks, I was hungry.

I forced Vince to take me to every museum that was open, and we slowly made our way across the city. Trying foods I've never heard of, while I could still enjoy them. Finding bars out in the open, girls and guys drinking liquor in the street. Vince opened my eyes to just how many establishments had a back room for those with a more distinct thirst.

Anonymity was easy in a city like this.

Our respite was soon coming to a close, and I knew that Vince would not wait much longer to begin exacting his revenge, no matter how I wanted to dismiss our troubles in favor of drinking and dancing—the two things I was best at.

So one night, I told him to stay behind, because I had something I needed to do.

"Are you going to join me?" I said, no louder than if he was already seated next to me.

His presence neared, summoned.

I was never one for smoking, but when he offered me a cigarette, I placed it between my lips. He held his lighter up, shielding from the wind as it caught. All the while our gazes were locked. His piercing chestnut eyes, dark ruffled hair. Just like the first night I met him.

I exhaled after a moment, ignoring the fluttering in my stomach that must have been nerves. "You've found me."

Marcel Brancato grinned, settling into the chair across from me. "I thought it was time we meet again."

"You've been hiding?"

"Hiding? No." He waved down a server, barking an order in perfect French. After the server ran off, he leaned back in his seat, a finger tapping at the edge of the table. "Biding my time, more like."

His gaze was penetrating, intense as ever. Like I was the only girl on the street, and I'd caught the eye of a bachelor in need. It wasn't my blood, couldn't be.

"For?"

"You." His finger stilled. "I've been waiting for you."

I averted my gaze to the passersby, watching as couples clung to each other as they walked, men laughing together and sharing smokes, as lively as though it were not nearly midnight. The streetlamps sent a yellow glow against the cobblestones, bright enough to scare away the stars blanketing the sky. This city did not sleep either, but it was decidedly not New York.

"So you've been following me?" I accused. I placed the cigarette at my lips again. "You could have revealed yourself to me whenever you wanted, could you not?"

He stared at me through his lashes. Too direct, too intense, and he knew it.

"No. Not without running into your *lover*, too."

I threw him a plastered-on smile. "Afraid of him?"

He scowled. "You know what he is. I did not care to go through the hassle of it. A *brute*, is what he is. But all things come to those who wait, yes? And here you are, falling right into my lap."

I ignored the image in my mind.

The server came, dropping off two glasses of greenish liquid, barely enough for a creature of the undead to feel a buzz. Absinthe. I took a sip, letting the liquor linger on my tongue, but the fire was gone, the burn, and left a strange taste in its stead.

"Where were you that night?" I broke the silence between us.

Marcel swirled his glass. "You'll have to be more specific, dear."

Dear. It grated on my nerves, a sharp jolt of discomfort.

"The night I..." It all came back to me so suddenly. "Escaped."

"The night you murdered your husband?"

"*Hush.*" I glanced around, but no one seemed to hear him.

"Oh, don't be ashamed of it *now*. You've got what you wanted, yes? And his life was the price. A small price, it seems. He was rather arrogant, I'll admit."

"You haven't answered my question."

His smile was cynical. "The Highsmith line has ended, because of you. All that remains is the Lady, though 'Lady' she is no longer. The Barony has gone to a cousin." He shrugged. "Just thought you should know."

I grit my teeth. "Should I lay out everything I've done for you to judge?"

"We have all the time in the world for it." He leant his elbows on the table. "I'm sure you have some scandalous stories to share. Your brother—" He whistled. "He sure thought you were giving it up to anyone who asked. One of the first things he spilled. He could not hold his liquor. But if you ask me, I think he was jealous."

"What are you talking about?" I recoiled.

"*I* was. Jealous, that is." He laughed. "Would you believe that I still am? I am a covetous man, and you were dangling before me like a prize for the taking. And yet, I've still not had you."

Taking a deep breath into my lungs, a lingering habit from my mortality, I willed myself not to be affected by him. There was a reason I'd come out tonight, and I could not forget.

"I should kill you."

"You'd be well within your right," he said, lips pulling into a smirk.

"You let me get away."

Marcel's eyes glimmered. He was quiet for a moment. Then, "I was repulsed by the thought of Wright's hands all over you. I'd tried ignoring it. Maybe it was the liquor that night, but after the stench of blood was overwhelming, I knew what you had done from halfway across the house, and I knew that now, at the very least, my only obstacle was Vince."

"But what of Making Wright? Did I not throw a wrench in your plans?"

He shrugged. "I'd be a fool if I didn't think you could somehow undermine me."

"You are not angry?"

"Of course I am. By all measures, I've failed."

"There's a reward for your head."

"Yes, I've heard." He tapped his finger on the table.

"What will you do then? Go into hiding for the rest of your life?"

He chuckled under his breath, shaking his head. "You and I both know I have no need."

We sat in silence for a moment, watching the pedestrians, hearing every squeak of a rat in the alleyways, every drip of water in the drains, the clinking of glasses and laughter spilling onto the street.

Marcel sat back in his chair.

His gaze jumped to my chest, then back, staring straight through me. The elephant in the room. "When did he do it?"

"Does it matter?"

"I would have given you this gift," he said. "You know I would have done it, if only you asked. But I see you begged him to do it instead."

"I don't beg."

"Are you sure about that?" Marcel's gaze flickered to my lips, that hungry stare the same he'd given me even when I was human—starved for my blood, my attention. He remembered our conversations at Whitrow: the bargain he wanted me to agree to, my affection in exchange for his protection. If only he knew how close I'd been to cracking.

He adjusted in his seat, glancing about the mostly empty street. "Where is he, anyway? Listening in? Can't leave you out of his sight, can he?"

I shrugged. Offered him the cigarette.

He leaned forward, his lips against the paper exactly where mine had been. The tip burned cherry red as he inhaled. Smoke came out of his nose like he was some demon, and maybe he was, what with how he was staring at me.

When I replaced the cigarette at my own lips, I ignored how they tingled at the indirect contact.

What if I had given in to him the night we met at the speakeasy? Would he have killed me then? Would he have made himself a candidate for my hand? He could have so easily wormed his way into my life; he could have seduced me, earned my brother's favor, and stolen me away from Vince, all before I even knew my dead lover was alive.

I thought he was going to taunt me, to say exactly what was on my mind. But instead, he said:

"We could've had something good, you and I."

"Could we have?" I blew out smoke towards the sky. Felt him turn his eyes on me. His stare unsettling, *always* unsettling. He could not hide his emotions behind those eyes. Never could. Not like Vince. Marcel wore no masks.

"You know we would've made some fun of it." He laughed under his breath. "I nearly had you once, did I not?"

"Maybe you came on too strong."

He laughed in earnest this time, loud in the midnight quiet. A couple passing by glanced in our direction. "You like to drive a man wild, huh? Make him earn it." He leaned closer. "Tell me, my dear. Did I come close? Have I earned nothing?"

Were I alive, my cheeks would have reddened, and not from the cooling evening air. I still could not look at him. "I think you know the answer."

Marcel, always striving to be the winner. In second place again.

His thoughts must have traveled the same path as mine. "Should have sunk my claws in you when I had the chance," he said, a low sardonic murmur.

I shuddered as though he whispered in my ear.

"You would have enjoyed it. This game you like to play, to string men along. I would have put that to an end. Perhaps I should have come on stronger, tell you exactly what I wanted from you."

"And what would you have said?"

The cigarette was burning dangerously close to my fingers. But I was frozen.

Marcel had come closer. He sat next to me, a hand hovering over my shoulder, as if to caress, like he couldn't keep from touching. His lips inches from my ear.

I shut my eyes.

"If you'd continued on with me that night, I suspect we would have danced. Drank ourselves to another bar. Somewhere along the way you'd find yourself with your skirts at your hips against the backseat of a car. Any car, we'd find one. I would have drawn every drop of pleasure from you. Make you mad with it. Tease you with the promise of more until you were begging. And only then I'd give in. You'd promise yourself to me. You wouldn't be able to live without me."

His lips skimmed my neck.

"That's what you could've had."

Fingers dancing feather-light along my collarbone.

"And now?" My breath came out a puff of steam before me, the heat from the cigarette singing my fingers. The smoke dropped to the tabletop.

He paused.

"I would never say no to you, Helena."

My traitorous heart fluttered in my chest, the organ still barely alive, and yet my prisoner.

I pushed away from the table, putting some distance between us. My blood felt hot and I wasn't sure why—and that scared me.

Leaving the cigarette butt on the table, our glasses forgotten, I fled down the street. Wrapped my shawl close around my shoulders. My heels clicked on the stone.

I knew he would follow.

As soon as we passed the threshold of shadows, he pushed me back against the alley wall, encaging me with his arms on either side of my head. Were I human, fear would have muddled my mind.

But I was not afraid of him any longer.

"You tease me," he said, lowering his mouth to my neck. His knifelike teeth skimmed my skin, sending electricity through my collarbones, down to my fingers, at the feather-light scrape.

"I'm doing no such thing." My hands against his chest, as though to push him away.

He grabbed my wrists, pressing them into the wall so that I could not move, trapped in his grasp. "You know exactly what you do to me. I think you like it."

I turned my head away.

"You like torturing me. You're a *vixen*. I think you wanted me that night. And you want me now." His tongue darted out, tracing my skin, teasing the flesh of my throat. "Just admit it, Helena. I can give you what he can't. There's a part of you unsatisfied. Let me satisfy you."

He wrenched his knee between my thighs. Pressed so close I could smell the absinthe on his breath, the tang of iron from one of his last meals.

Something burned hot in my chest.

This time when I wrenched myself free, he let me go. Grinning, sharp fangs on display.

I righted my shawl, straightening my skirt, my hair. "Not here. I am not an animal."

Perhaps he knew he was following me to his demise. As soon as we entered the bedroom, I locked the door behind me.

"Wait here," I whispered, pressing him to the door with my fingertips to his chest.

His teeth glinted in the dim midnight dark. "My patience has run dry."

He took a step toward me, and I backed away, step by step, until my hips hit the bed. My heart gave a kick, a rarity now.

He invaded my space, and I pulled on the lapels of his jacket, until he was standing between my legs, spreading them wide apart. Settling his hips almost against mine, almost there...

I traced my lips against his ear. "Will you let me have my way with you?"

He hummed, low in his chest, and with a flash of his dark eyes, Marcel stooped to connect his lips to mine. I pulled away at the last second, meeting his gaze. Pure unbridled lust.

"Anything you want," he mumbled into the space between us.

A flicker of madness. Eyes narrowing.

"Is he joining us, too?"

He'd caught sight of Vince, then.

My lover was reclined in a chair in the corner, encased in shadows. He'd been waiting, watching. Even with our preternatural abilities, he was difficult to see, the moonlight casting only a sliver of light onto the bed. Like a spotlight, illuminating Marcel's body against mine.

I knew how it pained Vince to remain still. He leaned his chin on his fingers. "Go on," he said, low and menacing, as though there was no room for argument.

"I wish I could say I'm surprised," Marcel's hands turned to fists on either side of my hips, gripping my skirts, tightening his hold on me with bruising fingers. "You two were always doomed for each other."

With a palm at his cheek, I turned his face back to mine. "Are you saying no to me, Marcel Brancato?"

I knew I won when hate widened his pupils. But he gave in all the same.

It ended in a cheap hotel room in Paris, the walls painted the same carmine as the blood that stained my hands, another cigarette at my lips and an iron tang on my tongue.

It was only after we'd had our fun, when the sun began to peek between the buildings, washing the room with rosy morning light, that it became clear the amount of blood spilled could not be hidden and no amount of money would buy the hotel staff's silence. A blood bath.

I cracked the window, reveling in the cool breeze, exhaling smoke. The same lighter from before, weighty in my hand.

"Are you satisfied, my love?"

I glanced over my shoulder to see Vince wiping a speck of blood from his cheek. The patterned kerchief did not belong to him.

"For now."

He came to me, cupping my cheek, his hunger burning and not quite slated, that monster peering out at me. I could see myself reflected in his eyes, could see the crimson at my lips, and I began to wonder—was I a monster, too?

"We are only getting started," Vince said, and he looked very well like he could eat me. I could imagine the taste of him on my tongue, could feel his pulse beneath my fingertips, familiar like it was my own.

My vampire, my monster.

"I am the heir of Andreas, after all."

Epilogue

Capri was sweltering this time of year. The sun was unbearable, the air thick, and the throngs of tourists on the beaches too crowded for my taste. But nothing money couldn't solve.

A wad of cash and a hired boat put distance between us and the commotion of the island, all the people at the shore turning to black specks as we floated further out into the sea —far enough to feel as though we were the only two souls around.

Though I couldn't shake the feeling of a pair of eyes on me, always watching even when it was *impossible*.

Vince reclined on the padded bench, his gaze hidden behind tinted glasses, reading one of the papers from home.

"MURDERER OF QUINTRELL
SIBLINGS STILL AT LARGE"

That had been the story—that I'd been taken, assumed

murdered, and now my brother was missing as well—some vicious predator still at large after our disappearances.

From the tabloids, I'd gathered that the "crime" was quite the sensation, and I wasn't sure if I'd be able to show my face in the city any time soon.

If only the public knew. If only *my mother* knew. What would she say if she could see him now?

It was just as well, we weren't finished with our business here on the continent, anyway.

After our stint in Paris, I'd wanted to travel *far* away. Just like Adam and I had planned all those years ago. And we'd decided the Mediterranean was far enough, for now.

Vince and I had gotten in the habit of donning only enough clothing not to be scandalous—it wouldn't have mattered, we drew everyone's attention as the rich enigmatic American couple. Checked in under an alias, and we didn't converse with others much, anyway.

Vince's linen shirt was unbuttoned, displaying the tanned planes of his chest, the sleeves rolled to his elbows. He wore swimming trunks, though he hadn't really enjoyed getting in the water with me, and his auburn hair shone copper in the midday sun. His pallor was long gone.

"It's much too hot," I sighed, shielding my eyes. I lay on the opposite side of the deck, propped up against some pillows under a parasol, but it did little to protect from the heat. I found I still burned easily in the sun.

Vince lowered his paper. "It's summer, darling."

"Maybe I don't like summer after all."

He raised a brow. "Shall I make arrangements to travel elsewhere?"

I rolled my eyes, huffing. "No, I am too tired to travel across the continent again."

"Then I suppose all we can do is try our best to keep you from melting." He turned his attention back to the paper.

"Perhaps we should invite Flora and Dixon to join us. Or we could visit Blackwell." I'd called a few times since we'd separated and while Flora would chat for hours, Lucy didn't have much to say, if she even came to the phone at all. Anxiety for her lingered in my heart. And neither of the girls had mentioned the contents of the case I'd given Flora. I put it from my mind, wanting to enjoy our respite the best I could, before reality came crashing back down.

"I'd rather not see the viscount for a while." Vince frowned. "I've spent too much time with him this year as it is."

"What about Séra? Or—ooh, Claude would love Italy, don't you think?"

The look Vince shot me was nothing less than exasperated.

"Where *should* we go next?" I mused, fanning myself.

He hummed, his head turning slightly as he skimmed the next page. "Stockholm."

I gasped. "Somewhere a bit chillier—for me?"

I felt his eyes on me, even though I could not see them through his tinted glasses. "Of course," he drawled. "Sinclair *advised* me last night on the phone that one of Marcel's sympathizers had run all the way up north to Sweden. I thought it best we started there and worked our way back through the continent."

We. Not *I*—not just him, alone—but us, *together.*

"Are we leaving soon then?"

"Eager for blood, my darling?" The corner of his mouth quirked.

My cheeks reddened, and not from the incessant heat encasing me. I shouldn't have been embarrassed. He loved me—*all* of me, I reminded myself. "Just wondering how many days left I have to relax."

His knowing smirk told me he saw right through my lie. "We'll stay for the week. Longer, if you'd like."

He paused, as if to give me the opportunity to refute it.

"Weeks have already passed since their exile, I don't think he'll mind an extra few days to live."

I weighed the two in my mind: hot blood on my tongue preceding death, or pretending for the next few days that I did not thirst for it.

Maybe one day I'd wear this mask well.

I exhaled another deep breath before standing and turning towards my lover. Though a slight breeze skated across the water, I was baking in the heat, every inch of my skin flushed. The wind did hardly anything to stave it off, resulting only in tangling the few strands of hair that had escaped my head scarf.

The memory of a particular iron tang had me salivating. Not all blood was the same—the flavor was affected by life-style, of course. In my short time as an immortal, I'd tasted the blood of only two men. And though Vince's lifeblood was rich, comforting, *ambrosial*, I often found myself waking to the vivid echo of another's on my tongue and a hunger aching in my teeth.

Was savoring a memory betrayal?

I shed the silken coverup, letting the fabric fall from my shoulders into a pile on the deck. I'd forgone my bathing suit today, knowing we were blessedly alone, and this far from shore no one would be able to see.

Months ago, I never would have dared to expose myself so boldly.

But I was not the same girl from months ago.

I couldn't see Vince's eyes through his dark glasses, but I felt them all the same as he drew his bottom lip between his teeth. I was more interesting than his scheming and reading after all.

"Indecent," he said, voice low.

My breasts peaked in the breeze. "Shall I put it back on?"

"No." He slowly set the paper down, coming to his feet. "I forbid it."

Some sort of compulsion, the urge to obey at all costs, made me abandon the idea altogether, the silky fabric a clump on the deck. He stalked forward, the boat swaying gently beneath us, the breeze making a mess of his hair.

"What is it," he demanded, low but firm. He stopped before me, not touching, though I could feel the ghost of his fingers at my hips, gripping and possessive. "You do not have to go to such lengths to force my attention. Though, I am not complaining."

"Hmm." Tilting my head to block the sun from my eyes. "Could have fooled me."

He was the murderer the papers looked for. And, I guessed, so was I.

If only they knew.

Strangely, there was no grief that that life was far behind me. One day, curiosity might get the better of me, and I might check on my mother. Might even visit my father's grave. But I'd never be returning to Chateau Gaultier. Not for a long, long while.

Vince peered down at me, his chest rising with a steady breath. "Do not be ashamed of what you are."

Of what I am.

Woman. Murderess. *Vampire.*

His fingers hovered over my cheek, but before he could touch me, I backed away, painting on a coquettish grin. For the briefest moment, I felt the thrill of being prey, knowing the predator was about to chase.

And then the water rose up to meet me, cool against my balmy skin. Sinking deep, deeper, obscured by bubbles, until I erupted from the surface, the waves undulating around me. Laughing at my scarf floating away, treading the clear water; letting it drain away the heat from my flesh, the worries seeping away until I was only radiance and joy and *hunger.*

He hesitated only a second, throwing his shades to the deck before he jumped in after with a splash. Strong hands finding me, pressing my naked body against his. Pulled together like two magnets. Two halves, one whole.

His sharp teeth glinted as he smiled. I couldn't help the laughter spilling from my lips.

I was weightless, feather-light, living for this moment and *only* this moment.

I could die happy, I realized. There were no chains around my ankles, no burdens to drag me down.

Though—the thought of sinking *did* give me ideas.

"You followed me in," I breathed, pressing closer, only an inch separating our lips.

"Of course." Vince brushed his knuckles along my

cheek, his touch an electric shock, still, even after all this time. "I'd follow you anywhere."

And I knew it was true.

I let my eyes fall closed. Felt the warmth of the summer sun on my face, shivered from the shock of the cool water. Knew that if I were to shut my eyes forever, I'd only need to outstretch my hand, reach for him, and he'd be there.

"Promise me."

Vince skated his lips across mine. "I promise."

ACKNOWLEDGMENTS

Oh my god, I did it. This book gave me so much trouble, it was a real work of blood, sweat and tears. (If you follow me on Threads, then you know) The universe did not want my sadgirl and her angry vampire to get their happy(ish) ending!

A massive thanks to each and every one of you who've supported the release of Red Masquerade and went on to pick this book up, too. The love my little smutty vampire books have found is more than I'd ever hoped in my wildest dreams. Thank you, and I hope you stick around to see what else I have in store!

Special thanks to my local indies for their continued support for this series!

To Dayna, for once again translating the gibberish I send you and making beautiful cover art out of it.

To Trey, for always pushing me to be my best, and for reading whatever chapters I put in front of you.

And if you've read this far, see you again next year in Blackwell 😈

ABOUT THE AUTHOR

Shaye Madison writes dark and stormy romances, and when she isn't lurking around book stores and drinking iced chais, she's conjuring up gothic fantasy worlds she (sometimes) wished she lived in. Based in North Carolina, she lives with her partner and their cat, Phoebe. Red Masquerade is her debut novel.

instagram.com/shaye_madison

threads.com/@shaye_madison

patreon.com/ShayeMadison

ALSO BY SHAYE MADISON

Red Masquerade

www.ingramcontent.com/pod-product-compliance
Lightning Source LLC
Chambersburg PA
CBHW030221120726
47903CB00005B/1317